Wild Honey Time is a first novel of extraordinary zest and power – fresh, funny, unforgettable. The author was born in Perth of Irish-Scottish parentage, was brought up in Carnoustie, and came to England at the age of nine when he was incarcerated in a succession of boarding schools before joining a magazine as a journalist and spending several years in Fleet Street.

M. O'Donoghue is married with one daughter, lives in London, and works as a freelance writer.

'A sweet, giddy, passionate book that leaves you tingling and beguiled . . . it is the style – delicate and rich as a rum cake – which will gladden those readers perpetually in search of a Writer.' – *Vogue*

'It conveys a sense of atmosphere, joy and sadness which should find a big following.' – *Sunday Mirror*

'Really splendid.' – *The Scotsman*

'Delightfully amusing . . . I warmly recommend it.' – *Annabel*

Wild Honey Time

M. O'Donoghue

Mayflower

Granada Publishing Limited
Published in 1974 by Mayflower Books Ltd
Frogmore, St Albans, Herts AL2 2NF

First published by Hodder and Stoughton Ltd 1972
Copyright © M. O'Donoghue 1972
Made and printed in Great Britain by
Cox & Wyman Ltd, London, Reading and Fakenham
Set in Intertype Plantin

To R.G.D.

CONTENTS

CHAPTER ONE

THROUGH THE CASEMENT

IN the beginning I was aware of an acrid smell which came and went in wisps. It was my grandmother's essence and some years were to pass before I discovered that the same aura surrounds an open bottle of whisky.

Meanwhile, it wrapped me round and picked me up and danced me a wild jig through the house of squalls, which was to be my childhood harbour. For some weeks it was my universe and, when it drifted off, I was content simply to doze and dream.

Then something heavy landed on my chest and, all at once, there was no breath. White heat scorched in my head, my eyes burst open to a sea of crimson and my woolly ears were violently stripped bare to the noise of life. A stubby finger poked its way into my mouth and I bit – hard.

As the room filled with screams, the weight was suddenly lifted and suspended over me. It looked down through a girdle of five other screeching faces and I saw my family for the first time; Granny Morag and Auntie Annie, sharing the burden of Calum in the air, Bella, Catrina and Lachlan – black-eyed, dark-skinned and bastards, every one.

They hurtled me over the crib-side to the floor and jostled round shrilly as I stood up, staggered and fell. Auntie Annie fell with me, to her knees, moaning, for I was two years old and had never stood, or sat, or even opened my eyes before.

They lavished sweets on Calum as reward for his attempted murder and, ever after, though he grew to a simple and gentle lad, only I could bait him into brutal, inarticulate rage, because he thought it was the right thing to do.

With the slumbering cradle hours thus defeated, I tilted joyously into the prism of living. Beyond the bedroom I found a lobby. Somewhere in the depths of its squidgy blackness lay a sea-serpent, which slid along silently behind me as I floundered against the wall in terror. Its giant heart drummed in my ears and each day I would erupt into the haven, just as its molars began to grind in anticipation.

The haven, the kitchen; hung with webs of edible seaweed and onions, smelling of broth and bodies, home of mad Uncle Angus and his dog, Deamhan (Devil). This was a place where anything might happen. Here, if a small boy's shadow crossed the black range, Auntie Annie would drop on her knees and scream, 'The loonie's shadae passed the grate. There'll be evil afore the week's oot.'

And, sure enough, before the end of the week, someone would fall sick, or the chimney would catch fire, or the school authorities would call and Auntie Annie would solemnly nod her head.

Here, under the scrubbed wooden table, were Lachlan's wooden roller-skates in which Granny Morag would scoot round the chairs, hooting with glee: whizz, whizz, hoot, whizz; wee, blackhaired witch in button boots and dirndl petticoats. Uncle Angus would look on from his thick chair-bed, fingering the packet of rat poison established in his pocket and thinking of the day when he would carry out his eternal threat and eat it.

Here, if I bounced hard on the harmonium pedals, I could make it squeal out curses; or, if I squirmed between the mass of tiny feet, I could pull long, coloured strands from the rag rugs; and, if I played either of these games for long enough, Auntie Annie would cuff me round the ear and a fight would start.

'Annie, ye clooted the wee'n,' Granny would shout, accusingly.

'He's a heathen. That's what he is – a heathen,' Auntie Annie would scream in outrage.

'He's Mairi's third and wi' fine blood in his veins. Ye'll no cloot the laird's son's son while I have breath.' Venom would pour through Granny's black eyes as she jigged round Auntie Annie in fury.

'Awwwwwwwwww!' And Auntie Annie would be back on her knees, swaying to and fro with her arms in the air, like one of the scraggy, wind-haunted rowan trees on the hills above. There she would stay and groan until Granny Morag stopped dancing and started throwing – turnips and tatties, carrots and leeks. The kettle would boil and the battle would stop for tea.

This particular fracas could start up another way, too; when Granny Morag cuffed me and Auntie Annie leapt to defend, for their affections were ever inconstant and their favourites among us children changed from hour to hour and minute to minute.

In the corner, by the range, stood a great wooden chair with slatted back and jutting arms. No one ever sat on it, for it was Rob Mór's chair and he had left for America in 1901, a year after my mother, Mairi, was born.

Rob Mor was a swarthy nomad and our grandsire. He had come to the village from a vacuum to find labour for the season on the fishing boats, or a farm. Behind the bar, in the only pub, he had met wild Morag, tempting as a nightshade berry to a child, and he had stayed and wed her.

For ten years he let her whirl him round a pool of Scotch and, when he left, sent money every month until he died. But maybe he felt safer in America, because he never came back, though his strange, restless spirit always glowered in that chair.

They had had four children; Robbie beag, who lived with a woman in the village and, being Granny Morag's first-born male, had an oilcloth laid on the bare table when he came for a meal. Tómas, their second son, who fathered Lachlan by a fishergirl before marrying a respectable woman. The fishergirl, in turn, had yielded up the unwanted boy to Granny Morag and married a respectable man.

Auntie Annie came next and, at twenty, produced Catrina, father unknown. Thereafter, she became a confirmed hypochondriac and never left the house again.

The last of Rob Mór's and Morag's children was Mairi; mother of Bella, by a fisherman, at fifteen; of Calum, by a farmer, at seventeen; and of me, by the laird's son, it was said, at nineteen. After I was born, she went to Glasgow to earn her living in the most ancient of women's professions. We heard from her now and then through letters written in an awkward hand, and then she, too, married and emigrated to Australia.

Maybe it was she who had driven Rob Mór away by her blonde hair and blue eyes. Yet, had he waited to view her offspring, he would have known she was his true daughter, for his Celtic features were stamped on every one of us. Sometimes, in the ocean of the nights, we three would see her face above our beds; fair and still as she looked down on her little cluster of dark demons; holy and pure, because she was our Mother.

In every year there were twelve supreme days for Granny Morag and her covey, one for each month. They were more important than birthdays or Christmas and more exciting even than Hogmanay. They were the days when the money arrived from Rob Mór.

Oh, the sweet apple glory of those shive to sheaf moments; those tatters to tinsel hours; those morsel to Midas days! Suddenly, our cheeks became rounded cradles to humbugs and winter mixtures and our fingers glued with icing and sugar.

Auntie Annie would be ravished by six brand new bottles of 'cures'. Uncle Angus would snort and sneeze with relish over an abundance of snuff. And Granny Morag pranced round her bottle, tossing the precious notes in the air and chanting, 'Rin doon tae the shoppie. Rin doon tae the shoppie,' while my brothers and sisters scrambled and fought at her feet for the privilege of going to the village shop.

They always went together, in the end, and left the veterans settled noisily over tea and medicine, tea and snuff and tea and whisky. For a little, I was left alone, the wee'n, too small to drag down the hill and back and so sat fatly on the track to wait.

Little merlin, nesting on earth, burst like a bullet after the great buzzard from the crags. Kestrel swept across to join in – bicker, bicker, bicker, till the buzzard, his bluff called, fled hoarsely back to the mountains.

The pebbles turned into crystals of ice under my legs, but the heather was steamy and thick. I lay in it and peat water, oozing up between the stems towards the warmth, made a puddle round me. The flowers were a crisp mauve bedspread, which I wanted to turn white with a wish and so create a lake of luck to give to Granny Morag. Yet, they always clung stubbornly to their colour and their roots, at last growing angry, would rise up and jab me out of the snuggery. The grey sky, balanced, like a sheet of metal on the peaks, would rain down spanks of cold upon me and, as I opened my mouth to howl, the clan would return.

Trumpeting up the track they came, lumpy with bags and satchels of candied frippery and I would be bundled under a spare arm as they whinnied into the kitchen.

'Och, look how the wee'n's soaket. Gis a towel and a bottlie o' yon dazzle, Catrina.' Bella would rub me dry and fill me with fizzy cherryade as the party began.

Tranquillity was booted out the door when Bella's feet trampled air into the organ and changed it into a strident cacophony. Granny capered and bucked. Auntie Annie was hauled into a reel and, under the ringing 'hoochs' and 'halloos', her soulful dirge mourned like the drone of the pipes.

'Aye, ye'll no be feeling sae fine in the morn, Mither. Ye'll no ... Och, Lachlan, let me go! ... be feeling sae fine ... ye'll be forgetting I'm delicate ... in the morn.'

The cauldron swung over the flames. Rugs skidded under the chairs and Uncle Angus pulled his feet and his dog to refuge on the bed. From the top of the dresser, where they'd stuck me for safety, I gaped and watched through the magic frame of infancy – high, curving cheekbones; slanting, black eyes; fierce, hooked noses and tangled, raven hair. Granny Morag had turned into the Queen of the Kelpies and my belly churned in fear as she danced with her own crazy 'wee folk' in the lamplight.

They crossed two besoms in the centre of the floor and watched her birling the sword dance over and over and round and round. Her skirts rode above the twigs in layer upon layer of tear-drawing colours. Her lace shawl flayed and shadowed us with mad, black sea-spray and faces darkened wetly under her spell.

The uproar grew with whirling and skirling and, as turmoil and pandemonium loomed to devour us all, Catrina plunged into a corner screaming – shrill, stabbing little screams, till Granny Morag slapped her and everything stopped for tea.

Later, there were songs, ferocious with clan history, bonny as the hills, and Uncle Angus came into his own. He sat, ripe and swollen with bass notes, which rolled away from his epiglottis and dropped grandly among us, like huge, purple melons. They were mighty to hear and he was splendid to behold and we marvelled.

Songs. Songs. Sweeter and sweeter songs. Softer and softer songs until, at last, we children crept each to his bed and our

13

Granny Morag would be left alone, weeping over the sadness enshrined by our forefathers in their lilting airs.

Amid this tempest of passions I spun, giddy as a flirting moth with Granny Morag as my candle flame, and gradually began to learn the order of emotions.

Tears were allowed to flow without shame for joy or rage, beauty or sympathy, love or sorrow — but never for fear or self-pity. They came as easily and frequently as laughter to us all and, if one cried another would join in while Granny Morag nodded, unperturbed, 'Let them hae their greet.'

Anger steamed free and scalding from adult to adult and child to child, from the bustling kitchen to the hummock behind the cottage. There, on the briny turf, we would tussle; livid, panting, punch-drunk, squirming, bruised and gory; Lachlan with Bella, Calum with me, Catrina with everyone, fingers twined in hair, fists rammed against bloody gums, puce faces pummelled into the sod, until the fury was carried away to the hills and laughter caught us up again.

I learned, too, the tales of the mountains, whose mystic white caps were ever veiled in cloud. Auntie Annie would whisper the dread secrets when the snows soundproofed doors and windows in winter and the 'wee folk' slept. She claimed she knew when it was safe, but never forgot to be canny.

'They're oot yonder,' she would breathe, pointing a knobbly finger at the frosted windows. 'Aye, they're there in the hollaes o' the hills and trees . . . waiting.'

She would pause and look at each cowering child.

'Waiting tae pitch bad loonies and quinies intae the black night and send their own wee'ns tae the hoose instead.'

As a bubble of fear burst in each face, her eyes would grow deep and knowing.

'Waiting tae turn the milk sour in the auld goat. Waiting tae bellow up the fire in the grate. Waiting tae pinch ye all blue and black in yis beds.'

There wasn't a movement or a draught in the room, but the range suddenly belched up a bouquet of flames. The familiar kitchen was swallowed by a pit of spectral glimmers and glooms and it was witching time.

We hugged ourselves in rapturous dread and Auntie Annie shrivelled and curled into a wizened hag before our dilated eyes. Her voice quickened hoarsely, until it loosed a torrent of devils and demons, ghouls and apparitions, warlocks and bogies, hobgoblins and banshees about us.

Evil became at once hateful and tantalizing. We felt ourselves turning into sprites and goblins with long, pointed nails, like Chinese mandarins. Our world became carmine and sable, olive and ebony. It was wicked – so wicked that even I understood and would have howled, if I hadn't been sat on smartly by Lachlan.

When, finally, her cracked voice ordered us to bed, the night began in earnest. For the wind had heard the forbidden words and carried the news to the kelpies. Down the chimneys they came, billion upon billion of spiteful, little people. If we moved, they would wriggle under us and bear us into the black outside and put their own children into our beds.

Scuffle, scuffle, scuffle . . . 'Where are they now?' Scratch, scratch, scratch . . . 'I'm glad they're in someone else's bed, not mine.' Each child lay rigid as a floorboard. Even Catrina was too frightened to scream. They tickled our feet and pierced us with needles. They blew in our ears and turned noses to ice. They banged our bones with hammers and tugged the girls' hair round the bedpots. They twitched off the bedclothes and wound our nightshirts round our necks.

Then, as the birds wakened over the sea, they mewed and grumbled and fled and we were left to unravel the mess, all gooseflesh and chilblains, but too thankful to be alive to care.

We knew very well that the only reason we were preserved at all was because Auntie Annie always left milk and bread outside the back door for the 'wee folk'. So, for a day or so, we would run her errands in gratitude.

Above her bed hung a smoked herring, dressed in coloured rags. It was brought into the cottage by the first foot on Hogmanay to symbolize a year of plenty and remained till the twelve months had passed. To me it was a dead kelpie, crooked and puckered, like a shrunken, henna body dug up after an aeon under the peat.

Fearsome happenings would take place if it were moved,

Auntie Annie warned us, and she was right, for the day it disappeared was a sad day for us all.

We learnt the news in the morning, when she ran into the kitchen, weeping copious tears and groaning. 'Oh, there'll be wailing and starvation among us the noo. There'll be bitter lamentations and grief the noo. We'll a' perish afore the year's through.'

She slumped to the floor in despair.

'Och, get up off yis knees this instant and start yis porridge,' snapped Granny Morag, without looking up from the range. But our auntie only pointed a fateful finger and went on with her prophecy.

'Aye, Mither, and they'll have nae mercy on you. Ye'll be trodden tae the ground wi' the rest in misery and anguish. Ye winna be laughing then, when they very walls o' the hoose are toppled round yis bones and the hurricane carries yis dust tae the waters o' the ocean. For the "wee folk" are terrible angry, Mither, and they've taken back their smoky. This is the end.'

Her voice was like a hell-fire preacher's, fruity with doom, and it sent us all scurrying from the room to search for the herring, but, though we hunted high and low, it was nowhere to be seen. We looked at each other and our hearts shone in our eyes. Catrina's radiated satisfaction like her mother; Lachlan was sly and amused; Bella hysterical; Calum, puzzled and me, witless with fright.

The postman should have delivered the money from Rob Mór that morning and, when he still had not called by midday, even Granny Morag began to think about the lost smoky. At first she said we'd better have another look, 'just tae make peace for Annie.' Then she joined in the investigation and, by later afternoon, she'd become obsessed by the whole affair.

Drawers were upturned and their contents chivvied and shaken. Beds were stripped back and the bedrooms became landscapes of tangled clothes and blankets. We waded through them, kicking, tugging, stirring, feeling, over and over again.

Auntie Annie was in a state of smug melancholia. This was the zenith of her career as an oracle and the fact that we had all to die in torment to prove her right was unimportant. So she lay, prostrate in an Eden of tribulation, all day.

Granny Morag, on the other hand, was sober and dry, forced into total abstinence by a herring, and the more she thought about it the more irritated she became. She kept opening her cupboard, in case even a dram had been overlooked, and her eyes would fall on the array of bottles, shining, provoking and empty – an alcoholic's nightmare come true. She ransacked the cottage in frenzy and virulent curses crackled through her lips as she went.

'Fer Christ's sake, whit are ye standing there for, ye useless load o' bastards? Git up off yis backsides and find that herrin'. It's easy seeing ye dinna take after my folks, ye muckle, great idjots!'

All under age, including the dog, smarted beneath waves of swift blows from her tough little fists.

'Rob Mór'll rot in hell for this day's work,' – whack – 'Aye, and you, too, Annie, ye fat slut, wi' yis kelpies, and kippers and cures.' – whack – 'They winna save ye from the fire doon there, ye whoring bitch.' – whack – 'There's not one will gang tae bed this night till that bloody herrin' is found, d'ye hear.'

But it was not found and, of course, we did go to bed, eventually, supperless and snivelling. Soon the humping bedclothes stilled, as we drew to ourselves that careless slumber which heals every child's misery.

I shared a bed with Lachlan and Calum. They slept at the top end and I, between two pairs of feet, at the bottom. Some time in the centre of that night, I opened my eyes and saw moonbeams filling a sheeted hollow with silver and jet. Lachlan had gone. I stiffened, like a starched collar, all the half-understood warnings of the day waking in my mind.

So this was what they meant. We were all going to be taken away in the night, like the herring, one by one, and Lachlan the first to go. I felt very sorry about him, because he'd never stolen any sweets from me, and wished Calum could have vanished instead, because he had. Then I wondered whether Granny Morag and the girls were still there, or were the 'wee folk' going to take both a loonie *and* a quinie each night. Then I wondered whether to cry or not and, as I considered this problem, Lachlan came back.

'Hey, Lachie, where've ye been?'

'Hud yis wheesht!'

'Lachie, I thocht it was the kelpies had got ye.'

'If ye tell a soul I was oot the night, I'll slit yis throat, d'ye hear? Now get back tae sleep.'

He made a graphic gesture across his throat with one hand, while his eyes glittered at me ominously in the stark light. Calum moved in his sleep and I ducked my head back to the pillow and forgot about the whole baffling episode as fast as possible.

Next morning, the smoky was discovered, hanging in its usual place above Auntie Annie's bed. She announced that we'd all been reprieved and, sure enough, the postman arrived with the money from Rob Mór before noon. Our faith in her pronouncements was secure from that day and it was many, many years before I suspected Lachlan's part in the affair.

The village was bred into superstition and legend and few had the courage to deny the powers of the supernatural. We lived in a fortress of mountains and forests and moors and, from our earliest days, were aware of these immortals massed over us. They were indivisible, wordless and remote, the all-seeing viceroys of some supreme authority. They held the secrets of Time closer than the sphinx and were our gods.

Below us, in eternal motion, lay our almighty Mother, the Sea. From her we inherited our mercurial ways, our ugliness and our beauty, our loves and our hates – each one a dark, salt droplet of her passions. She ruled us all by her moods, for, when she was pleased, she heaped wealth into our arms and, when she was angry, she stole the food from our mouths.

Before I had even seen her, I knew of the sea as part of my being and the splendours of the land too. We all did, and eagerly grasped the lesson they taught and believed in them above all else.

If a rainbow ended on the Satan Rock, the fishing boats stayed on the shore and the wives of those already out at sea would gather together to mourn for the one who would die. That there would be a death was indisputable and if, by chance, all the men returned alive, it was because our eyes had been deceived. The rainbow must have ended behind the rock, not on it.

If an inland bird flew over a boat at sea, the catch would be lost. If you ate bearberry roots and seeds, or carried fern seeds in your pocket, you would become invisible. Didn't Mary Neilson do that every night. If you built over burnt ground, the fire would rise again and destroy your house. If you left no food at the backdoor, the 'wee folk' would steal all you possessed. These things were so and we knew them.

Gradually, I grew closer to the earth and soon only her smells and sounds filled my wakeful time. There were roots buttoned up in her corners, waiting to be dug out by chubby, prying fingers. They were chocolate-brown and crumbly outside, but each bite polished up their secret colours – ivory and sorrel and saffron and claret. They were juicy and filling and the grit that went down with them never harmed me a bit.

There were grasses which scratched quick, repelling cuts in my flesh when I pulled them and grasses with sticky nectaries, which I could suck. There were beetles to chase, or race, or bury, or tease, or dissect with detached interest. I looked deep into the flowers and leaves and saw their meanest tinctures and each pig-ment-filled canal. Small things were great to me. Great things were incomprehensible and so I would walk into a tree while gazing at a grain of sand.

The stone cottage began to creep away from me as I played and often, when I turned, tired and cold towards its happy dis-order, I would find that it had wandered to the other side of a hillock and left me to climb wearily after it.

The days were limpid and limitless. The mild sun blushed perpetually. The blue sky was as blue at bedtime as it was when we awoke and I forgot I'd ever known an evening in those first spying months. Being the wee'n, I went alone to bed, before the others, and, as I slid between the chilling sheets, would throw my mind through the window to the heavens and try to capture their warmth. Slowly, their misty hue would filter down until it closed my eyes and nose and mouth and ears with the opal dust of sleep.

This was a blithe and bonny dreamery, full of dulcet, sensual times and, one day, as I meandered round, it was gone. On that day, I suddenly realized that all the immense boulders and crags and glaciers and floods and waterfalls and jungles were only parts of the little garden behind the cottage. I could see the end of it: a high bank of reeds.

I ran towards it with eager, foolish steps and scrambled, clawing, to the top and looked.

There – a magnitude of blinding lights, beating into the passive sky and roaring thunder; outrageous, foaming explosions erupted off mammoth rocks towards me. I was arrayed in a veil of pearls. Tears were enticed from my eyes and my babyhood was snatched away in a moment. It was Omega and Alpha. It was the immemorial and the hereafter. It was everything that ever was and is and will be.

I saw the Sea.

CHAPTER TWO

TIDAL TIME

NEW horizons were opened to me by that first sight of the sea. It was like being born again; abruptly and painfully being faced by the vast, radiant, gusty, clangorous world again and my senses embrangled with shock. I could only lie panting and waiting for them to learn to accept it all and, when they did, I realized that the water was really very calm.

Below me, the bronze soil rubbled into tawny clods, which dribbled to a kyle of cream and boulders sprawled from this into the gurging tide. Beyond the flaunting waves and cockle boats, the ocean lay in lazy abandon with the sky. She was starry-skinned with love. Her greens and blues were his greens and blues and, as they clasped each other in the distance, they covered themselves with a blanket of gold.

At the close end of the bay, shadowed cliffs jagged up to meet a heathered mountainside, then plunged back, like a cruel beak, into the water. These two had battled since Time was an embryo and the water had gouged great holes in the rock, its prison wall. But if the cliffs had relented a little, they had left behind an indestructible warden to symbolize their strength.

This was the Satan Rock, which hunched about half a mile from the shore, like a Mososaurus left over from a prehistoric age. The black, horned face, which seemed to leer from its slime-covered surface, gave it its name and it incited the breakers to such frenzy that they never ceased bashing themselves berserk against its bulwarks. No boat could safely pass within five hundred yards.

The fishing people watched it for omens of woe. If its hood of sea-moss shone too green beneath the sun, the fish were driven away. If they could see the white surf round it from the village, a boat would be lost. If a rainbow ended over it, a man would die. Yet, the day it crumbled to dust would be catastrophic for us all.

They feared it, the gulls avoided it and I looked and was afraid, too, for it was an evil thing.

On my other side, the narrow strait of sand shrugged off its rocky shackles and widened into a milky beach, which wore a bonnet of bride's lace and couch grass. It curved, luxuriously, for over a mile, ending in a hog's back and I could see no further.

For hours I stayed on the bank of reeds and heeded the sea, entranced, yet dared not even trespass on to her fringe. I had discovered my first mistress and found her too fair to touch.

The sound of my name came faintly, like something from another sphere; but, gradually, it badgered me back to consciousness and I sat up.

'In heaven's name, Micheil, whit are ye doing lying there, pinched as a naket wee rabbit wi' the cold! I've been seekin' ye half the day.'

It was Granny Morag and, suddenly, I hated her. She looked down at me, perplexed, and then her eyes cleared.

'So ye've found the sea, bairnie,' she said, turning to scan the waters for a long moment. 'Aye, but she's bonny, the auld witch, though today she's stolen my last wee'n away.'

I loved her again and she took my hand.

'Come away, my weary loonie, and ye can come back in the morn.' She never called me a wee'n again.

I was too young to know about pirates or the seafaring heroes of boys, so my dreams that night were abstract and strange. A white gull rose from a backcloth of heaving water, crying bitter lament. Its arched wings sped relentlessly towards me, till every feather flashed clear for an instant, then blurred from focus. Its lifeless tongue and inky eyes bulged and merged into the grinning mask on Satan Rock, who opened his mouth and laughed; a booming, vermilion laugh.

I could see the beauteous sea, smiling and inviting, through the cavern. But, when I stepped inside, I found myself on top of a pointed, yellow fang, the first of thousands which sprang that second between me and my vision. I jumped wildly from one to the next, to the next and on. Their spikes jabbed my feet while more and more burgeoned ahead. My lungs seemed to tighten and block the air I thrust into them and I began to sob with exhaustion.

Then, all at once, the water was there, smoothing my forehead with a cool, liquid touch and the sea spoke.

'Wheesht now! Wheesht now, Micheil, and rest. There's no cause for greetin', Hinnie. Be still awhile.'

How soft and certain was her voice as she drove away the taunting spikes and images and lulled me to innocent sleep. I never thought it strange that the sea should sound so like my Granny Morag.

Morning came brimming over the night, like a rosy shower, all spangles and fuss and I dispatched my porridge rapidly and somersaulted into the flow. It swept me up the reedy bank and tipped me over the top. I hovered and slithered and lay. Gold dust covered me from head to toe and, when I threw a fistful into the air, it fell back to grate my teeth and sting my eyes and teach me my first lesson.

A man came bobbing and stooping, like a winged brown bird, from the shadow of the cliffs. It was my Uncle Angus and I ran towards him, longing to show off.

'Uncle Angus! Uncle Angus!'

'Wha'? Wha'? Och, it's you! Will ye awa'!'

'I'm by the sea, Uncle Angus.'

'Git awa' wi' ye! Awa'! Awa'!' He picked out a piece of driftwood from his bundle and brandished it. 'There's nae peace, nae peace. I'l be takin' ma powder soon. I'll nae be here for long. Git awa'!'

He lumbered past me, muttering, and I stuck out my tongue after him and yelled, 'Ye're daft! Ye're saft! Ya!' Then bolted away, in case he set Deamhan on me.

He disappeared back into the shadows and so it was always to be. As I grew up and roamed far from the cottage, I would still meet him in the loneliest nooks and he always swore and shambled off with his dog.

He collected seaweed and wood, seacoal and berries, herbs and fir cones and peat. On fine days he stayed near his kitchen, but in the heart of a storm he mght stray fifteen miles or more.

He was a slow, shy man, who had spent most of his life with his mother in a harbour cottage. When she died he had moved into Granny Morag's kitchen and gradually grown more and more eccentric. We children teased him mercilessly into spasms of baffled rage, but Granny Morag and Annie left him alone with Deamhan. His only two desires were a little snuff and solitude and, for the first, he would give us his rich voice at our ceilidhs and, for the second, he went off into his own wildernesses.

He never did take his rat poison, but died of good old age on a sunny hillside near his home one day. We were all grown up by then, yet each one felt the wash of sadness at the news. He was so much a part of the earth that we had almost believed he would live for ever.

The tide was out that morning, so I clambered over the rocks, slipping and stumbling on their blanket of bladder-wrack. The crannied pools were filled with delicate hues. Golden-fronded oarweed and pink sea fir dripped and massed over their cavelets. Red and green anemones ceaselessly searched for titbits with silken tentacles. Minute sea slugs ruffled their orange and yellow plumes in the stir and pea crabs, each a bright, new colour, bustled through the ferns.

I saw them all and sat agog and blinking. I was slack-mouthed with wonder, tingling with curiosity and soon could control myself no longer. My hand plunged in. The water shied. Its inmates flinched and fled. My feet skidded and hands clutched and I scrabbled, squeaking into the puddle. There I squatted, like a plump frog, and giggled.

Something wriggled beneath my palm and I pinched it out of the water. It was a peach-coloured pea crab, which waved its tiny claws at me in helpless anger, and I forgot to giggle and screamed with delight.

Then I tramped back towards the sand, feeling like a dragon slayer with this, my first catch. Limpets and bladder-wrack tried to scratch and bind me as I passed, but I kicked them aside, contemptuously. This was my victory march and no petty obstructions could stop it.

But they laid a trap for me, a concealed hollow, and I fell again. The pea crab dropped into the dark and hied crazily away and I erupted with frustration.

Granny Morag found me later, damp, sandy and still bawling. She ran me back to the wash-house, stood me fully clothed in the empty boiler and flung a bucket of icy water over my head. The sand deluged away and we both went into the cottage, saturated.

I think the sight of us, glowing and wet, must have given Auntie Annie the idea, for she said, very casually, 'I'm hearing that salty water wid be guid for the feet.'

We all looked at each other in alarm. Experience had taught us that our aunt's statements about aids to health were auguries of added toil for the rest of the family. She became inspired in this way about once a fortnight and lengthened her already measureless list of 'cures' with the new fancy. We waited.

'It's a thocht that ye might each tak a turn at fetching up a wee pailie for me in the morns,' she said.

'We'll a' be in class and Micheil's tae sma',' grumbled Lachlan.

'Och, but ye could fetch it afore ye went, surely,' answered Auntie Annie, assured of success.

Granny Morag butted in, irritably, 'I'm hearing that fresh air wid be guid for a body, taw. Could ye no be fetchin' it yersel'?'

'Now, Mither, ye ken verra well I'm delicate. The air's aye bad for the chest.'

We resigned ourselves in silence to years of pail-dragging. Already each roamed the shore and moors in search of herbs for his aunt, so one more chore made little difference.

We grew parsley and rosemary for coughs and 'nerves'. We flung sticky burrs at each other, then carefully uprooted the burdock plant for her to use on spots. She made us chew the bitter leaves of scurvygrass, 'tae gie yis all fine skins', and drink dandelion tea to purify the blood. Bearberry from the moors eased her rheumatism. Sickly, yellow rue flowers were dried, stewed and drunk as tea for indigestion. Fennel was boiled with fish to stop gripe and extract of monkshood cooled our fevers.

Each dose meant an hour of shudders and each child had run vomiting from the room many times after the daily medicinal rounds. As Granny Morag's burning loaf poultice (her standard remedy for every ailment) was dreaded every bit as much as Auntie Annie's mixtures, very few dared to cry sick. All the same, it was a minor miracle that no one was ever poisoned and we must have had the purest blood and clearest skins in Scotland.

So it began that, on every day not annulled by snow, two

children were sent with buckets for seawater and, before long, my name was on the duty list, too.

I still have nightmares about those burdened, farcical journeys; the lopsided hobble back from a tide, which might be half a mile out; water sploshing over boots, which clogged and chafed with sand; fingers like frozen cod roes, knees webbed with chaps. Nothing was ever more hated than this wrenching, squelchy, aching, sweaty, clumsy pantomime we performed daily for the benefit of our aunt's feet.

However, if it did nothing else, it roused my interest in women's legs and gave me a severe shock in the process. Until then I had never really thought about them, other than to take it for granted they they were all brown and woolly. But, on the morning Lachlan cursed in the first full bucket, I was there, watching.

Auntie Annie disappeared from the kitchen for a few minutes and, when she returned, slid her feet quickly and bashfully into the brine, I stared, fascinated, at her sawn-off legs. They were ashen under a ravelling of blue veins, like two thin snakes which had left their sloughed skins in muddy lumps on the floor. They were most revolting, but I had to see more.

I drew closer and looked from Bella's plump, bare calves to the hint of Granny Morag's russet-encased sturdies, between boots and skirts, and back to those wan exhibits.

'Granny Morag, when *ye* tak off yis skin, is yis legs like yon?'

She let out a cackle of laughter. Auntie Annie rose, cruelly mortified, and made for the door. The forgotten bucket toppled with a rabble of clangs, taking feet, legs and woman in fearful display to the floor. There they lay, utterly still before us and we saw that, in her shame, our Auntie Annie had pretended to faint.

If we assumed this marked the end of her latest whim, we were wrong. It only drove her to tend her feet in the privacy of the wash-house and I never saw them exposed again.

Every highland cottage had a wash-house which stood, like ours, outside the back door. It was a grey stone hut holding a stone boiler, a wooden wringer, a tin bath and a junk of pails. It was windowless and the sharp smell of carbolic and soiled clothes was trapped forever behind its door.

On washdays we would rattle, in order of strength, down the track to the pump, where Lachlan seesawed on the handle and hypnotized himself with motion. The spout, like a giant udder, freed oval splutters of smoky water tinged with rust into our buckets, or over our feet. We drank this water, too.

Those waiting their turn brawled restlessly, twisting out heather roots to switch each other's legs, pulling the girls' long hair in boredom, pushing heads under the spurting liquid and crying with rage. Stones jerked and cracked away from our aimless toes, the pails buckled with shock as we swung them together like cymbals and Lachlan never stopped pumping, like a dancing puppet, till he had fettered us all with burdens of water.

Subdued, we carried them back to the wash-house and tipped them, ten cascades of relief, into the boiler over the fire. We hung over the edge as they met in a fizzle of suds on the melted soap at the bottom and simmered there an hour or more under a crust of foam.

Then we harried the washing through the bubbles with wooden poles, ruthlessly bludgeoning clothes which ballooned to the surface. Sheets, sarks, curtains, cloots, bloomers, breeks and bodices whirred unwillingly towards cleanliness. One by one, they were snatched out as Granny Morag purged them vigorously on the washboard and mangled them into purity through the ringer.

More water was heated in the boiler then poured frugally into the tin bath. As every sprinkling was precious, each bath, one third full, was used by two of us. I, as the youngest, was subjected first.

It was always ultra-cold on washdays and the door of the wash-house had to be left open for light, so the whole act of ablution was one of searing discomfort. My bottom and legs pulsed under water, so hot that it felt icy, and above the navel was numb in a wintery gale which burned.

Eventually, I would escape, axed in two at the waist by extremes, and Calum, who had waited over me, stripped and quaking, always found his bath cold. The rest followed us in pairs, Catrina and Bella, Lachlan and Granny Morag, alternately boiled and frozen. Despite her views on hygiene and health,

Auntie Annie never bathed, but sponged herself mysteriously and secretly when we were in bed.

However, there was no mystery about Uncle Angus. He just never washed and would have remained reeking happily forever had not Robbie beag ejected the women from the kitchen occasionally and forcibly scrubbed him. This happened three times a year and it took about as long again for the old man to recover. 'Tell Angus tae be here when I come up the morn,' Robbie beag would say, suddenly, over the oilclothed table. As he was the only one of her relations Granny Morag could not beat into submission, his word was law. We all knew what the message meant and it was always delivered.

Uncle Angus became loudly incoherent at the news, shaking his packet of Rodine at us, bouncing convulsively on his collapsible chair and bellowing reproach. Deamhan, seeing his master's distraction, would lift his long muzzle to the ceiling and howl; measured, tuneless howls. But they were both there, meekly waiting to be tormented, in the morning.

'Come on, ye dirty old bum,' Robbie beag would grunt, pulling the rags off our great-uncle and pushing him into the tub by the range. There he would stand, five foot two, still wearing his cap and looking like a timid grey spook someone had laughed at.

As the soap was greased on, he would shake his head, abjectly, and mutter, 'Aye ... aye ... aye.' and, as he was ruthlessly scoured with a large brush, he would add, 'I'll nae be here for long ... aye.'

'Gis the ither leg and hud yis tongue!' His nephew, brutally unimpressed, scrubbed the harder and soon had the old man out on the rug, wincing under a rough towel.

When he was dry, he was dressed in a clean, long-sleeved semmit and woollen drawers, which reached to his ankles, a collarless shirt, his old, stained waistcoat and, once a year, a new suit. This was always a cast-off secured by Robbie beag in a hopeless attempt to encourage his uncle's appreciation of sartorial elegance. It was tatty and torn within a week.

After being dressed, he was polished. A cut-throat razor pared away weeks of beard. The few tufts of growth on his head were trimmed. His drooping moustache, ginger with snuff, was pruned back and, finally, the long hairs sprouting from his nose and ears were clipped.

Throughout all he suffered, helplessly, without making the slightest effort to dissuade or assist, and, when at last the whole operation was over, he would lean back in his chair and sniff, sadly.

'Robbie beag, I canna help thinking ye're a mite lacking in respect.'

Robbie beag would draw a packet of snuff from his pocket and hand it over.

'Och, but ye're a guid lad, aye, a grand lad.' Uncle Angus forgave all disrespect in a moment and the two sat over a pinch together.

Everyone relaxed and when Robbie beag was quite sure we were settled, he pounced again; this time on Deamhan. The scurfy old collie, convinced he was forgotten, would forget to skulk under the table and emerge to lie brazenly on the floor. It was a mistake for, in that second, he was plunged into the cold bath.

Like his master he never struggled, but, having more spirit, yowled protests to the world. Lather might ooze into his closed eyes, or up his nose, and water could dribble down his ears, but his mouth remained a rounded hole through which the whines merged into one long yodel, a barbed strand of sound which did not break until he, too, was dried, brushed and returned to his corner.

The disagreement between nephew and uncle over the importance of baths was the only one they had and Robbie beag had a strong affection for the old man. The two went poaching together on the moors and in the forest and, as both were practised shots, their expeditions cost the laird many a fine brace of birds.

However, they always acted honourably and only organized these forays when we were all virtually starving; this being more often than not, as Granny Morag never knew when to stop buying liquids and start buying solids. So it happened that, when we were penniless, we thrived on delicacies we should never have tasted otherwise; game soup, grouse, ptarmigan, snipe, plover's eggs and, rarely, mutton. Our kitchen was a Ritz of smells.

Robbie beag was a past master at catching sheep, a skill he never bragged about, and his method was pure athletics. When his quarry chewed its way over the brow of a hill, he simply discarded shoes, socks and trousers, wriggled into a suitable position and started running. The sheep, seeing a silent man in underpants hurtling towards it, would run, too; down the hill. The race was invariably won by our uncle. He swiftly cut its throat, recovered his clothes and lugged the prize away with Uncle Angus. Sometimes they hid it under a bush for the night, but usually it was brought straight to the cottage.

Granny Morag, wakened by the tapping on the window, would let them in and the three would sit up all night skinning and chopping the mutton. By the morning, the kitchen was in its natural clean confusion, but the cask at the back of the washhouse was gorged with salt meat. Some time later, Robbie beag would present us with a brand new sheepskin blanket.

'Now, for why should a body wi' a great flock miss one wee, sma' lambie?' he would ask and we never thought to tell him, when our stomachs were stuffed for many weeks through his innocence.

Our uncles brought home other spoil as well; eagles' eggs, baby weasels, a dead adder which we skinned and, once, a cast antler. All priceless treasures to us children.

Years later, when Lachlan went to work in the slaughterhouse and the need for their poaching was no more, the two drifted apart. Uncle Angus retired and Robbie beag was left to carry on his unconventional hobbies alone. But it had been a fine partnership.

The sea changed at the end of my first summer with her. Her colours submerged under a leaden coat and everything around turned grey. Golden plover fled from the moors as silver, speckled ones flew in. Dun, hooded crows mysteriously deserted the woods for the shore and seized winkles, crabs and fish from the sombre rocks. Pearly moths flittered round silvery hair grasses and even the sand seemed like ash. I would sit, cowled by this cloud, for hours, and yet it was not depressing; only soporific.

She was resting before her winter passion and I drowsed in her lap. Throughout the long months of the sun she had shown herself to me, a little and a little. She had answered all my thoughts and taught me urgently. Now we were both tired and she sang me a soft grey lullaby.

From the moment I tumbled over that bank of reeds I had become one of her floating islets, isolated and detached even from the delta of my family. I had been brushed by the paint of solitude which never wears off and I grew apart.

The sea-serpent had perished in the lobby and the kitchen had concentrated into a small square jumble. I could dress now and open the bread bin and leave the cottage before anyone else was awake. I could lift once riveted rocks easily and build miniature crofts of my own. Fish had convulsed and died in front of me and a ewe had dropped a lamb.

I spoke the strange, literal poetry of young children.

'Granny Morag, look, the washing's cryin' on the line.'

'The birds are waving tae me.'

The baby love, welling on a full stomach, had gone and was replaced only by tolerance and liking. People were no longer indispensable; but they were intriguing and slowly I had learned how to play one against another and how to charm my will past them.

If I listened carefully as they spoke, complete phrases lingered on in the mind to be produced later for effect.

'Annie's a limmer,' said, suddenly, over a bowl of broth brought a salute of laughter and probably an extra humbug after dinner.

'Auntie Annie says ye're an auld cow,' whispered in Granny Morag's ear, decided a prime row.

I grew crafty and persuasive and sly. I watched their eyes marbling with reveries and strove capriciously to change their expressions. I was touching power for the first time.

With my brothers and sisters, however, there could be no such subtlety. They were too close to me and too sceptical to be fooled and we jostled together, casually and harshly primitive, encouraged by our Granny Morag.

'Whit did he hit ye for?'

'I said he was having a snotty nose.'

'Well, be hitting him back then, instead o' greetin' and, Calum, wipe yis nose!'

So I hit Calum and, after the battle, he smeared his nose along his sleeve, or picked it with a blunt, grimy finger. We scratched and crunched and belched and pulled at scabs automatically, and Lachlan was excessively proud of being able to spit from one side of the track to the other.

It was achievements like this, meaningless to adults, which were essential to each child, if he wanted his existence recognized by the others. So I practised winking for months, until I could flick either eyelid perfectly on an otherwise impassive face. When I could alternate them at speed, I had not just performed a clever trick, I had passed a vital test. Being able to waggle one's ears and slide one's scalp over the skull, to and fro, were every bit as important.

We had rituals, quite separate from adult superstitions, which we believed ensured our survival. The girls bobbed curtsies and the boys bent their heads to the lone cypress tree, which poised gauntly on the cliff edge. It would have killed us otherwise. We touched the old goat each day for luck, maybe because her white hair and pink eyes seemed magical and we dared not offend her. We clutched on to our collars and kept our fingers crossed for hours of dread if we saw a blue hare, which was really a witch in disguise, and even when I was alone for days, I obeyed these laws of youth.

Of the world outside the family I knew nothing. True, there was talk of 'the village', but that was three miles away. Although nearly six years old, I had never seen a shop, or a church, or processions of houses, or a harbour. This 'village' must have been an immense, warren-like cottage, full of rooms which housed the postman, Mary Neilson, Bauchie Nell the fishwife, Mrs. Mackenzie surrounded by her cupboards of shop, disagreeable old dominie who ran the school, and many others. In all my explorations, I had never been attracted to the village. It was too alien; but my enisled life was nearly over.

Little by little the dusk snipped sparks off the days and decay on the forest floor nursed forth a yield of toadstools; innocent-looking Death Caps, slender Inky Caps, scarlet and white Agaric and puffy Earth Stars. Thorny brambles, crawling over ditch and dyke, dropped rich black kisses into our palms. The hares of the mountain changed their grey coats for white and waited for the snows. And, as beaters flurried the game on the moor, the outsiders began to converge on me.

When I went down to the sea one morning, a stranger was there. He sat, knee-gaped in a wind break, smoking a pipe through sweeping whispers.

'Good morning, young man.' His voice shocked me to a halt. It was unlike anything I had ever heard and I looked at his florid face, doubtfully.

'I said good morning,' he repeated, shaping white eggs of sound, identical and indistinguishable.

'Eh?' I said.

'Good morning!'. The man looked irritated, but this time I heard.

'Morning,' I said and began to move away.

'I haven't seen you before,' he continued, loudly. 'What's your name?'

'Eh?'

He enunciated each syllable slowly again and I picked up the last word.

'Micheil,' I answered, suspiciously. 'What's yours?'

'I am your laird.'

So this was the laird, the Sassenach whose name drew acetous comments from Granny Morag. He was wearing brown plus-fours and the look of a man who had just made an impression. I did not like him either.

'Granny Morag says I'm the laird's son's son.' It was a polite attempt at conversation, but I might as well have fired an airgun at his backside. His eyes bulged like pale gallstones. His jowls quivered and flushed, sorrel as one of his own setters, and he lurched down on my neck with a heavy, splayed hand.

'What did you say, you guttersnipe?'

He shook me till the sand and the sea and the sky shimmied into rainbows.

'. . . the l-l-laird's s-son's son.'

He bellowed and ovoid words fell, like blind, curled hedge-hogs, round my ears.

'You insolent puppy! You lying brat! Take me to your mother! I suppose she sent you here, you snivelling mongrel. Where do you live? I'll put a stop to these bloody lies, if I have to break her neck. Take me to your mother!'

He stopped and laboured for breath, almost black with choler and I twisted away from his hold. My face blundered into his hand and my teeth seized a lump of flesh. It was thick and rubbery and, though I gripped till my head almost burst with pressure, the skin would not break. At last, he flung me off and I ran screaming into the dunes.

There I hid, choking on gulps of terror, till he had gone and I could whimper back to the shelter of the kitchen.

The whole incident was inexplicable to me, but not to Granny Morag and Auntie Annie. United for once, they spun into twin tempers and fluently cursed the laird and all his issue (bar me) into obliteration.

'His own grandson! Did ye ever hear the like?'

'Aye, but his time's not far off. He'll be going doon in fire and water.'

'Burning and flood and the grand hoose wi' him.'

'Aye, and his fine wife and . . .'

'Jist a few wee ashes left and the wind'll soon be blawing them awa'.'

'His fine son. Him that was casting toil on poor Mairi . . .'

'And the wee lambie here.'

Auntie Annie's cheeks were hemmed with tears and Granny Morag crashed her pots and dishes as they intoned their high, almost religious-sounding responses.

'Jesus, I'll be tearing him up in sma' pieces when he comes by the door.'

'The heavens'll open and billin' water poured ower his head.'

'He's no workin' man.' Granny Morag, a strong Socialist, rejected anyone not sporting a cloth cap.

'The black fiend of evil!'

'The fat Sassenach bastard!'

But, though the laird never came by the door to reap his fate, he discovered where I lived and, all at once, the authorities were watching us all.

First, there was trouble over Lachlan and Bella playing truant. Then Robbie beag and Uncle Angus were forced to go canny on the poaching. Calum was caught stealing chickens' eggs and there were insistent demands that I should be educated.

Granny Morag fought with customary fanaticism; denouncing the school and dominie, abusing all gillies and taunting the only policeman by loudly airing her grievances over droppies of Scotch in the pub.

But one night she did not return, though we waited and waited. Such a thing had never happened before and we waited till the range embered out and the night wind rose. The food stayed raw and Auntie Annie rocked and moaned.

'Mither Mither! Whit can have happened? Half after nine and no yet home. They'll have dropped her over the harbour wall. Poor, defenceless old woman. She wis aye tae brave fer them. Ah loonies and quinies, remember yis Granny Morag. She aye had the courage . . . Murder! That's whit it would be. A poor, defenceless old woman.'

We even began to agree with her and, early in the morning, went stern-faced and scared to bed.

Premonitions of disaster lay cumbersome and chill on my stomach and my heart beat misery in my throat. I grew older as the snows fell that night.

CHAPTER THREE

DEMONS AND DOMINIE

NEWS arrived at daybreak with Bauchie Nell, the fishwife. She crowed it triumphantly over her creel, then fled away down the track under a shower of stones. She left a backwash of fallen fish and Auntie Annie was not too angry to have them picked up.

We muddled shapelessly from bed and, still dressing, followed the old woman towards the village. Breathless and bloated faced we arrived where the streets were instantly smooth and the severe purity of the hills suddenly smudged by jostling houses.

And we ran on, clatter, clatter, past eyes and noses and mouths twitchingly set in peculiar, unknown patterns; people I did not know, pushing carts, fluttering curtains, slamming doors, shaking rugs and aprons and heads, all prim and curious with tight-lipped stares.

At last, we stopped at a door and knocked. 'She's gone,' said the woman. 'Ten minutes past.'

Clatter, clatter, on again down the main street and by the harbour; jungle of boats and sheds, sequinned with fish scales, smelling of death. Up, climbing above the water to where the cottages bowled by like white marbles.

Then, all at once, we saw them, walking together along the dusty road.

'Granny! Granny! Granny Morag!'

She turned her head, but still walked on with him and did not stop.

We caught them in a panting mass.

'Where are ye goin'?'

'Whit's happened?'

'Wait, Granny! Wait!'

She just shook her head and stuck out her chin and we fell back.

36

Then we saw a terrible thing. Our Granny Morag was fettered to the man by an iron wristband and chain.

'Whaur's he takin' her, Lachie?' My stomach fizzled with fear. 'Why're they wearing yon bangles?'

'That's the poliss,' Lachlan muttered, hoarsely. 'That's whit they dae tae *prisoners*.'

We all stood in the road, a bundle of embarrassment, watching them walking away.

'Will she no come back ever?' asked Catrina and, not waiting for a reply, started her piercing scream.

'Stop till I tell them,' said Granny Morag to her captor. 'Stop for the bairns.'

We circled her again like swarming bees.

'It's tae the station I'm going with the polissman here. We're tae be having a special reserved carriage fer usselves only, all the way tae Dornoch,' she laughed over us. 'Like a grand lady travels and the same this night for the return. That's correct, isn't it?' She looked commandingly at the fat man.

'Aye,' he agreed, sourly.

'Now, Lachie, ye're tae be at the bobby's house at half after six fer certain and carry word frae me tae Auntie Annie . . .'

'Wid ye be trying tae miss the train, woman?' the policeman growled.

'Och, not at all, not at all.' She might have been answering a very small boy and, as they left, I heard her again.

'Ye ken, Mr. Duff, ye worry aye much fer sic a young lad. Now, I've always found mysel' that there's nothing like a wee bottlie or two fer setting the heart at peace. Wid ye not agree?'

I did not hear the reply, but Police Constable Duff was not a drinking man.

We dawdled back, trailing our shoes through the grass and wondering.

At the first group of cottages two women stood, arms folded, at their doors.

'Drunken at the harbour, she was.'

'Hurling fish at the poliss frae the sheds.'

'Whit a disgrace!'

Their lapping chins quivered indignantly as we came by.

'The destruction of the transgressors and of the sinners shall be

together, and they that forsake the Lord shall be con-
sumed . . .'

'. . . In everlasting fire. Isaiah One, Verse Twenty-Eight,
Amen.'

In the harbour below I saw with milky surprise boats, cottages
and fishing sheds bouncing on the waves like Hallowe'en apples
in a water butt. Men spilled the silver of the night over the
cobblestones, while their women knelt to fill rush baskets to the
rim. Nets heaped together like eagles' nests and trawl lines wealed
the harbour wall. Tackle and dead jellyfish, old men and drifters,
sweat and chilled sun rhymed with the sea at this early morning
time.

A knot of children came warily up the brae. They hinted of
face flannels and watery combs and, even to my vacant eyes, their
glassy boots looked queer. These were no urchins of the hills. But
I had other problems.

Like a grand lady travels, she had said; but Granny Morag
wasn't grand. She was thinner than Auntie Annie, so why would
they be putting her with the fat ones? Prisoner, Lachie had said.
I didn't like the sound of that.

'Bella, why . . .?'

'Fishers loons,' hissed Lachlan and suddenly it was too late to
ask, for they were hooching down the hill and I could only
follow.

Handfuls of earth from a roadside garden, whoops of excitement and yelps of pain and the ancient strife between highland
and plain drummed out again with lust. Bella was swinging on a
fishergirl's plaits. Calum was shredding a lad's hairy jacket and
Lachlan, pounding away like an engine, surfaced and dived
through a mess of limbs.

Catrina screeched me off the sidelines as a flabby opponent
shoved her face in the hedge and I kicked at a pair of thick
ankles, then hunched my shoulders for the blow. To my astonishment, the big girl turned and burst into barks of raucous sobs
and the cottage door opened quickly behind her.

'The wifie. The wifie.' Within seconds the street was empty
and the shindy over.

On the safe side of a corner, Lachlan stopped.

'Dinna dae that again,' he said to me.

'Ay?'

'Ye dinna fight wi' the lasses, man,' he went on, contemptuously.

'But I'm aye fighting wi' Catrina and Bella.'

'They're no lassies. They're yis sisters, ye daft loon.'

So my first battle was dishonourably victorious, but everyone felt very refreshed and charged with new power. Had it not been so, we would never have gone near the railings.

The yard inside was a shaking kaleidoscope of children patterning the concrete playground and the grey stone school stood stolidly behind them.

'Hey, Lachie!' a boy called from above. 'I saw yis granny the night past, down by the sheds peltin' fish at the poliss.'

'Aye,' agreed Lachlan, stoically. 'She's frae Dornoch Court the day.'

'Man, whit a grand sight. The bobby a' smeary wi' guts and stink and the fishers folk shoutin' her tae stop. She wis singing! Dancing wi' armfu's o' fish and singing right enough.'

And he echoed like a shrill bird:

> 'They say the laird's a dandy lad
> And so's the braw young master,
> But the laird's fine ma didna wed his da,
> So I'm thinking he's a bastard.'

The tale of our grandmother's performance unrolled to the accompaniment of her now notorious song, sung to the tune of 'The Piper o' Dundee'. It was a tale which led from hostelry to herring shack, along a trail where streetlamps were smashed and ribaldry shouted and the worthy Mrs. Neilson received a black eye; where the one village policeman, a staunch lad who was only doing his duty, was rendered so distressingly fetid that his own wife would not allow him to re-enter his own house.

'Then whit happened?' asked Bella, never satisfied.

'I dinna ken, for my Mam took me home,' said the boy and his choirboy treble soared again.

Suddenly, he fell off the rail with a squeal and we saw behind him the skull of the dominie.

'Run,' cried Lachlan, but it was too late. The dominie, like an upright snake, struck through the gate and caught him. Without a leader we were lost.

'Well, well, well, the school is honoured that this collection of insurgents should return in such eager search of knowledge.' The soft voice sounded almost friendly and the eyes in sallow sockets glittered over us. 'What? All here?'

'Yessir.' Lachlan wriggled under the bony grip.

'A miracle, no less.' The dominie swayed on his heels, his black gown arching behind him in the wind, like devils' wings. 'And this? What is this?'

I was seized from Catrina's shadow and held aloft for scrutiny.

'That's Micheil, sir, our wee'n.' Even Bella's voice trembled.

'Another! Is there no mercy!' Jaundiced lids closed over the learned eyes for a moment and the dominie sighed. 'However, *non omnis moriar*. No doubt you will regretfully agree, Lachlan?'

'Sir!'

'You imbecile!' roared Sir. 'Translate!'

My brother answered very slowly, 'You will soon be dying, sir.' And Calum and my sisters looked up with sudden interest.

'You illiterate moron!' The nostrils of the dominie flared as he pulled each of us through the gate and clanged it shut.

'I shall *not altogether* die. In fact, I shall have the pleasure of strapping the entire Sinclair family in ten minutes.' With that he rose into the air before my eyes, flew away across the playground and into the school.

We followed him in sullen, silent submission.

From the window in the narrow corridor, the railings looked endless and, beyond them, my own wherry of liberty was adrift, wavering away on the white sea mist; and it never came back again.

Lachlan and Calum and Bella and Catrina lined up with arms outstretched and pink palms up. Three strappings each by the dominie, maliciously dignified: Lachlan airy, Calum expressionless, Bella resentful and Catrina weeping. Over and forgotten soon, because it was due. Besides, our Granny Morag hit much harder with her bare hand.

A gaunt woman took me to a classroom packed with eyes,

hoops of curiosity which rolled after us as I was led and moulded to a desk. Before long, the air became floury with chalk and chants, like pendulums, nodded me though curtains of interest and distraction, doubt and boredom to a rosy alcove of sleep.

And my grandmother fandangoed with the dominie in that first hour at school and the flabby fishers' girl ate raw fish, like a seal, while sitting on top of the blackboard and little did scrawny Miss Ogilvie know that she was sailing out of the harbour in a creel, just as she shook me awake.

The same sleepy stupidity was to screen me through all the class-bound years to come and, when at least I was released at fourteen, I could read and write and count; no more, but that was enough. With coercion gone, inquisitiveness returned.

Of my classmates, few were to use much schooling, and the mathematics, geography and Latin learnt so laboriously were soon lost for ever among the farms and animals and country tumble.

Yet, perhaps not all was wasted, for the dour, cynical discipline of the dominie prepared us well for the rigours of adult life. We did not collapse under its tests and injustices, because they came as no shock. We had already met them on a smaller scale at school, where most found a way to adjust.

So the first day ticked out numeral and alphabet, coloured bead and slate squeak, confusion and snigger under the wintry hands of Miss Ogilvie, till Granny Morag's case had been heard at Dornoch Court and Bauchie Nell had sold all her fish, till the church chimes and tea gongs and Big Ben of London town rang us back to timelessness. Till four o'clock, that magical hour when children are turned into crackles of leaves and bunches of balloons tugged free in a breeze and all race down to the harbour.

There the women tittle-tattled in a row, brown bosomed, bunned and belling with striped petticoats, waiting for their men to bring in the day's catch.

'Were ye hearing . . .?'

'Well I never!'

'Ye'll no believe it . . .'

'Did ye ever!'

While those with menfolk far away for another day or two, prattled more dizzily still, to cover their terror of the sea and hide their secret prayers.

We played tig round trestle tables in the sheds, slipped on severed fish heads, sat in ocean dross. We discovered a hundred hideouts and started a dozen new games. We skirmished a couple of times over territorial rights with the natives and, finally, were chased away by menacing Mams with bared teeth. But then it was time to go to the policehouse.

When we arrived, Robbie beag was already there and the policeman's wife trembled as she showed us into her front parlour where he sat.

'Get out,' he said, without looking up.

'But Granny Morag said . . .' Lachlan started.

Our Uncle Robbie beag gently picked up a china peke from the fireplace and pitched it like an expert. As it glanced off Lachlan's head and smashed against the door, we turned as one child and left.

Once safely in the passage, we scrummed past poor Mrs. Duff to the street and they exchanged appreciative shrugs.

While they debated the conflicting orders of grandparent and uncle, I was pulling faces at an old woman on a nearby doorstep, who peered at us from under a straw hat, ripe with artificial cherries. All at once, she scuttled into her house and, within seconds, a large cardboard notice appeared in one of its windows:

GET THEE BEHIND ME SATAN

It was then that we saw the prisoner stepping spryly up the street, with Constable Duff a weary trudge behind.

At once every house was chinked and cracked, and open-keyholed, twitter-curtained and I-spy-with-my-little-eye. Our grandmother, aware of every fidget, waved graciously to each and cruised on without pause.

We tucked round the side of the policehouse and listened.

'How much, Constable?' said Robbie beag, softly turning the title into an obscenity.

'Five shillings fine, five shillings damages,' replied the police-man, bitterly. 'And the fare.'

Coins clinked and Robbie beag left without a backward glance. He was rock-faced with rage and Granny Morag, abashed for once, meekly crossed the road behind him.

There, in the cottage window, we could see the cherries boggl-ing excitedly above the talismanic edict. Through the still-open door a congregation of texts gloated on the walls and, with treacherous silence, Robbie beag sprang inside.

In a moment, his twisted face appeared beside the fruit and he gave an infernal roar which wailed and hung, shaking the coffins of the righteous across half Scotland and bulleting the old woman across her room. Dumb with terror, but still clutching her sprouting bonnet, she began insanely to climb the wall as our uncle advanced. He crooked his fingers against his head and turned the roar into a snarl, inspired by old Nick himself. Then, laughing with villainous melodrama, suddenly danced wildly backwards into the street.

Granny Morag's delighted cackle filled the air as she fell on him, boxing his ears adoringly, and, when we jumbled from our hideout, they pulled us into a crazy song-and-dance team and bantered triumphantly home to Annie.

The combined force of Robbie beag's authority and our Aunt Annie's howls that night undoubtedly persuaded Granny Morag to mend our ways. Certainly the return from Dornoch Court began her crusade for regular schooling, which she was to resume spasmodically over the years, following each masterstroke of delinquency. Sending the bairns to school became atonement for her own frailties and, when we grew too old for this, she transferred her conscience easily on to Uncle Angus and sacrificed him to the bath.

It was at the beginning of this penance by proxy that I remem-ber waking up for the first time. Before then, no one actually awoke. We had simply stopped sleeping when the light brought sight.

Now the act of waking became earnest and we schemed and wriggled to escape; pulling our heads back into the indulgent smell of the night beneath the covers and their safe cocoon of dark, muzzily shrinking from the terrible daily choice between her hot bread and poultice and the dominie's institution. Was it worth playing sick? Morning pinpricked relentlessly through the blankets, the seconds pierced with disjointed panics. And, as her footsteps clicked in the lobby, we drivelled over which of us would be kept at home to help.

Was it Monday, Lachlan's day to hump water for Tuesday's washing and Bella's day? Was it my middle day to run errands? Had Miss Ogilvie found the scrawl on the wall? It couldn't be Saturday. My thoughts staggered drunkenly into a delirium of excuses and improbable plots.

Sometimes, they would drag me up and through all the slow frustration of buttons and sleeves and into a kitchen of scalding porridge and freezing milk before Granny Morag shattered the fantasy by pulling me brutally from bed.

She was Amazonian at daybreak, plundering our blankets and biting our dreams in half with her harsh voice. The soaking cloth in her hand fired icy drops recklessly with each swing of her arms and finally slapped like a wet haddock across Calum's defenceless buttocks, because he was always last to wake and because his nightshirt slid up to his armpits in the night.

She was supposed to have a bed in the back room, but we had never seen her sleep in it and I didn't believe she slept at all, just stayed awake all night thinking up new tortures to inflict on us at dawn. She raged with such relish.

The gall one felt at sun-up habitually bore out these suspicions. She wasn't one of us at all, that's why she never slept. Probably the real Granny Morag had been snatched away as a wee'n and this old harpy put in her place.

I glowered daily at the others drooping over the table; Lachlan spirtling the slop noisily round his teeth. Calum chewing and smiling and chewing, Bella gulping and Catrina pouring her bowl of milk over her porridge and mechanically stirring it into a grey mush. And they looked back at me in docile dislike.

Spoonful by spoonful, I became aware that they were all usurpers and I was the only mortal, just waiting for the power to unmask them and take revenge. They burnt witches in England, I remembered and malevolently tied my family's future to the stake.

'Will ye stop that loitering and get oot o' here, ye brainless lummock.' It was Herself ranting again, but the crack of her wooden spoon on my skull only hardened my beliefs and images of English flames were comfort all the way to school.

Even now, each morning arrives as a merciless conspiracy against me and I never wake without that old childhood feeling of being the only human in a world of monsters.

Miss Ogilvie viewed me, as she viewed all her pupils, with enduring distaste and a strong sense of duty. Children, with their dirt and snivelling, their clumsiness and giggling, were obviously germs in need of a lethal disinfectant. Unfortunately, our teacher had to find what satisfaction she could out of being a good detergent.

She was the colour of a London smog and years of indigestion and suppressed disgust had clamped her nostrils together, breaking most of the blood vessels on her nose. It shone unfairly heliotrope, although she never touched a drop. A few curls were hourly kneaded into a bun and defeated by a scaffolding of pins and we infants knew she was more than a hundred years old. Strangely enough, when we officially left school she looked no younger.

For twelve months Miss Ogilvie scoured at our sinfulness with hard work and God, correcting our ignorance with a pointer and answering all misunderstandings with the strap. Yet it was not the punishment which frightened me. It was her complete lack of emotion.

'Three errors, Micheil. Hold out your hand,' she would say, handing back my slate and picking up the tawse with precise dispassion.

Perhaps she strapped a little harder because I wore Calum's old clothes and small boys in saggy breeks were particularly offensive; perhaps not. But her expression remained one of sealed indifference and it paralysed me with the kind of fear that crushes rabbits under racing wheels. Granny Morag's scarlet shrieks and wild-cat face seemed loving in comparison. What were they but the first breath I'd gasped and the first sound I'd howled, as natural as life itself; and, beneath Miss Ogilvie's tissued eyes, I used to long for some reassuring wrath.

But her crowning accomplishment and, I think, her single

pleasure, too, was an ability to impale humanity with a look. She could fossilize a child from fifty yards and pole-axe local adults at as many paces. Even the dominie hesitated when she turned and the laird himself was never so effective.

Beyond this first waited a number of teachers, like post-office sorters, who stamped us with their individual dyes before delivering us up to the last room in the corridor, where the dominie rejected every one. They governed square buff and bilious-green islands in which earth's elements were denied and the only climate, too hot or too cold, was the temper which was not sparing the rod that year.

They taught us through rhythms of repetition and fear. Yet the lessons were engraved on our brains for ever more: A B C, 1 2 3, *amo, amas, amat*. Never use a preposition to end a sentence with. You could snap your fingers and tap your feet to the jazz of those schooldays when Bonnie Prince Charlie was Scotland's pure hero, with no one to mention that he died of drink, and Mary was our Martyr Queen, although she never bothered to learn our language, and Robert the Bruce provided the true example of Scottish perseverance. Who knew then that his blood was Norman and that the only real Scot was his spider?

They taught the girls to knit and the boys simple woodwork. We learnt at last why the English were wicked and that there were Presbyterians and Catholics. All those who were not Catholics, were Presbyterians, and all fisherfolk were Catholics. We did not like each other and the little Catholic church, which stood back off the harbour road, was the spring of wickedness to me then.

The few descriptions of hell I'd heard tangled with my Aunt Annie's solstitial yarns of sorcery as I scampered past it in my infancy. Behind the studded wooden doors were creatures with claws, faces like apes and snakes for tails, who scratched and lashed at any Presbyterian who rashly strayed near. There was heat, which scorched the hair off your head and the skin from your bones, and things called brimstones, huge bitter pills which you swallowed till they tore your stomach open. The Devil himself lived in there, stupendous on a throne of fire, laughing as babies were shovelled into his mouth.

As I grew older, I began to pause opposite the place, daring myself to creep up and look through its narrow, stained windows. By then, the monkey faces and fiends had gone and the Devil had exchanged his blazing volcano for the sinister blackness of the cloth. In there now was a cage of lions, which the priest fed with Presbyterians shanghaied in the night. He smiled at me one day and I bolted away, but wished I was a Catholic so that I could see the beasts.

It was later still that I longed to trespass in the first rutting days of my youth, for there, in the Catholic church, I knew, were nuns, naked beneath their dark habits, who locked Presbyterian boys in stone dungeons and raped them every night.

When I finally went into the little church, many, many years later, its ordinariness came as a relief, but faintly mixed with disappointment.

In the village school were boys with ears like teapot handles and minds like poster paints, with square heads and pithy tongues; boys, who wrote 'shit' on walls and faced scrutiny like cherubs; thin boys, who blew stinging peas through toothless gaps, and a fat boy with six toes on each foot. Squabby, stumpy, squiffy boys, who smacked of other tribes and one skirted stiffly round them at first, because they were not brothers.

Until one of Bug Renwick's nits came home with me and Dug Sauchan's squint became merely a weapon to taunt him with and Cracked Bill thieved a comic and Warty Walter's growths were eclipsed by their own permanence and I could tell which Sturrocks twin was which.

Smoke-rings from cinnamon sticks puffed secretly in the lavvy link us together and we gang to a corner of the playground, aimlessly kicking the wall, or at a football earnestly.

'Goal!'

'It's never!'

'Y'is aff side.'

'I wisna'!'

The minutes are stuffed with invented squalls and swift, white-hot clashes make our mouths taste of salt. The little girls walk by, self-consciously; there for us to heckle and we do, watching their shocked faces as they bustle away. The pretty ones turn up disdainful noses and walk by again tomorrow, but Cracked Bill is hit by a plain one and we all swagger and nudge over our own daring.

In class we drowned, groaning, together in incomprehensible facts, or crowed silent spite at each other's blunders. When one was sent to stand behind the blackboard, the rest writhed with damned-up mirth, till our turns came and each sensed the ridicule behind him and the embarrassment twitching at his calves.

We would meet later as men and distrust the alien traits again, but, as boys, we were clanned by our stars. Two years ahead stood our perpetual superiors and those two years behind were ignored. I suppose we were intolerant, but our memories were short. We were certainly more cruel, but it was easy to call 'barley's' and in our world of swank and guile and whoppers and cheek there were no real Judases.

The sky pressed against the high windows and the shifting landscape pushed at the walls. There were forests of fortune waiting outside and the sweet air from the pines slipped by the teacher's guard to fill our heads with whispers of adventure.

I knew the locked shed on Gregson's boundary was a treasury of toys, with skittles and footballs, claymores and shields, boxing-gloves like the ones Jack Dempsey wore, bows and arrows and a chieftain's feather headdress hilled in its corners. And, against the centre wall leaned a bicycle, black and silver, with hardly a scratch on it. My belief in the shed was absolute. It had been padlocked for the war they kept talking about and, by the time that had ended, before I was born, no one could find the key. But I would find it. Visions of new hunting grounds drifted across the arid day, until an hour at school seemed slower than Hogmanay eve.

'Are you not writing, Micheil?' The words plash as softly as sulphur bubbles.

'Eh? Yes, Miss, of course, Miss.'

She comes my way between the desks. Fleshy, edgy and agile this year, and the class rests, smugly.

'What are you writing, Micheil?' Behind her the chalk copperplate blurs on the board and becomes a cotton wool wad in my brain.

'Well, boy?'

'Mmm . . .' Sudden frazzle of words. 'Culloden, Miss. We've tae do an essay on Culloden.' She turns away to rap Bess Piercy across the knuckles, and we slump back again to plots of scape.

It was the Sturrock twins who spent a whole morning break rubbing their cheeks with rough bits of towel, till they looked like peeled tomatoes. When the bell went, they were sent straight home and old Doc Fergus diagnosed an exotic disease which kept them off school for a week. They basked in our reverence for ever.

My own brainstorm was to scar me for life, when I sucked my arm till blood erupted like a jet of oil and spattered the floor with rust. It was a display which impressed even me and the other children oohed with awe, convinced I'd burst an artery. In the lightning glory I saw myself driven home in the doctor's trap to die with wan grace in Granny Morag's arms. Lachlan, Calum, Bella and Catrina wept by my coffin in the churchyard and Auntie Annie, festooned in mourning weeds, flung herself inconsolably into the grave, where they buried us together.

When the dominie arrived, he agreed it was a boil and Miss Ogilvie provided the plaster.

Humourless, sad little grannie house of women without poetry, and a discarded scholar, yellowing like an unread book. Spirits, lamed through lack of rhapsody, hiding from fables to be frightened by shadows. They explained away rainbows and denied the crocks of gold. Decaying dominie soured by realism, crabbed Miss Ogilvie trying to live without moonshine: we passed through their retreat, where thick walls stopped the heavens, and were too callow to care. They taught us without joy, which seemed the natural order of things and, if they unwittingly fed us poison sometimes, the narcissism of youth protected us.

'So my intellectuals are finally forsaking me, determined no doubt to spread culture to the rest of Man without a sciolism of erudition between them.' It was his parting remark. 'What shall I do without you?'

Unhappy dominie. He stirred our pity at last, for beyond the school railings a whole world waited and our dreams were still intact.

CHAPTER FOUR

TINKERS OVER THE WALL

THE cottage next to ours was delapidated. It housed a
rusting plough, an old pony harness and the glass remnants of a
hundred nights' drinking. Moss dozed on its damp walls like
small green hedgehogs, and spiders had fixed thick flexes of black
web to the ceiling. It was a place we enjoyed for its debris of finds
and eery decay.

In the early winter its tenants arrived with shouts and neigh-
ing, bleating and cursing and ferment. Men, urgent with quick
blood, and their women, sluttishly primitive. Bottles exploded
against the wall, rangy dogs attacked the goat and a shipful of
noise was suddenly beached at our door. They were a dirty,
savage people, whose brood looked out through secret eyes and the
wraiths of the ruin were routed in a trice by sheer, ugly life.

They came in the evening, riding carts top-heavy with the
pickings of endless migration; iron pots and orange boxes, a bird-
cage and mouldering shoes, abstracts of coloured rags, half a
bike and an old chair. Soon ponies, hobbled at the fetlocks, were
stumbling about in exploration, while smoke from the fire on the
kitchen floor recoiled through shattered windows and hung
gauze curtains down the walls. A dust of children blew over the
grass.

'The tinkers,' rejoiced Granny Morag, and our Auntie Annie
groaned.

They came for shelter every year, the Foleys, the MacGregors
and the MacPhees. Summer rolling tumbleweed across the north,
winter in the old, cold cottage; this was their calendar. Clothes-
pegs, farmwork and thieving; these were their living.

To us, they were bards bringing tales of fantastic lands beyond
the mountains and mesmerizing us with wisdom. Their eyes were
burnished by the light of great lochs and their feet had walked
through cities where all the houses were higher than the laird's

mansion and the rich drove round in carriages bigger than the local hearse. Their voices were winnowed from a dozen counties and they had passed the castle where the King and Queen lived. There were places, so they said, where there wasn't any sea; but it was the ease with which they said it which impressed us most of all. They were sophisticated and they had been to Aberdeen.

Oh, the coming and going of it all after they arrived, with the women in a fine bustle of borrowing and lending and our excited grandmother handing out 'wee presents' from her flask to all but the babies. To and fro, swopping prizes for booty and spoils for treasure till we all felt swollen as pawnbrokers and the tinker bairns' scorn leaked out in happy sneers. Who else but a tribe of greenhorns would have bartered gold for glass beads? And, back in the cottage, rubbing our hands, we were thinking the same of them.

They were the inventors of disorder with the whole world as their untidy palace, spotted with ashes from discarded nights. They moved in a confusion of children, who were everyone's children, and women, who were mothers of all. They carried no papers and signed no census and officialdom turned away with a shudder as they bumbled by.

Only the Church, drawing on nearly two thousand years of patience continued to worry over their abnormity, for the Catholic tinkers remained untouched by marriage rites. They greeted the local Father with regular subservience and promises to mend the situation, but Bess stayed on with Tom Foley and Katra with Alan MacGregor and Moira with MacPhee; and the banns were never called. Each woman took her man's name and I hardly remember noticing that they weren't Presbyterians.

Yet there were weddings. The MacGregors were married one year, with three gaunt infants tussling at their feet and Katra's belly heavy below her breasts again; warm through her skirt for a child's cheek to press on and mine was held against it to feel the unborn kick.

Frost lay over the earth and halter bells clinked from the shadows where ponies nosed the grass. Through my sleep-sticky eyes the stars spread into yellow splashes on the sky and wind, grunting in the rubble, sucked up a confetti of litter to blow around our heads and in the dark we melted and crystallized as ghosts to each other. Alone, behind a lamp-lit window glass, our Auntie Annie mouthed damnation.

Katra stood in a corner of the ruin with the women about her, pulling trinkets from their secrecy of pockets and bosoms to dress her for the marriage. There were ribbons in her unbrushed hair, which she covered with a scarlet shawl, and someone had run rings of bangles up her arms. A brooch from Granny Morag was pinned at her throat and, when she laughed, it flickered different colours in the firelight, although two stones were missing.

Calum and I, with our eyes on Robbie beag, circled the men, warily. They were throwing coins on to the ground as wedding gifts and laughing, too. All baying voice and brawn and richly male. They seemed like giants to me, but Lachlan swaggered between them with irritating bounce, because he was nearly grown.

The man and the woman came together by the fire, where the smallest finger of his left hand was tied to the smallest finger of her right hand by a piece of string, and they were married.

Then, Tom Foley's melodian soughed its first chord for the wedded pair to begin the 'swaree', a gala of ragged dances, a lingering of our reels. Roll, shuffle, flounder, skip; feet over the mirthful earth. So the women grew giddy and pink and sapphire sparks flinted off the stone floor and the young were nudged gradually out in the air to play among themselves.

Lachlan joined sweating trials of strength, to lift the heaviest rock, to jump the highest bar, to wrestle another into a grovel, but all to catch Jeannie MacPhee's eye and to prove he was a man. Robbie beag revelled away on his own, bottle tilted to mouth and ale running down his neck with every jolt; while Calum and I and our kind spied, clambered, teased and sprang on girls' giggles gathered in the velvet alleys of the dark.

'More o' that and there'll be less of it.' Our Bella was pert by the cart and Barry Foley's voice quickly covered his hands till she squeaked again in pleased dismay. 'My, ye've got a cheek, ye've got a nerve.' And then they both saw us.

Under the wall, an acre away, Catrina was chirping in baby surprise, but the boy who had touched only stood back and grinned and her first vagrant look slid over him, for she was twelve.

Tin mugs of whisky heated by the fire and our Granny Morag grew bawdy in her cups till the gleam in her eyes shone young and young and the men at the wedding pushed their ways to her side. For the lads recognized and their fathers still fancied and the tales she was telling were gems of disgrace. So the retorts spat brine, like olives, and the cracks jabbed quick; the wine-like-scandals spilled deliciously and our grandmother trapped secrets in her slit black glance, then crowed shamelessly back into their hot faces.

And, when she lost interest in the men, she settled with Bessie flush in the smoke, where with tipsy relish they screeched ribaldry to each other with a rawness known only to women. Oh, the spice of her charm was timeless and she was cock-a-hoop this night.

Tom Foley's squint eye slid further and further into his head as he sweated music and there were songs I'd never heard before, which were not for family singing. We turned into puppets, with limbs jerked only by threads of early verse and eyelids burned open by the flames, till tempers were lost and tears came too fast.

'But I'm no weary . . . no, Granny, no-o-o-o.'

'Och, leave us a while, aw.'

For it was tantrum and pouting hour, time to whine our way home leaving the tinker loons still jigging. But, suddenly, our toes were tucked resentfully into our nightshirts and the sounds from next door were melting down our dreams like candle ends.

Weddings went on for a further day and night, times so long to me that they still seemed as vivid as yesterday. Other tinkers would arrive, from shelters on the far side of the village, carrying stories of friends and friends of friends, till the trickling news became a gabbled swill of interruptions.

'He was wanting a winter squat, so . . .'

'. . . the Craigs are away tae Glasgow, for permanent she said, but it'll no last . . .'

'Can I have a piece, Ma?'

'. . . he smashed the Sheriff's window in Aberdeen and made the jail . . .'

'Ma, can I have a piece?'

'Bonnie Aileen, the Nichol quinie ye mind, has taken hersel' a fancy at last.'

'. . . three months and out in March.'

'I was hearing . . .'

'A piece, Ma!'

'. . . and I sold the pony as a leaper, him that would jib at a blade of grass.'

'Ma!'

'Fer God's sake, give him a piece, woman!'

Tinker wee'ns slumbered in cosy heaps as they tired and big MacPhee snored on, unaware that two were pillowed on his bulging paunch.

Great clan wars were refought over the heather, in plaids and kilts of salvaged rags, and, all in a morning, I could be Rob Roy and Cameron of Locheil and the Stewart of Appin and Macbean of Kinchyle and Duncan.

Even our easy days seemed painfully squared against this drifting, schoolless freedom and, when the party was over, it took our aunt and grandmother a full week to deal out enough blows to bring us back to the shambling order of old.

As each summer cornered us tightly together, so each autumn set us free, with 'over the wall' as the pass phrase after the tinkers arrived. It was as though our own cottage tilted over each day and emptied us into theirs, where lifelong friendships and blood brotherhoods were sealed in minutes and lavishly tossed off for others within hours. There were plenty of tinks and plenty of us, so, for a few impetuous days, we could all afford to be extravagant.

It wasn't simply the novelty of having new neighbours which drew us out. It was the special pleasure of finding other people like ourselves in a village generally hostile. With their artless fancies and lawless ways, the tinkers came upon us like next of kin and, in our anxiety to escape the suffocation of each other, we forgot all other years.

The division between us, when it became obvious was always a shock, as though the whole fraternity had been a hoax and we'd been cunningly deceived by a band of frauds. There was no warning, just the rancid smell of hot cow horn making our Auntie Annie retch, as it did every morning, and sucking us towards the ruin, where the men moulded spoons to sell and the women were heating water in the boiler.

Perhaps there were thick oat bannocks for breakfast, to be eaten impatiently in the race to get out, and Uncle Angus's teeth would be an abandoned grin on the table as he softened the biscuits with bald gums.

Over the wall we could hear their daybreak of crying babies and fitful talk, a jabber of shouts and a flush of quiet as we were scraping back our chairs to leave. Granny Morag stood by the range with her first whisky-tea of the day, placidly warming her feet at the vent and apparently immersed in contented self-indulgence. That she spoke at all came as a surprise.

'But ye'll no be going tae the tinks the morn.' And we faltered at the table with mouths full of protest.

'But . . .'

'Whit?'

'Not the morn,' she repeated with bland decision and Auntie Annie edged in virtuously from the corner.

'Well, Mither, ye've taken long enough tae see the disgrace of mixing wi' pagans like yon. Wasn't I forever telling ye they're no fit fer human society.'

'Aye, Annie,' our grandmother nodded, amiably. 'And now I've no doubt ye'll find a use for the bairns, seeing ye've aye so much tae do.'

And, having treacherously sold us out to her daughter, she returned to the warmth with a benign little smile.

Over the wall the quiet changed to a strange, long silence which brought the drum of the sea to the door and made the reeking air more reasty. Gooseflesh crept at our necks and we tensed into statues of alarm without knowing why. High on the mantelshelf, seconds purled faintly from a hidden clock and the day waited to be wronged.

It was a cracked tongue of hate which tore us back to life, and, in the rush to the window, Granny Morag's fierce, 'Get yisselves ben the hoose!' faded into a futile whisper; for, over the wall, big Bess Foley stood in full-throated, inarticulate fury.

From their seats by the fire the men were watching carefully. The children had oozed away and, framed by the crumbling gap to the wash-house, Katra was an ominous mountain of threats. They shuddered darkly at each other, these women of mighty bosoms and shoulders like girders and heavy red arms, which could haul a laden cart or lift a calf from a field; these women of burden turned rabid with rage.

And Katra seized a hissing rope of cloth from the boiler and sent it seething across the raw air, and it trapped Bess Foley round the head with crucifying savagery and dashed into her face like a flameless torch, burning white hot forever through her skin. Pitilessly, the woman thrashed the woman who floundered and screamed, till the sheet became a living thing which lunged with a frenzy of its own and her face became a sadistic blaze and her face was a furnace of terror.

The men had filtered beyond the walls when Bess was driven against the fire, deformed into grotesque blubber by her agony, clawing hideously at the logs. And, as we flinched and cried at our window, she reached the black pot of waxing horn; she flung the black pot of spitting horn and, with its crash, foul, hungry blisters spewed over Katra's bare feet. Unbearable screams of pain as they, locked closer than lovers, became a heaving female pulp, where tortured hand gripped bulging neck and eye looked bleeding through the hair and only these poor fragments showed that humanity was there.

Terrible beyond expression: the whole valley seemed tempered in horror; and only tears moved.

Lurching, stumbling, tottering shambles. The winding sheet brought them down at last, still clasping each other with feeble fingers, struggling slackly to dredge up breath. Slower and slower, mauled to a quiver, weaker than ewes top heavy with fleece, whimpering as they crawled away.

We were all sobbing when I looked round, and pleading at Granny Morag's skirts. But she wept, too, mutely ashamed, and stroked our heads with helpless hands because we had seen the squalor of things and were her innocent bairns.

'That's not the way it is,' she said, and she said it every year.

Sometimes it was a fight between men stripped to the waist and hobnailed with boots, which shocked us into hiding for days. Because, whatever the crisis, the same electric brutality was there, lighting up the difference between us and, when it was over, we kept to our cottage and dared not even look out at theirs.

It was bewildering for a while, a riddle to brood over when one was alone and never find an answer, for we lived in a circle of warmth and the tinkers lived in a jungle. Harried by law and shunned by folk and punished by the elements from the day they were born, their need to keep moving had made them outsiders and the world of the outlaw is a merciless world.

My brothers and sisters straggled back, warily, one by one, missing the old jantying and hanging about and I went, too, but with new spiky senses which rubbed on edges I'd overlooked before.

There was a famine about the place. It was the kempt on threadbare trousers and the unstitching of worn shoes. It was unwashed bodies and diarrhoea in the sand and mildewed mattresses bulbous on the floor. The foxy look on children's faces was its mask and, when they cried for food, it was the bottle of stout which made them quiet again.

Babies died quite often over the wall.

'Oh the wee'n, Holy Mother. Oh my babbie.'

Cries, keen as songs, spreading slivers of primeval pain and tears of dear pity among the women. Even we children felt the instinct to be kind and stopped playing to look for a minute, soft and uncomprehending as cows. How suddenly frail the big, strong mother seemed, wandering bewildered round the cottage, blinded by the little grave, lonely as an orphan.

'Spare the wee mite, Mother of God. Oh my wee'n. Oh my babbie.' It had happened before and would happen again, but each time was a reachless sorrow.

Buried the same day, brisk and practical, and mourned a few hours more with classical wailing and gestures of grief; perhaps remembered later in solemn, half-proud tones. Death was no novelty.

Babies were born regularly, too, and the living babies worked. Moira and Bess and Katra shawled their youngest to their backs and took them begging in the bleakest weather. It was only common sense when people who would give nothing but lectures to a tinker on her own, pressed food and maybe money on to one with a wee'n.

In fact, the women toiled hard, hawking the few odds and ends their men produced, gathering rags to sell again in bundles, posing as gipsies to tell fortunes sometimes, and begging. Often

57

they would be out from sunrise to sunset, returning with a pittance and, in the evening, they cooked; bone stew often, or fish, when they could filch some from the harbour, seaweed and, on the ruby days, chicken. Folk said they ate squirrels, and it was probably true. Certainly a dead horse was never wasted.

A smooth, round stone, the size of a rubber ball, lay at the bottom of the pot 'for flavour' and into the water with it went the lickings of the countryside; berries and mussels, and roots and kernels. All the sealed seasonings and seeds in our cold earth were known to the tinkers and in went myrtle, mustard and clove plants and peelings and racy pennyroyal. A spinach of deadnettle floated on top and, through it, rose hips bobbed from the simmering thickness below. The main ingredient, fish, bones or rabbit, was added last and the broth looked as slimy as a bog.

Yet it must have tasted good for we often had bowlfuls and I remember finishing every scrap, but even boiled potatoes had special gust over the wall.

The tinker men were loafers, shiftless and indolent, who spent their days in vegetation round the fire, lazily whittling at a few clothes-pegs or modelling shoe-horns and spoons. They were big talkers and held impressive conversations about past sales and the horses they were training for the future, but the thin, dull-coated beasts listened listlessly and knew it was only bluff. They were more demanding and petulant than their own children and with their children they were irascible. Rare, winsome moments were reserved for harder times, to wheedle hot meals for themselves out of silly old maids, who spurned the women and babies. Each man had the temperament of a prima donna and a selfishness quite virginal.

Contact with their families during the day seemed to bind the three like triplets. It was as though each was afraid that an un-allied move or thought would destroy his position of authority and leave him on equal and unprotected terms with his woman. But, on the way to the village at dusk, selfhood returned like a disguise.

So, red-haired, wall-eyed and warped as a mandrake root, Tom Foley would sit in a corner of the inn and boil his heart nightly in bitter beer, chafing at the winter which had stalled him in his tracks and brooding sweetly into his mouth-organ. His frustration was as blatant as a birthstain and his own crooked frame taunted him constantly, until he rocked to and fro like a weaving, bronze lizard and the men at the bar edged towards the door. But, when the time came, Tom picked his foe easily and, swarming up the strongest drinker present, would butt him sense-less with a head like a sandbag. He was the only five feet tall man ever known to leave our six foot four Provost unconscious; but there were other times when MacPhee and MacGregor had to carry him home after a beating.

Evening revealed Big Drew MacPhee as a woman-hunter, handsome as Tom was crumpled. He was a man who loved all women, from the little highland maids to their respectable mothers and, even, sometimes, their god-fearing grandmothers. And he loved them because they loved him almost as much as he did. There was a dynamic about his weak features which enthral-led them all and, although he was reticent about the small, cracked mirror in his pocket, he never passed a darkened window glass without honouring his reflection. All round the bay, stories of his free roving were traded by unlovely goodies with greedy envy, for there were children with MacPhee smiles and curly brown hair in the most unlikely families. Big Drew's was that coarse charm fatal to cold matrons and nice girls.

The three men were gamblers, as most tinkers are, but Chance was Alan MacGregor's quarry which he stalked through all seasons. Truth to him was raindrops racing down a pane, falling leaves and stuttering dice, pitch and toss, twist and bust, icicles melting penny by penny, pigeons homing like tired, white gloves. Men and dogs and cocks fought for his fortune. Cards, nervous as the Red Queen's gardeners, flipped and skidded alive from his hands, then gathered and cut and shuffled and dealt and fanned and separated with the silken precision of a minuet. His hours were full of omens, his pockets were full of mascots, his head was full of systems, 'infallible as the Pope', he vowed. He found the Lady sometimes.

But I was aware of these men only vaguely, for then we were nearest to their offspring. The tink children were bony and be-devilled by two forces. Hunger and cold ruled the tides of their days like moons. They pried and scratched and thieved and hated for food. Cruel as ferrets and voracious as weevils, they could hear food, juice gurgling and rind crackling, in empty winkle-shells and taste fire, hot as paprika, in old, damp wood.

We were hungry, too, sometimes in the night, with bellies as dried out and screwed up as raisins, but it was not the fixed craving of over the wall. There was piece-and-jam in our kitchen and warm brose in the morning. Their hunger was as nagging as a missing limb and it left them taut as cats.

The entrances and exits to every warren echoed for them across the glen and their traps watched, lidless-eyed behind the bait.

Winter was stern, with days so short that it seemed the light was hardly there before it was night again. We were beaten by leather-tempered winds and the sky rolled down from its height, thick as fur and wetter than rain. The prey hibernated safely, folded between summer fat and autumn stores, and the stoats which shrieked in the traps died needlessly, their ermine coats petrifying in the ice and rotting in the Spring.

Led by Barry Foley, the boys raked the pinewoods, lupine under the black Spruce branches where the cones lay sugared with frost, then past the village four miles from home with full sacks like sins on their backs.

'Hey, Missus, are ye wanting . . .?'

'Tinkers!' The message of the slamming door was clear.

'Aw, go and crack yer nits!' shouted back Gus MacGregor.

And it was Geordie MacPhee's turn next. 'Cones, Mistress, fer the fire?'

'Aye, put them ben the shed and here's threepence to yersel' and a bannock, ye poor laddie.'

Wherever they travelled, Geordie freeloaded on his lucky face, for its honey-brown eyes and pale, delicate curves were beautiful and never blotched by the scabs of want which crusted the others. His beauty was mystery, certainly not inherited from his plain, meaty parents, and it bagged him more perks and snacks than the rest of the squatters together. Old women patted him and spinsters mothered him. He was the do-gooders' delight of tasteful poverty, sensitive and saintly-looking as a Vermeer girl, and the women stopped short of kissing him only because even beautiful tinker children have lice. But, when he was grown, one dared to at last, pulling him over her threshold and off the road for good.

Humped as a caravan of dromedaries, they would trudge towards the cottage, collecting pennies and curses on the way and followed unhappily by wee Eck MacPhee along his own road of private pits and booby traps.

Heavy-headed and purblind, Eck had had a month of paradise once, when spectacles, like Catherine Wheels, had found the whole world in a smudge. And Eck had seen that the world was trimmed and pleated, striped and dimpled, and to his amazement, reasoned. Its peaks had geometry. Its masses dovetailed and he could keep up with Geordie.

There were places to go now, but he did not hurry. On the way to the village he could stop and look, and, when we returned, he would still be there, motionless in the afternoon dusk, looking at the mountains, or at a snail's shell, or at his own footsteps in the snow. What he couldn't identify by sight, he remembered through his hands and he seemed to have forgotten the cold.

Then one day Geordie put the glasses on, peering through them with head on one side, parroting Eck and jumping back from his groping hands, until they reached out quickly and the brothers collided against a wall.

'That was daft, wee Eck. Ye've smashed yis specks,' said beautiful Geordie and ran on across the years, for no-one thought to buy wee Eck another pair.

They killed time with Lachlan and Calum and me and borrowed our sisters, shadowing Bella for her haphazard kisses and toying with Catrina until Auntie screeched. God, the Devil and the little people were invoked to destroy the randy lads with pox and then her excited daughter was roundly plumped and sealed into the cottage.

But Catrina grew eel-like and eldritch and sidled, paper-thin, through cracks in the door, or surfaced from the chimney in the smoke. She whisked through mouseholes, or slid down sashcords, whirled out on a draught, or just melted through the stone. Soon, only a poltergeist haunted the rooms with shufflings and taps, for Catrina had escaped through one of a hundred pores and was over the wall again. Sly among the girls she would sit, pretending she loved their small brothers and sisters, too; kicking her heels and hoping someone would come by.

Bare-bottomed babies squealed over them, all like piglets, and rode stickily on their hips. Infants took the place of dolls and were the girls' first masters, despotically damming their movements, until they almost forgot how to run and walked more passively than women. Our dotty, darting sisters seemed like tearaways by comparison and were more likely to answer the wee'ns whims with slaps than obedience, but, for a while, Catrina tried hard to change and lingered, fidgeting, in their circle.

They unstitched old sweaters and put the wool into a box, where it squirmed and unwound and knitted itself into a bird's huge nest and was never used again. They sifted the rags into coloured heaps and fetched water from the pump, not in our one-armed, crippled way, but balancing the full buckets on their heads. They were neglected and unformed, with welts of blue cold down their spindly legs, but they stepped over the rough ground like a wand of queens, and, although I didn't know it then, I was seeing a grace of centuries. To the women of the village it was worse than blasphemy.

The tinkers were as much a part of my childhood winters as snowballs and chilblains. They came in on the first hoarfrost and were chased away by the first flower, but, for those few months each year, their dizzy schizophrenia kept us all in a state of shock. The cross-currents of their savage fatalism, their lolling restlessness, their meekness and violence, flooded my Decembers as surely as the snows drifted, so that, even now, when the leaves have fallen, I expect everyone to become freakishly fickle.

They were illogical and clever, ugly and glowing. They were as picturesque as a Christmas card. But, although Granny Morag poured her golden spirits down their throats and padded out the wee'ns with baps, we didn't envy them very much.

One or two left the camp as they grew older, but rarely for long. They withered in the cities, where houses smothered them and the clocking-in and clocking-out routine of days became a treadmill. At the foot of the street was another and, beyond that, a brae, then a road and a lane, a field and a long, new path running over the hills. Most of them followed it in the end.

They were slummy and unhealthy and crawling with bugs and

a lot of people thought they shouldn't be allowed. There were protests and even petitions. Occasionally a local authority would stump into action and fence in a wood, or move them on, or carry off a child and lock it up in school.

But the tinkers went on being tinkers, the tattered ends of humanity, and they thumbed their noses at us all royally.

CHAPTER FIVE

AT HOME

FOR more than two hundred years our cottage had crouched in the seabank like a child's forgotten block. It was small and square, and miraculous because our family of eight managed to fit into its three rooms and breathe. There was a bedroom for us boys and another for the girls and Annie. Uncle Angus had the kitchen and in a cupboard (impressively named 'the back room') our Granny Morag slept.

An old woman had lived alone in it all before we came and before her no-one could remember and nobody cared. Whoever its first occupants were, they had left no trace of their lives and no sense of history whispered from the corners and crannies. Our grandmother's arrival as a bride had swept out the last wisps of other personalities as surely as if they had never existed.

The baby scrawls waxed on the walls were ours and the stain, like a brown frog, above the kitchen door was where Annie had aimed a tin of boot polish at our mother, Mairi, once – and missed. Countless family tantrums had slammed a crack in the back door and the front door was cemented by disuse.

The slates blown down by a storm-wind one October came from above the passage, for the damp patch on its ceiling was as big as a fooball by November and the icicle, which hung there every year after, grew like a stalactite.

Uncle Angus had once dropped snuff into his oil lamp which had exploded into an indelible black splash on the floor. It was covered with a mat later, but we knew it was there. We knew, too, the dent behind the discarded cot made by each one of us bucking into our earliest mornings. The lintels over the windows had woodworm and a floorboard in the girls' room had ominously vanished into the limbo below. There was a small, inexplicable hole right through the wall in the scullery and an echo lived in the lobby.

Each flaw was a familiar old trespasser and we might have built the cottage ourselves, it was so completely ours.

We took our bloody knees and bruises to it and pruned it with appetites, sharp as sickles. It was the place to hide private disasters in and where our torn sweaters were darned. We were physicked and fostered and reinforced there and it closed strongly round our weaknesses like a horny carapace. Muttering windows and hasps confirmed its permanence and every day, as we pelted from the North Pole of our beds to the tropics of the kitchen, the milk boiled over the range.

'Mercy on us!' Auntie Annie's squawk met us at the door.

'Och, hags and tatties!' That was Herself gathering élan.

'Ye didna give tae the kelpies last night, Mither.' Which was why the milk had burned, of course.

'I've better things tae do wi' good food than waste it on a load of loony ideas, Annie. By jings, but ye're as cracked as old boiler— Hell! damnation and cuss!' The toast was in flames and she kicked the dog.

Muffled by snowdrifts into the cauldron of this place, our lives constantly spumed and fizzed and fumed and spluttered, but now I remember its days of tight love and grow homesick.

How they danced, with Granny Morag beating the dust out of their mornings with besom and buff and sending the thunder of her scrubbing brush across the floors like the daughter of Zeus, tossing mattresses, throwing bedclothes and rugs out of the windows, turning the brass knobs on our bedsteads into golden mirrors. Chairs somersaulted and tables walked in this hooligan Highland Games and I suspected that she really hated housework and would have been more at home in a wrestling ring.

Then the clock struck twelve and the furniture was all in place, with feather beds rolled up like English pancakes and the glass panes polished clean away. The last spider was crawling up one in disbelief and food smoked, gravy-rich and nutty, in our plates. It was afternoon.

Easy, slippered time of recovery and nodding peace; we drew together and gentled in it. The dishes were stacked unwashed in the basin and Auntie Annie took out her ironing and Granny Morag opened her cupboard at last.

Tea was infusing in the pot and there was a fire in the grate. Uncle Angus was out in the wind somewhere, but his moustache cup was waiting on the table. He would come in later, looking like a snowman, and shuffle across the room as though it was a summer's day.

Annie would tut over the puddles of his thawing; but now she hummed importantly, smoothing an old blanket over the table and testing the flat irons heating on the kitchener.

They were fine foils to each other, my grandmother and aunt; the one as restless as a haywire magpie and the other a natural mourner. Auntie Annie liked nothing better than a good death to pick over.

'That's Andy Barnet gone, Elsie was telling me; passed away in the night and took a terrible time in the going. An uncommon agony, she said, and his face still black when they called her man.'

It was no accident that Elsie Pate, the local undertaker's wife, was our aunt's best friend.

'Of course, I was saying he didna look fit the last time he was here, ye mind.'

'Away and chase yerself! That wis a year ago and ye say the same about a'body,' interrupted Granny Morag, unkindly.

'That's as may be, Mither, but there was death in Andy Barnet's eyes and I knew it. The poor soul . . . Mind you, it'll be a grand funeral. There's a few bawbees there, I shouldn't wonder, and I suppose it'll all be going tae that wifie o' his. I never had time fer her.'

Her iron buzzed over the last crease and Calum's Sunday shirt came up like a crisp shroud. Bilious with forecasts of catastrophe, she had no pep for the labour of housekeeping, so the sedentary chores her mother was too impatient to bother with were left for her. She mended and knitted, socks like gumboots and bullet-proof jerseys, and, long before women's magazines said it was the right thing to do, Annie sat down to her ironing.

She collected books by quacks and faith healers and knew the medical history of everyone in the village without ever leaving the house. She steamed open letters and her prophesies of death usually coincided with her quarrels, which were bitter and frequent. She could spend all day spying at the window for someone to pass along the track, when, on a swift rattle of words, she would wreck his good name.

'There's Billie Stronach wi' his new suitie on and they owing four weeks' rent. His wifie's doon wi' the "flu", but there he is gadding aboot just the same.'

Our Auntie Annie could make a perfectly respectable man sound like an ogre.

Strangely, it was my brother Calum who found something in her which no one else could see. In his slow, sad way, he adored our aunt and nursed her gravely during her attacks of *lurgy* – a sickness which struck when someone opened a window. In turn, she treated him with a surreptitious gentleness that almost matched his own and never laughed or ranted at his clumsiness. It was a special, speechless intimacy which we accepted, but could not understand.

Calum was the exile among us, grown large and taciturn in a family of noisy pigmies. He seemed to have been born old and planting things. Already the earth's callouses were hard on his hands and his pockets were worn through by corms and seeds. Crockery fled to pieces from his blunt fingers, but the slight, moonwhite first eyelash of a tree grew staunch and branched at his touch.

Because he lived with us he added his weight to our teams and battles, but he was clearly beyond them and far happier in his potato patch or helping the pig to farrow.

Now, in the tolerant afternoon, he pored over a heap of farming journals, dated by years, but treasured since a neighbouring crofter had turned them out of his attic. *Farmer and Stockbreeder* and a few brand new *Farmer's Weeklies*, as exciting as science fiction to my brother and in their Utopia of rapacious machines and mighty horses he saw his life.

'I'll have they Percherons on my farm, fine fer the ploughing, and Friesians fer the yield,' he murmured to himself, alone at the table. 'And the byre'll be here, wi' the dairy by, and the sties there and a silo next the barn.' It was a time-honoured routine and, through my drawing, I could hear him moving cups and jamjars into position.

'And I'll have a muckle great new thresher.' The crash of another dish interrupted us all for a moment: 'Och, just Calum at the make-believe again.' But he made it all come true in the end.

Lachlan was working now, down 'at the Slaughter', and sweet, wild Bella was in service at the Manse (six days a week, come all weathers, with mercy but no money on Sundays). Catrina was with us, I think, puckish in the chimney corner, mooning over tinker loons, though pretending to play with her old dutch doll.

'Now eat yis dinner, there's a lass. Look ye're dribbling! Now eat it up. Och, ye're that bad, I'll skelp ye, I will!'

And, belabouring the doll, she forgot the lads and played after all.

The rocking-chair was carrying Granny Morag over the us-quebae waves and bobbing in time to her dreams. She was curled up and purring, mild for once; beginning to sway with it, sleep-ily, so that her feet just left the rug and when she opened her eyes the room was at sea. Seesaw and the walls rolled, too, and her skirts lifted and dipped as the ripple swelled. A strand of hair fell over her face and she swung more quickly to toss it away; back and forth and blow it on the downbeat, lurch and pulse. She was wide-awake now and swinging ecstatically, reel and pitch, 'Wheeeeoooo!' till the chair stood on end and rocked her to the floor.

'That's cooled the room,' she said and began to tell a story. Her tales were short, disjointed and hopelessly confused, but we always listened just in case she got one right; though we knew she'd give away the end long before it was due.

'... And the auld witch said, "If ye can guess my name, ye can keep yis bairn, but, if not, ye maun keep yis promise and give the wee'n tae me." The wifie had promised, d'ye see ...?

'Micheil, pass the bottlie, there's a laddie ... now, where was I? Och aye, the auld witch's name was Whippity Stourie and she used tae sing ... whit was the song? ... my, it's thirsty work, the story-telling ... I canna recall the song, but it disna matter. The wifie heard it anyway and kept her babby after all ... Aye, aye, but this is a fine drop.'

Steam condensed down the walls and we were still and sep-arate for a while, no longer 'them', lumped together with a shud-der, but each one unique and given place in the smoky gloam of the cottage. Under the pulley of drying clothes we scribbled and nibbled and yawned, drank tea to Annie's endless malice, saw fortunes in the tea-leaves and found ourselves.

A vitrola had arrived on the dresser from God knows where with a few warped records, thick as plates. Now Catrina wound it up, but 'Goodbye Dolly Grey' never sounded like that.

'We could steady it wi' paper. Get's one from the room, Micheil.' And I went through to the bedroom to find an old newspaper.

Outside it was lollipop land where trees were flapping new-feathered limbs and stones became coconut cakes. A tipsy judge in a tilting wig stood where the wash-house had been and the bushes round his feet had turned into cotton-wool lambs. The cottage next door was rolling in flour and the gardens were bubble-baths and all the stars had come down from the sky and landed as winks on the path. I pressed my face against the glass and longed to paint the white moor from butter to plum.

Then I would see him, or Catrina would look out of the kitchen door to catch sight of him crossing the hill, or for Calum he would appear implacable and duty-bound for our cottage, and we dropped our trances and ran.

'An inspector! An inspector!' What anarchy in the kitchen at the news, with Auntie Annie bursting into prayer and Catrina into screams and Calum demolishing the rest of our cups in an effort to get his magazines to safety under a cushion. This time, I goaded my chaos in alarm and thrill, for inspectors were the bloodhounds in our lives.

School inspectors, sanitary inspectors, the gillies and the factor rummaged through our hair, scullery, the housekeeping purse and the outside water-closet and left us the poorer for their raids. Even missionaries were sent to inspect our souls; though Granny's proved to be so irredeemably black that these rarely returned, which was a pity because they were the only ones she enjoyed.

But in our afternoons of crisis, she dozed on in her chair while the rest of us roiled over her. At last, when I shook her, crying in her ear, she came up like an Irish navvy.

'Where? Where is he? I'll no have another of they long-nosed buzzards tramping over my hoose wi' his Kaiser boots. Where is he? . . .' All at once she sobered. 'An inspector did ye say? Well, what the de'il are ye all footering about for? Get the blinds pulled and close the shutters, ye daft half-wits.'

Catrina's screams were slapped and the door locked and Calum's cushion thrown at Annie on the way to the window. 'A fat lot of use you'd be without me, I'm telling yis.' The shutters were banged together. 'Get yisselves hid.' I was hauled after her by the ear. 'By Christ, they'd have yis all inspected intae coffins. Doon! Doon!' And she would crawl under the table.

Auntie Annie disappeared round the harmonium, and Catrina made for the cabinet. Calum always bumped into Rob Mór's chair in the dark before scrambling behind it and I was sat in excruciating discomfort next to our grandmother.

There was a long, long pause.

We all tried to stop breathing, but the silence was loud with jitters and soon my shoulders would begin to ache and Calum's swallow resounded across the room, like a drain.

'Sshh!' spat Granny Morag and tugged my ear, because I was nearest, and we cowered on in acute distortion.

My backbone was turning to stone and my legs had fossilized into the floor. If I didn't move soon, they would crumble away, but another tug warned me of fates worse than that. My ear grew bigger than my head. I was old and dead and embalmed and this time I couldn't stand it.

'He wis miles away . . .' I began and wondered why the room seared with lightning and bells. But, at that moment, his feet crunched outside and all my skin fell off.

He waited and knocked and we could hear him listening in the choking hush. He walked round to the window and rubbed at the glass.

'He must know we're in here,' I thought, with quick, desperate visions of the Black Watch coming to his aid and battering down the back door with a caber.

He was outside it again, stamping in the snow, knocking, rattling, pounding, hammering, deafening, even more persistent than usual. Then, just as he seemed to have given up, the kettle screeched and spurted over the fire.

As the kitchen filled with yelps and steam, Lachlan's voice came bellowing through the keyhole. 'What the hell are ye doing in there? Will ye open the bliddy door!'

We let him in, blue as bleach, and it was days before the sight of me didn't drive them all to rage.

However, although we flagrantly exaggerated visits from the few determined officials who forced entry to our home, its three-mile isolation from the village kept most invaders at bay and our own guile did the rest. Thus we were able to preserve our curious cast in a way that would be impossible today, when platoons of bureaucrats are employed turning unicorns into donkeys. In fact, our cottage with its panics and peace was a very private place.

When I was born it was squat and stone, typical of the high-lands. Its grey walls were dappled with green pools of shadows which filled their hollows and, although it was rough and thick, it looked soft in a dusk of years. On damp days, bewitched by clouds and the low sea mists, it evaporated and only the lan-terned windows were left, bobbing like glow-worms.

It had been so since it was built and so it remained for a further six or seven years. Then someone (Robbie beag, probably) whitewashed it and Granny Morag discovered a paintbrush. Every fortnight or so afterwards, she prowled round with a bucket, coating over the flaking patches until the whole place crystallized into a cake decoration and she became very proud of her painting.

Before long, forgetting to stop at the back door, she carried her brushwork across chairs and window frames and in daubs and highlights down the lobby to the front door. There was the oc-casional side trip into the bedrooms on the way and, with little warning, we were living in a kooky hospital where the remedy for every squeak and leak was paint. It took our fingerprints in chalk before each drubbing and covered our clothes with calamine and even our secret thoughts were psychoanalysed in tell-tale streaks across its surfaces. It seemed an interminable time before our grandmother dropped a bottle of raspberry flavouring into the bucket and invented colour.

Colour. At first it was pastel and pretty, faintly tinted to catch the light, pink and primrose, prim and pale and we approved. Her hand grew bolder and, like all true artists, she began to allow the experimental phases to run their full course.

Granny Morag, too, had her 'blue period', as tactfully powdered as a royal coat in its early stages; later deepening somewhat into cornflower, which merged into aquamarine, then turquoise, and finally emerged again, brilliantly, as an ultramarine which insulted the whole shoreline.

Her red years followed with horrible stirrings of dragon's blood and cochineal and a puce climax which shattered the view for weeks. Thereafter, and while I grew up, the cottage was variously ginger and tangerine, emerald and mustard, chromed and lipsticked and livid. It became a landmark and radiated across the heather like a dayglo sock, though how such theatrical results were achieved we dared not ask. It was enough that she mixed colour as preposterously as she cooked: and no one ever lost his way to our home.

Others, besides inspectors, came visiting and sometimes brought news of foreign happenings beyond our glen, and Granny celebrated for a week when all women over twenty-one were given the vote. She was an ardent suffragette.

They talked of the General Strike when I was seven, but I only remember Bauchie Nell sitting in the kitchen in her galoshes assuring us that Ernie Keir, the local notary, had driven the train to Dornoch with Elsie Pate's husband as his fireman, and all we boys knew that must be a lie, for a start. How could a wee bit baldy like old Ernie drive a train?

The war had ended before I was born. Means Tests and the Dole and Ramsay MacDonald were abstract words to us and for years I imagined the Labour Party to be a universal, beery debauch, a sort of pickled revolution which would precede the end of the world. It was easy to see why Granny Morag was so anxious for it to start.

More often they gupped about each other. Nell whispering to Annie about Elsie and Annie passing it on. Scandals scurried round their chairs, like mice, and the libels and rumours begun by these three could have launched a gossip column and kept a court in full-time session. Inquisitively, I stretched my ears to meet their busy voices.

'Of course, the bairn's no his, ye know.'

'Is that a fact?'

'Not at all! I've seen it mysel', not a whisker of a likeness.'

'Och, I'm no surprised, no surprised at all. That Bertie from Gregson's stedding was never off her doorstep last summer.'

'Aye, and there's been some carry on wi' John's brother, I shouldn't wonder.'

'Mind you, they say they're not married onyway.'

'Would ye believe it!' Our aunt shook her head, incredulously, completely forgetting her own past naughtiness in the fillip of this new sensation.

Then they exchanged symptoms and twinges, until we were all qualified anatomists and every disease was known to me: I knew a lot of unknown ones, too.

'It starts wi' a burning in my chest and palpitates the heart something fearful. It's my liver, d'ye see, and I'm telling yis the pain isna awfie, it's gie.'

What a ghoulish trio they were: Bauchie Nell, with the fish-scales rotting in her hair, and Elsie Pate, anaemic as one of her husband's corpses, and Annie. Our grandmother detested them and they only dared to share her kitchen when the bottle was an hour or so emptier than full.

In fact, all Annie's friends tried to make their arrivals appear accidental, though it was perfectly obvious that no one ever walked miles into the middle of nowhere without a reason.

'Just passing,' they used to say, and salaam round the door, eyeing Granny Morag uneasily to ensure that she was temporarily tame, before they scuttled into the shadows like cockroaches. It was a hard choice they had to make between her temper and being the last to know the latest in the valley. But our aunt was so consistently well-informed that they usually took the risk and sat blissfully aghast in her corner. It was better than a visit to a fortune-teller.

At five o'clock they creaked and scratched regretfully at the tops of their stays, remembered their husbands without enthusiasm and sighed their way into the cold. Bella was coming home and Granny, surprisingly restarted, was deep and demented in peelings in the scullery.

'D'ye ken ye canna tell the difference between an apple and a tattie if ye hold yis nose, Lachie?'

'Och away! Ye can so.'

And the peeler caught me a dunt on the head as we stole slices of raw potato for the argument. They didn't taste like apple at all, but I wouldn't have admitted it.

'Yon Fiona Renwick was up at Battie's Den the day and I wouldn't mind having her, I'm telling ye,' said Lachlan to no one in particular, then leant back with a hearty laugh and put his feet on the table.

Calum and I looked at each other and shrugged and Auntie Annie clouted Lachlan for not taking off his boots first, and for being coarse.

I thought about Bug Renwick's sister for a while. She was a roly-poly teenager, who always yelled at Bug and me when we needed her curlers for cannon ammunition and they were usually in her hair, anyway. Most people I knew thought she was soppy.

The hustling from scullery to fire grew faster and the invective louder. China was skidded into place and a mound of bread and butter landed miraculously dead centre. Herself was late for the evening excursion and it took more than a blizzard to stop that. As she lived on bottled protein and didn't eat with us, the matter of our high tea was a source of daily vexation and tended to vary in quality from uncooked to ashes. We had to accept the fact that she made it at all as a sign of great affection.

Dumb with melting aches, Bella was holding her hands to the flames and shaking ice out of her veins. Hoyden and gracile, more than beautiful, she was our bell, book and candle girl with spells in her hair. Tidal waves of her kissing bubbled over my childhood and her hugs were impulsive and generous. We adored her.

On Sabbath, freed from the dismal presbytery, she streaked up trees and tore her clothes, stood on her head and cut her knees and galloped the tinkers' ponies across the sands. Little tomboy chit, turning the day into a switchback: lads sweltered when they thought of her and she scarcely noticed, just took a little longer coming home some nights, if she met a favourite on the way.

'Yon Iain Peitrie said I was bonny today and I made him lift two eggs frae Ma Soutar's just tae prove it. He's that soft.' Her laugh, as she handed over the eggs, would have cut his lovesick heart in two. But she went on, wistfully. 'He gave me a hurl on his new bike and it's a grand machine, with a three speed, even.'

We stuffed ourselves with hot, brown smokies and tore into the bread. The smell of fish and snuff brewed under the ceiling and Granny Morag pulled her head ito her shawl and lifted down her lamp from its hook. She didn't waste time on farewells, just closed the door and the afternoon behind her.

About a week later, we woke to find a bicycle propped against the back wall. It was third-hand and worn, but it was for Bella.

This was an act very much of our home, where presents were shaken over us without reason and official anniversaries were usually forgotten. Any birthday falling the week before Rob Mór's money arrived was certainly ignored and it was almost an offence to have been born at all at such a time. I came into this category and, even now, discovering my age means searching through dog-eared documents or a clutter of arithmetic.

As children we knew how old we were through the surprises sprung on us by Granny and aunt. They gave bashfully, leaving the prize where it would be found and not caring for thanks: a fishing-rod for Calum, he must have been eleven, and long trousers when he was fourteen; a pair of patent leather shoes with straps for Catrina, twelve years old and needing beauty; tobacco for Lachlan, a man at seventeen, and for fifteen-year-old Bella, off to her first dancing, an imp-green dress sewn secretly by Annie over weeks.

For me, the infant years became boyhood and each night, crushed between the nether ends of Calum and Lachlan, I wished a wish which didn't come true. But it dominated my sleep, filling it with collisions and shocks, so that I was always dreaming of walking into walls or being the ball in a football game. And, as I grew bigger, the walls pressed in, closer and closer, until they became a little box with me inside and the wish became a symbol of identity.

In the morning of that day, our grandmother pushed us off to school, half-asleep and with heads singing as usual, and in that afternoon it was me she raged at and sent on impossible errands until her temper reached its climax.

'Get oot!' she howled. 'Get oot o' this room tae yis bed and nothing d'ye eat this night.'

And I slumped off, snatching a hunk of bread from the table in passing and muttering all the curses she'd ever taught me, all the way down the lobby; and there were still some.

For a second I didn't notice that the room had changed, but the marble-topped washstand was gone and the chair had been shifted behind the door. The great double bed was by the window now and at the far end of the room in the dim corner was a new single bed, with blankets and a sheepskin and black, shiny bars, and my nightshirt lay on it.

CHAPTER SIX

GRANNY MORAG

AFTER their marriage and in the first quicksilver of passion for her, Rob Mór gave Morag a honeymoon. He took her to the black, teeming squalor of the Gorbals and there they slept the daylights away on a working friend's bed and drank red biddy nights for a month.

The city reeled up to them, fou and loving, topheavy with tenements, thronged as a freezing India. It mobbed and swore at them in sing-song stridor and flourished arcades and emporiums tipsily in their faces. Its sweaty musk blew into their nostrils and alleys opened up where policemen never strayed, but the Salvation Army gave out soup and prayers.

Ships bayed on the Clyde and carriages rattled up Kelvin Side, where the newlyweds watched Scottish bankers and merchants step in and out to a rich silk rustle of wives.

Our grandmother was enchanted. She noted every detail, from the white ribbons on the maids' aprons to their mistresses' modish bustles. She peeped through windows at drawing-room teas and saw the starched children prepare for bed. She cut her own visiting cards from a sheet of white cardboard and was on the point of stealing a top hat for Rob Mór when he saw her.

But he was too late to stop her soaring imagination. It had already decided that gracious living was for her and she developed delusions of grandeur which only intensified with time and led to my being her favourite grandchild, because through me she was related to the laird. That she also detested him was irrelevant.

From Glasgow on, our Granny Morag never walked if there was the slightest possibility of riding in any kind of vehicle from which she could incline her head to passers-by and favour friends with acid little smiles. She was a woman of stunning condescension, when the mood took her, and I have seen her make a haycart seem like a royal coach. She bought packets of paper doilies by the dozen, brandished a glassless lorgnette on those special occasions when she wore a hat, and distributed her handmade visiting cards for the rest of her life.

They had taken a honeymoon day trip to Dunoon and watched the trains in St. Enoch's station and spent most of their evenings in a chocolate-brown pub, where too much dole was spent and nips chased wee heavies in dizzy confusion. Women with whining bairns argued at its doors and, as the nights deepened, the mirror reflected a bar full of triplets through its winding gilt flourishes. Corks and knives were drawn there. Men of drouth gathered there, garrulous men, conspiratorial men, men. It was a place where the lived-in faces grew.

One evening as they sat still with the happy astonishment of country mice, a bearded man with a sheaf of paper under his arm walked in. He bought a black pint and took it to their corner, where he stared at the young Morag so hard that Rob Mór shifted aggressively. But the stranger ignored him and, taking a piece of charcoal from his pocket, began to sketch.

For a whole hour she sat, flattered to stone, while her husband preened himself in the reflected glory and kept the painter's pint filled and frothing. They grew silently rosy together and the picture darkened on the page until it was done and the artist's bow tie was undone with the effort, and he stood up and bowed unsteadily.

'You have a beautiful profile,' he said to her and was gone.

It was the highlight of their holiday and, like all other events, was woven into the mythology which became our grandmother's version of her early life.

That little month became a year, two years, then three, during which she had actually lived in Kelvin Side and owned a carriage and pair and been the toast of the country's artists, who had fought for the privilege of painting her portrait.

'They travelled for miles just tae see me, ye ken. Sitting outside the gate for hours they would be, waiting for a glimpse of me stepping from my carriage,' she would tell us, her eyes inspired with memories and dreams. 'It wis my profile, d'ye see. The bonniest profile in all Scotland, they used tae say.'

And, tilting back her head till her chin jutted out like a

fighter's, she would stand sideways and force us to agree that the beauty of her profile was matchless. Our Granny Morag had the spirit of a duchess.

In fact, she was the daughter of a shipwright and he had been renowned for a thirst, which led him, one mad, red, three-bottle sunset, to mistake the brine for wine and leap gleefully into it over the side of one of his own boats. He surfaced for the last time still hiccuping to his cronies to join him; but they were not so sure.

As most of his boats had been just as unseaworthy, he wasn't greatly missed, but a photograph of himself in pouter stance glazed out at us from his daughter's cupboard, where it was hung for ever as an act of respect.

The wife he left behind was a meek, birdlike woman, whose joy was her shy son, but who was slightly afraid of her ferine daughter. I remember seeing her once, smoothed on to a drift of pillows and quite transparent. I could stare right through her and, although she held my hand, I knew that only the tissue wrapping of a person was there. The rest had already gone.

Our grandmother grew up random and unschooled, more at home fishing than in her mother's kitchen. Her father's friends took her out in their drifters and, in the house, she rebelled so vehemently against all restrictions that the family found it easier to leave her free. Yet, when they moved from the boatyard to a croft behind the village, it was Morag who spent six months clearing the boulders and stones from a great patch of land to make another field.

We were marched round it once to see its sculptured edge of rocks. Our grandmother's acre, but blonde with the whiskers of someone else's barley, for sickly stock and ruinous weather, inexperience and her mother's loneliness had driven them back to the village in the end.

She grew without time for the other girls, with their simpers and fads and scheming chastity, and they must have found her arrogance unbearable. She had learnt her curses from skippers and was still scrapping like an urchin long after they had resorted to other wiles. Her unladylike escapades must have been the subjects of scandal and heartburning, especially as they seemed to tug the lads towards her, rather than turn them away.

'There's a few folks' husbands round here didna get the lassie of their choice, I'll tell ye,' she would gloat at the beginning of a tale of some long-buried romance. 'Yon Johnny the Baltic signed on wi' the whalers and wasna seen for three years after I turned him down and Steaphan Peitrie's never looked at another woman since me, not to this hour. Conn Barnet proposed tae Teenie-frae-Troon just two days after he'd had my "no": on the rebound, ye would say. And, as for that Dollopy Kirst's Billie, was he not trailing after me, like a wee dog, for weeks, threatening tae do away with himsel' if I didna have him.'

No wonder the village daughters hissed over the griddles and mothers plumply guarded their sons. Not a house in the valley would take her into service and she refused with her usual determination to help in a shop. But the family was poor and her brother, Angus, had started labouring at twelve, so, at last, she was sent to work in a local pub.

It was lamplit and sawdusted in those days and proof against females until our grandmother became its first barmaid, but we gathered that she took it over from the night she strode into it and her sequent marriage to Rob Mór only meant moving to the other side of its bar.

She had been a wild young maid before, but, in the salty climate of this drinking room, she matured into an eccentric. It was there that she developed her taste for alcohol and golfing umbrellas, and there she began carrying a small hammer and a fistful of nails in her skirt pocket for unspecified 'emergencies', the way other women carry safety pins. She could not pass a loose board or broken fence without proving her ability as a carpenter.

In the pub, too, her cranky political opinions were born of half-heard conversations and her own biases. She was *for* strikes and *against* trade unions ('a man maun fight fer himself'), *against* collars and *for* scarves, *against* foreigners, which meant anyone living south of Berwick, and *for* nationalization, which meant free goods for all and the shop of her worst enemy, Maggie Chalmers, being seized for the people.

Massacre the middle classes, but Up the Aristocracy! With sweeps of Celtic rhetoric and oaths and harangues and snorts and lectures and traitorous threats, she slammed her view through our childhoods: at times she would even wake up one of us in the middle of the night to deliver a scorching sermon on the rights of women and the most reactionary politician of the day would have supported her ideas for the sake of peace alone. Her quarrels with opposition were fanatical and enduring and we all knew that the first Labour victory in 1892 was due solely to the countless letters of advice our Granny Morag had sent to Keir Hardy, M.P.

My grandmother never would admit that she could neither read nor write and a pair of spectacles were kept especially to prove that she could do both. They had belonged to someone else and were always lost. But she could have seen a flea in a black blanket, anyway.

Her mania for writing letters was almost as troublesome as Auntie Annie's daily footbath and, as we learnt the alphabet, so we learnt to run from the rustle of paper or the ominous sight of a bottle of ink. She was habitually preoccupied with advertisements rediscovered in old papers.

'What does that say, laddie? I seem tae have mislaid my specs.' She would grab one of us slipping by, to translate 'new miracle laxative, sample on request', or 'mend that tear forever with Robertson's unbreakable thread'. And then there was the letter to bungle and blot.

Dear Mister Wartsgon,
It was with amazment that I read that you have cured yourself and many others this morning and it would be a great obligation if you would be sending me a sample of your cure for the wart I have had for five years ('No, loonie, we'd better make that ten') for ten years and exceeding discomfort.
Morag Sinclair

Wartless for as long as I knew her, she also sent for horoscopes and recipes, corn-cutters and hair-tongs and, once, at the cost of a week's food, for the latest anti-wrinkle creak, 'secret of the East, now used by the crowned heads of Europe'. Their photographs could have told her it didn't work.

But her essential genius was reserved for official letters; stews of fire and ginger which she simmered for days over grievances, until her indignation reached its peak; then the oilcloth was whipped out of the kitchen-table drawer and Robbie beag was summoned.

He was the only one considered grand enough for her attacks on authority, which were dictated with dash and a punchy phrasing all her own.

'I'll thank you to mind yis own interferences in future,' she snapped at the Education Office in Dornoch during one exchange, and assured the district provost that the next water engineer she saw would be 'malagarused' – this, after an inoffensive man had made the mistake of straying into our garden, while measuring a village boundary, and she had been convinced he was going to dig it up for pipes.

A letter from our grandmother was also also sent to the Prime Minister one autumn, when he joined the laird's shoot for a few days.

'Seeing ye're in these parts,' it read. 'It's right that ye should know that the man calling himself a survayer is a spy for a bolshy foreign government and hasna survayed a soul since he came.'

Monstrous tirades and accusations and jabs and melodramatic pleas for justice anticipated the angry generation by thirty years and were penny-stamped to the Establishment of the time. And, occasionally, to her delight, a formal reply was received, signed by someone's secretary's secretary, to be treasured and grow sooty behind the clock.

With her screams and whoops and tempests and sudden songs and voltaic, crackling speech, Granny Morag was a preposterous old rebel. Strangers were scared by her and authority plagued and the village offended. She was obstinate and prejudiced and frequently absurd, yet her eyes saw right into a boy's heart and understood everything. No one knew better than she how to oust the vampires of childhood. She was a pillow of sweet dreams when I was very small, the fireside of my growing and an ally ever after. She could enter our world at a moment's notice and completely, balancing on walls or walking the plank, playing chain-tig or hide-and-seek or leap-frog or blind man's buff, swinging, dodging and jumping; and she could exit just as quickly with a swift adult blow.

She cried; though it happened so rarely that her tears were shocking. For a whole night they fell during the crisis of our Auntie Annie's one serious illness. And the hot drinks and bottles and meals were made and medicines were given with hospital precision and we were washed and tidied and steered through our evening and the nanny goat was milked and the hens shut up, and all the time her face drowned in a ceaseless, silent flood.

Her sense of pity was deep and generous and little happenings touched her till she wept unpredictably; turning away from Lachlan's first wages, held out in a knotted rag; gasping at the sink sometimes, when Bella came in, blushing and satin with cold water from the wash-house.

'My, but these onions are strong!' And, a few minutes later, 'Ye're a fair quinie, right enough, Bella.'

Hurt by our hurts, sobbing because we sobbed, she was half ashamed of herself and hid her secret sadnesses deeper. Yet I saw her crying once by the sea her husband and youngest daughter had crossed and where her father lay.

Impossible brainwaves gripped her without warning, the results of scraps of information picked up in the night and half-remembered in the sober dawn. So she had learnt a new way to set the girls' hair, then angrily cut off all the curls which didn't come to order at once. It was weeks before the bald patches disappeared. She cultivated carrot tops for decoration in dishes of water, until there wasn't a plate left to eat off, and for a day, she believed in the freedom of pigs.

'It's no right tae keep they creatures cooped up all the time,' she declared opening the sty where an old sow had been nursing litters contentedly for as long as I could remember.

But, by the end of the day, when she'd been knocked over by two piglets and their mother had trampled a line of clean washing into the mud and eaten one of Annie's semmits, and it had taken us two hours to coax them all back home, our grandmother had returned to her original conviction that the only use for pigs was bacon, which she ate thereafter with a look of airy satisfaction on her face.

Unfortunately, her other vagaries were not so easily defeated. The old materials we cut into strips of rhythmic preparation for

83

a rag rug, which would have covered the entire moor, had it ever been made. The jam pots we collected only made a glass mountain in the garden and were never filled with the mythical bramble jelly only she knew how to make. Those dawn announcements of new orders, which we learnt to dread. The time she entered us all for a highland dancing competition, when none of us really knew the steps.

'Well learn them then, ye lumbering tattie pickers, drrrrrrat-tattarattattattarattatata! Get to it!' With a week to go. 'Whee! Point yis toes, laddie, point yis toes!' Beating Calum's great boots with a stick. 'Diddlydiddlydiddlydum. Get yisself off the ground, man! Hooch! Och, dearie, dearie, that'll never do.'

It was left to Catrina to save the family name by being part of the team which took second prize in the foursome reel; and we survived somehow.

Granny Morag grew no taller than four foot ten and her figure was never more than a girl's. As she aged, she minified, growing smaller and more tinderish, until there was a hot blue smoke at her heels and it seemed as though she would spring into it one day with a final whistling shriek and disappear for ever back to the kelpie thicket she undoubtedly came from.

That she managed to have four children and rear a further five was remarkable; that she could also lick even the heftiest of us into obedience was heroism. But the taller we grew, the better she controlled us and, although I could have lifted her with one arm when I was fourteen, I wouldn't have dared.

Her lack of height was a limitation she schemed against with deceitful shoes, high-swept hair and a lifelong irritation. It offended her autocratic soul that the mob should be able to look down on her and that she had to climb into the wardrobe to reach her clothes. Pedestals of boxes were placed strategically under all the heights in the house; the chimneypieces, the dresser, below the antlers in the lobby where she kept a spare kettle, and under the clothes-line in the garden. She kicked and guarded them resentfully.

Her slightness, too, was a reason for her hats, ecstatic cuckoo salads of moonshine and seasons, curdling with feathers, gimcrack with fruit, crowned with weeds and blossoms in crescendo every year. She wore them when she went visiting and she went visiting when Rob Mór's money arrived.

We all went visiting in those days in choking collars and sulks to strange second cousins in the hills and unrelated aunties, or terrible Uncle Tómas. They were days of parade, baths, lavender water, blisters, feuds and the status symbol of a hired pony trap.

Bandaged into our suits and crippling shoes, we were hustled from soap to hair oil, with no time to eat and unable to sit down, perforated by our grandmother's hatpin, while the girls panicked through her maze of hooks and eyes: until, at last, we set off under the banner of her bonnet, leaving Auntie Annie waving and wailing at the door, convinced we would never return. For once, this was not unreasonable.

Stimulated by her belief in the horse's superiority over the laird's motor car, our Granny Morag expected a souped-up performance – and got one. Farmer Gregson, who hired out the pony, used to boost it with extra corn before our expeditions and the pony, recognizing of old the brandished umbrella and screeches, always made off before the last child had time to squirm in. That scramble over the rumbling wheels left me shaking and dizzy every time.

Then hares flew and trees pelted by with frowning barks as the valley rocked on a seesaw and trackside gullies widened into ravines under the trap. And we were toppled into each other's arms, churned into junket. And our ears caught fire and the girls lost their ribbons and popcorn stones fired at the hound of dust behind us and the earth became a trampoline on which we bounced higher and higher until we jumped the sun with our grandmother spinning lyrically above us, singing in a whirl of plumes.

Gorgeous rainbow bird of a grandmother, flaring across the cider sky, carrying us away on a gale of flowers and fringes. We gulped down fizzing clouds until the world rolled past like a butter-gold bead and stars fell into out mouths.

... We landed in a hedge of lather outside the village, where she reluctantly handed over the reins to Lachlan and seated herself on the best seat in the trap, while we four were squashed on to the one opposite and sternly ordered to make ourselves inconspicuous.

From then on, the advance was slow, often progressing down quite unnecessary lanes to give her the cachet of passing the cottages of traditional enemies and inferiors. She wielded her lorgnette for gestures of insult or favour and viewed those natives not exalted by her acquaintance from under arched eyebrows.

In the High Street, we would draw up to buy presents for the visit.

'When I was in Kelvin Side, a lady would never be calling without taking a gift, a wee token of manners fer the wifie, d'ye ken.'

So she asked for the impossible, a length of silk at the local draper's. 'What! D'ye no have silk? By Christ, man, I don't know ye keep open. Well, lace then. No? Times are not what they were and that's a fact.' And she gave him a lecture on days of gentility and style and bought a hanky.

Shortbread and woolly pom-poms, potted hough and a teacosy were accumulated with the same aplomb and a sadistic indifference to our blushes and smirking friends. She must have known Dug Sauchan and Jack Soutar minced past with wiggling hips every few minutes and the Sturrock twins stuck their tongues round every corner.

'Toffee nose!'

'Farty breeks!'

'Would ye not say the one in the middle was bonny, Jackie?'

'Och no, the one on the side's a wee picture, Dug.'

We'd slump in our seats with shame, while the girls tossed their heads and patted their dresses and pouted kissably at older lads.

'Look at that Maggie Kirst in thon old ganzie. She's been wearing it since Hogmanay. Did ye ever see such a sight!'

'Quick, Bella, Iain Peitrie's coming up the brae. Och look, he's gone all red, he's that sweet on you.'

Bright eyes and giggles and cheeks like petals, how adorable our sisters were in their first dewy days. We couldn't have guessed they were dancing away from us and so we scowled and thought them daft.

On to the pub to pull up in a drama of flinting hooves and harness jangle as Jamie MacDonald hurried out with a pint of stout. Our Granny Morag downed it like a parched gentlewoman.

'Ye'll have time for another one, will ye not, Mistress Sinclair?'

'Well, maybe ye're right. I'll be needing my strength. We're tae be visiting Tómas, and his Alice is a fanciful talker. Och, and if ye wouldna mind putting a wee drop in the flask against the cold.'

And, when we set off again, she was up to 'Mairi's Wedding'.

Uncle Tómas was a barbarous man, who had sired a browbeaten clutch whom he leathered nightly for the crimes he hadn't discovered and the sins they were going to commit in the morning. He seemed to have inherited all the worst elements from Rob Mór and Morag; their kink of violence, their fever and sudden cataracts of rage, their drunkenness. But their pity and love were not in him. His was a house without laughter and where no one sang.

We feared him. But it was Lachlan, his bastard, who harboured the deadly hatred which was to climax in bloody struggle years later, and leave our Uncle Tómas unable to beat up anyone ever again. What Granny Morag thought of this man, we never knew. But he was her second son.

For her, the glee of visiting was in preparing and once she arrived, it went sour. The house was as wintry as a workhouse in the barren mountains, where cries were twisted into echoing chuckles and there were no neighbours to come running.

Tómas was always in bed and his wife shivered round her kitchen in a long whisper till he called.

'. . . Malcolm's away fer peat and wee Angus is lying in the shed. Och, I had tae send him there after the night, Mistress. Tómas is a hard man.'

'Alice!'

And she'd wince away to his room.

'Semmit! . . . breeks! . . . grovit! . . . What are ye footering about for, woman!'

He'd sit on the edge of the bed while she dressed him.

'Fag!' And she'd place a cigarette in his mouth, light it and tie up his shoes.

Our grandmother looked at her with freezing contempt and turned back to the kitchen.

Then, one by one, our cousins would come in like charred sighs, to shrink dumbly against the walls, waiting for their turn to sit at the table and, when it came, they lapped at the broth and listened nervously for his voice.

'Yis mither's been putting maggots in the soup again. Can ye no see them creepin' about in the bowl? Ye were out at the dung heap this morning, were ye not, Alice? But they slide down that easy, ye wouldna notice. Dolly maun have had four in that last mouthful just now . . . and ye didna notice, did ye, lass?'

So he turned our stomachs with sick-making pictures, grinning as our cousins turned white in their places and trowelling smells and nightmares into their plates until Granny Morag lost patience.

'Will ye leave the bairns alone, Tómas,' she'd snap, but it was usually too late. One by one they put down their spoons and ran away. Our Uncle Tómas scraped their leavings into his bowl and ate with relish.

Our grandmother drank her tea and fidgeted, ruffled by Alice and incensed by Tómas. She had no time for chattels or bullies and wasn't good at wasting time in one place for long, anyway, especially when her flask was empty and the tea was neat. Gratefully, we would see her working up to our release.

'And when will ye be getting out the welcome then, Tómas?'

'Well now, mither, the fact is that ye're calling at a bit of a bad moment . . .'

'A bad moment!' This was what she waited for. 'So it's bad fer a wifie tae visit her son, is it?' She slapped her bonnet back on her head and silenced his protests with a swift blow from her umbrella. 'I can see when we're not wanted. Indeed I can. Come along, bairns. We'll not be staying a minute longer in this midden.'

And we were withdrawn like princes.

What a relief to escape into the dappled night, where we could stuff our ties into our pockets and chase the black sheep shadows down the hills and blow the airs and mims into the trees like crumpled scarves, until she became our own darling Mother Morag again and crowded us into her arms.

Then someone would discover the last full bottle under the

seat and we'd swallow its fire in the frost-cold dark, until our bellies were hot as forges and we were tripping and stumbling over baffles of words. Bats dived by with torches for eyes and an octopus swung its tentacles, where only a gorse bush had stood before; but, cocooned in my grandmother's shawl, in the nest of her scent, I was voluptuously safe and would wake up in my bed in the morning with her songs and stories still in my ears and without ever wondering how I'd got there.

She lived a life constantly spurred by tides of extravagance, for thirty days ebbing in a current of rehearsals and wishes, which measured us for clothes which could never be bought and coined promises which could never be kept. We would have fur-lined coats and football boots and six-course meals three times a day and she would put by enough every month to make us tycoons in a year.

So she borrowed and pirated and ran up impossible debts, happy as Santa Claus, and, on the thirty-first day, she surged in with banquets of trifle and marzipan, completely forgetting the bills as she squandered the little allowance on pantomime and eye-catching nonsense. When I look back, we were like vaga- bonds with a monthly wedding cake and, although notches riddled the tally stick like woodworm, she never came down to earth. She locked the front door on creditors and chased out the back way after floating dandelion seeds.

She wafted home with china pekes and brass candlesticks and silk tassles for curtains of jute, and humiliated our long-suffering grocer when the price of last week's sugar was nervously men- tioned.

Periodically, she would insist on a family photograph and chivvy us into the village to line up in identical sailor suits, looking like the merchant navy. More often than not, she became so overheated with the idea that we all burst into tears and it had to be abandoned: or one of us would go missing and the picture would have to be taken without him. But the successful efforts were rewarded with issues of pandrops and beaming smiles all round – and paid for by a long diet of pure oatmeal.

Now they lie in an attic for the nostalgia of rainy days, to be smirked at by her great-grandchildren and dreamed over by me.

For there she is, grandly posed in the centre, transfixing mankind with imperious eyes and still clutching her umbrella.

Evergreen witch-woman who never mellowed. It is impossible to think of her placidly. She explodes back into the mind like a firework, with her tantrums and dances, her quirks and cackles, her salt and songs still sparking.

Often, it is the edge of her voice which badgers me awake and hers is the face that appears in the fire. The long, unholy nights of her magic capture me again and she is there, whirling us through the steam and lamplight, taunting Annie and massacring the harmonium, Rabelaisian with stories and gently covering old Angus with a blanket.

I see her frisking in with the morning milk, while the rest of us were still half-asleep, pole-vaulting round the boiler, smothered with suds, cuffing Lachlan, kissing Catrina, strutting to the village in a new frilly blouse. But, most of all, she is in the last low glow, rocking in her chair, deep in her own solitary world.

For my grandmother was an alcoholic. The little cups of her girlhood overflowed down the years, until a bottle of whisky a day was not half enough and she was astray on a desert of aching thirst.

In the mornings she would rise, still drunk from the night before, her hands shivering after the stone-dry hours, stretched out for the glass that always waited on the table and without which she could not have started the day, although only a dram restored her.

Whisky was her life and her escape from life. It glossed over the frustrations, which constantly goaded her, and made the disappointments bearable and, above all, it cushioned her spirit, which could not compromise, against the reality which demanded terms.

She drank to get drunk, because she liked it and, later, because she couldn't help it and, in my childhood, I can't have seen her sober very often. Yet, she never grew sottish, or vomited, or overbalanced, or fell into stupor, or carried hangover. There was nothing disgusting about her drunkenness. It was just an indulgence which made her shake a little in the morning, sway in the evening and grow sweet and sad late at night.

She was lucky, I suppose, because Big Jamie at the bar was an old friend, who looked after her in the late, blind hours and never refused her on penniless days. Because of him, the craving seemed a petty weakness, without need for begging or shame and we were not corrupted. But I sometimes wonder what might have been without him and if her natural arrogance would have rebelled in time.

As it was, no one, apart from Rob Mór, had ever suggested abstinence and she would probably have thought it was a new curse, if they had. She chuckled over her own forgetfulness and scolded herself mildly for the breakages; the cups that were left till they cracked on the range and the plates, thrown at early irritations and which grew more slippery as the day progressed. Plastic was in the future and we never had saucers. It didn't occur to our Granny Morag to vex herself over a problem, which was only a problem when the bottle was empty, and she was well content to ripen up to the routine Bacchanalia when it was full.

And, later, when the pot of lights boiled over, bubbling a troupe of gremlins and hobs and greybeards and beasties across her way, she treated them with the same basic logic. The imps were pushed summarily off the range and hairy gollochs were plucked from the basin, without quarter. She used to row with the cat, that was supposed to follow her home in the dark, and complain that an old man kept tapping on the pub window.

But the phantoms grew bolder and more intrusive, so that we used to hear her damning and blasting at familiars who wouldn't let her sleep; and, at about three o'clock one morning, the whole family was roused by a pandemonium, which sounded as though the house was being demolished round our ears. When we rushed into the back room, there was our grandmother, philosophically nailing bits of wood into the walls.

'It's they bliddy serpents,' she said, crossly. 'They keep creeping through the cracks and it's more than a body can stand. I'll have tae write tae the factor in the morrow.'

She grew more bizarre and mercurial, crewed by invisible hands and veering in secret winds, tack and tack, until it was impossible to tell the course of her moods from one minute to the next. Her face, always apple bright, mantled with too-vivid heat and her breathing grew rapid and shallow.

She was ill and her only answer was to live the faster, as

though there would never be enough time to cram in all the feasts and impulses and emotions and gusto she needed to taste. She squandered her passions over us, gambling for action with precious drops of blood, for, as the great arteries feeding her heart narrowed and hardened, she scoffed at the idea of visiting doctors and to the end she did not slow down.

And down in the village the hostility grew and, as far away as the distant county hall, the problem of our granddam was discussed and plans were laid. But, as the community turned its back, so she pulled its other outcasts into her fold, swelling our family with rejects and misfits, giving without sense of proportion: money to Tattie Boggle Dan, as rich as a sheik despite his old clothes; mutton loaf to Fat Eck and her bed to Bertie, whose own was only a mile away.

It was no rare event in the kitchen to step over Bible Tam's body, still sandwiched between its wooden texts, asleep in the steam from the rains he had stood in for hours the night before.

'There'll be weeping and wailing and gnashing of teeth.' Forecasting Judgment Day, even in his dreams.

She moved at the head of a weird procession of strays, who came after not only for the windfalls, and only her censors were too blind to see that our grandmother was utterly pure. She gave loyalty and fun and truth and fierce protection without thought and somehow turned fear into a mouse and men's worries into feathers. Her instinct of right and wrong became a guide I will never be able to follow, because in her path there were no greys. She was a woman, all woman, and a life, all life.

But, greater than all, our Granny Morag gathered us to her with a love so warm and strong that we never knew we were five unwanted children.

CHAPTER SEVEN

WITCHES AND HAPPENINGS

I NEVER saw the valley of my childhood, though I lived in it for eighteen years. It was a place cloaked by the eclipsing seasons in snows and clouds and rains and mingling mists and dews and summer haze, shadowed by highlands and sprayed by surf. It emerged and submerged through veils, its shapes and edges a thousand hints, but impossible to see clearly. It was uncanny and magic and mantled in eternal purdah. A place without beginning or end and the people and events it bred often seemed touched by the supernatural.

Among us were heavy-headed children, rapt in chimes and poems, whose mothers sometimes hid them till they grew too old or they freed themselves to wander the braes, seeing lifetime lands of raspberries and clocks and crying over stones.

There were seers and healers and visionaries and a witch; weird women, who passed by leaving a trail of spells and hauntings and gramarge behind them like exploding crackers. It was said that they mixed potions, full of the moon and rat's gizzards, which turned lovers into husbands and cold wives into hot-water bottles and childless widows into mothers and even husbands into last wills and testaments. They cured growths and rheumatism and livers and baldness; tomorrows were their yesterdays and no one doubted for a second that Mrs. Crook could stick pins into wax dolls *successfully*. 'Look how Maggie Chalmers' old man died so convenient sudden!'

Queer, numinous females and made the more sinister because, apart from Mrs. Crook, who looked every bit a night hag, they appeared to be normal; grey hair respectably bunned, benevolent, middle-aged eyes like faded perse, and shopping bags. Some were even married and mothers. Most were in our aunt's circle and, although she stressed that they were all impostors, I heard trees splitting and smelt roasting toads in their presences and was left with the sensation of walking on snake bites.

Among those with second sight who did not visit our house was one Martha Neilson, a distrait Lilliputian, who may not have come because she preferred her own company, or perhaps because she was not invited. Certainly her reputation, as one having the 'gift', was spread over a hundred miles, which was more than could be claimed by Auntie Annie or her fellow harpies; and did not gratify them at all.

People journeyed like pilgrims to consult Martha Neilson, and usually had to go home disappointed, for she lived in complete seclusion, as frightened of her own powers as a ghost of its reflection. Yet, before we ourselves reached them, our futures broke into her isolation and distracted her.

Everyone knew how her wreath had been delivered to the Keirs on the day their boy was killed in the war and before they had even received the news; and how she'd snatched wee Tam Pate from under a tree the very moment before a bolt of lightning sliced it right down the middle and left it in flames; and how every one of Soutar's pigs had dropped dead in a row of hams after she'd warned of a great family loss to come, and them all hoping it would be Granda Soutar, who'd been lying snug on his money-filled mattress for near quarter of a century.

Her mana was beyond doubt, a legend and official, and the village held her in that special fearless esteem reserved in the north of Scotland for a genuine seer. They guarded her staunchly against outsiders and her privacy was so respected that, although her cottage was the last one on our side of the village, I had never seen her before that night.

Gordon Nichol had been missing for a month. He had done it before, yearly, in fact, going off his food for a week each March, disappearing for three days and returning as cadaverous as a love-sick old tom cat to face the fury and useless cross-examination of his wife. But it was Autumn now and he'd been eating fine and so, after allowing a few days for the possible frailty of man, Constable Duff organized a posse. It searched along the coast and over the moors to the mountains, where word was spread among the crofters, who passed it to the shepherds, but Gordon Nichol was not found.

94

So, after a week without sign of him, the local keening chorus began consoling his wife with the idea that he'd left her for a jade in Aberdeen and, after a fortnight, everyone began to forget about it.

That night, when we were wakened by the pounded door, it was raining as though the sea had tipped herself over us, and there was Martha Neilson, near to fainting on the step.

'It's himself, Gordon Nichol,' she whispered. 'He's gone back tae her. I saw him by the Minnie Burn below Taran Crag. He's gone back tae her.'

We wrang her out and curled her up quaking over the stove, but she wouldn't say more than that and stayed so agitated that, finally, Lachlan was sent for Robbie beag, who sent him to Constable Duff, who, as a believer in the 'gift' besides being a dutiful policeman, put on his uniform and arrived on his bike.

The Minnie Burn flowed through a remote corner of the glen and was named after a young girl found hanging there many years before. No one lived within miles of it and it was a long way from our cottage, but Lachlan, Calum, P.C. Duff and I set out, a line of sleepy moles burrowing through the woolly night.

The torchlight weaved drunkenly ahead, leading us into pits and lighting up impossible eyes until we all moved closer together, pretending not to see, and Lachlan's insistent whistle slid down our nerve endings like the wail of the last banshee.

With the sea roaring behind us and the dawn spurting beacons across the mountain peaks, we came to the burn, slurping across its bed of stones, slow and thick as blood. It filtered through mud-clogged weeds and carried roach to the jaws of waiting pike and young trout to their cannibal parents. On its dark banks, the vampire plants drank their victims dead and, in that first patch of day, a sundew folded its red leaves round a greenfly and smilingly ate it. We wished we were back safe in our beds.

One of my brothers found him, Gordon Nichol, half-fallen in the water beneath Minnie's tree, just as the seer had told; and, as we stood looking in fright, the current rubbed his dead bit hand back and forth against the tree as though he would never stop reaching for it. For it was Minnie who had been his love and Minnie he had strangled and hanged there full twenty years before.

Death by natural causes, they said, and the church took his remains and Martha Neilson went back to her solitude without another word. Strange, though, how that confession note had been found in his pocket: almost as though he'd known it was his turn to be taken . . .

Eery currents like this ran under our normal lives and left us tuned to auras of mystery and myth. We saw Roane, the sea-princess, disguised in every seal and there was no boat launched without at least one thole-pin of rowan wood to protect it from the sea-devils, and there were many, many other things we knew, for the laws of magic had ruled us for generations and we were never incredulous.

So, the day Catrina was brought home covered in blood and crying deliriously of yellow witches in the woods, we believed and the whole village with us. Her arms were scratched into tatters and skin and her clothes had been mauled with such ferocity that they hung in shreds from her shoulders. There were bare patches on her head where whole fistfuls of hair had been pulled out and in her neck were three deep holes, which could have been made by the Devil's trident and had mercifully just missed the jugular vein.

They had found her, lying unconscious at the edge of the wood. It was a wonder she was alive at all and it took her days to recover. She came out of shock with us all round her bed and the tale was told.

They'd been dancing, she said, the witch and Black Donald in the air above a black circle and she wouldn't have seen them at all if the witch hadn't laughed and made her look up. Then they'd both leaped on her and all she could remember was running out of the wood with the witch on her back; a witch with a yellow cloak and golden eyes.

If there were those who doubted the story, they held their tongues when strapping Sim Bruce was found in the same spot a few weeks later, with wounds an inch deep. He whispered that he'd seen the Earl o' Hell and only a madman would have walked in the woods after that.

Months went by and Catrina and Sim grew well, but kept the scars for the rest of their lives, and through the winter people would come across red stains and hair in the snow near the trees and tales were told of strangers who'd passed that way and were never seen again.

At night, the sounds of pipes and screeches could be heard for miles and, in the Spring, lambs were stolen for black sacrifice, it was said, until Farmer Gregson took down his gun and, with never a word to a soul, walked into the woods and was gone.

Two days later, there was a shot and he emerged with the witch over his shoulder. She was about four feet long and yellow indeed, with black-lined face and pointed ears, ferocious-looking, even when dead. She was the last wild cat ever found in our glen.

So, when I look back on my childhood it seems to sing with violence; not senseless, corrupting havoc, but immense explosions of temperament and sensations. Each event, however small, was an extreme in itself and never to be forgotten or matched; the terror I felt on seeing my first train, drowning me in sirens and scrambling people and steam, like a thousand factory tea breaks; the nausea of sinking my teeth into a brilliant, scarlet apple and discovering my first – and last – tomato; the falls and fights and fevers and Granny Morag, all so intense that I would have finished up punch-drunk, but for the rock-solid love and safeness within the cottage.

Yet, even the cottage almost saw its end during one of our grandmother's economy drives. These periodically slashed essentials and later invested twice the savings in repairing the damage.

A new leg was added to the table once, to such effect that, by the time it and the remaining three had been sawn in turn to achieve the desired stability, we were left with an object more suited to a Chinese teahouse and had to sit on the floor to eat off it, until she relented and bought a new one.

This time, it was the chimney sweep who was peremptorily 'cut' and replaced by a brush, which Granny Morag had bought fifth hand for two shillings and assured us, as she bore it off to the roof, would last our lifetimes.

It rasped down the chimney, like a giant cat's tongue, and the room filled with sooty birds and plates and bronchitis and night and last rattles and our grandmother's triumphant howls echoing down the flue. With more and more vigour she plunged from above and, suddenly, the end of the brush whirled off its pole, scything through the sponge of soot like a great hairy golloch, and I remember quite distinctly a whole chestful of gold doubloons cascading before my eyes as it hit me . . .

I came to in a room full of Negroes and dinosaurs humped under black sheets. A woman was mourning over a brush and 'Just lie still, laddie, we'll get the doctor,' they said, The walls breathed in the lamplight, closing in on me and expanding in time to the drums in my head, and I seemed to be inhaling through chocolate, when a lump of carbon came blazing on to the floor.

'Christ! The lum's on fire,' shouted Lachlan and Granny Morag dropped the brush and skeltered out to the wash-house, leaving the back door wide open, and the draught which blew up the chimney had fanned the embers into flames by the time she returned with a heavy earthenware pot in her arms.

To the accompaniment of Auntie Annie's doleful prophesies and Catrina's screams, she began flinging handfuls of salt from it up the flaming stack and more salt was tipped into the coal scuttle and my brothers sent with it to the roof. Then, as I lay deserted on the floor, the cottage fizzed and crackled like popcorn, as salt met fire and filled the kitchen with sparks. The doctor was long forgotten.

An hour later it was over but for a night-long vigil, and Lachlan and Calum descended without eyebrows and someone slapped Catrina at last.

'We should never have cleaned the bliddy lum in the first place,' I heard Herself muttering, as they carried me off to bed.

Not all our dramas were catastrophic, however. Each year was cornerstoned by its holidays, which kept us in a state of excited anticipation for months beforehand and talking for months after. The Mayday fair, the Highland Games and Hogmanay swept us all, shallow- and deep-water fish together, into the same net, where we forgot our differences in the cheer. And, on one exotic, always-to-be-remembered night, the moving pictures arrived.

We didn't have a cinema then, so the first show took place in the village hall, a windy, low-ceilinged barn used more for ceilidhs than local politics. But it did have a piano and the walls outside had been plastered for a week with posters of heroines with rosebud lips and spaniel-eyed heroes in turbans.

A man had come from Dornoch with the picture machine and even a special pianist had arrived and we started queuing outside about two hours early, because the organizing mister, Hector Keir (that would be Ernie's brother), was a methodical mannie and wouldn't open the door one minute before the allotted time.

When that arrived, most of the chairs were knocked over in the scrum and not everyone managed to get in anyway. Of those who did, half had come in 'round the side' without paying, and then the performance was held up for three-quarters of an hour by an argument between old Keir and Dollopy Kirst, because there wasn't a seat left for her and she'd reserved.

The film was *The Sheik*, with Rudolph Valentino sweeping innumerable maidens across the desert to the flat trilling of the piano. Yet, all I remember of it is sitting in the front row, hypnotized by black and white flashes and the sound of everyone reading the dialogue out loud at different pace. Those who managed to reach the end each time whispered it, during the next piece of action, to those who hadn't and the selfish kept up an angry 'Shhh!' from beginning to end.

In the middle, the projector broke down and the necking couples at the back sat up like a row of pink owls as the gas mantles suddenly lit up, and although the front row wasn't greatly impressed with Rudy, we all took our half-sucked humbugs out of our mouths and whistled and stamped our feet till he was back in his tent with another female.

We were rewarded for our enthusiasm by the second picture, *East Street*, and cunning Chaplin, hilariously pathetic, tumbling across the screen and, all at once, I understood that I was in the *cinema*.

Later, they built a proper stone one in the village to which we went every Saturday and saw *The Four Horsemen of the Apocalypse*, the three Stooges and Our Gang, *The Hunchback of Notre Dame*, Buster Keaton and, later, *Treasure Island* and *Beau Geste*, and I became a fan for life.

The Mayday fair arrived, in fact, a week before the first of May. It had to be in Aberdeen on Mayday and only visited us at all because we were almost en route from Dornoch. But it arrived with bray and ceremony just the same, rolling up in brightly painted waggons and slapping posters covered with Big Wheels and Shoots on to every wall along the way.

That it had neither a big wheel nor a shoot didn't matter a bit. It had three roundabouts, a small one of outsize rabbits chasing double-decker trams so slowly that the mothers could walk round hanging on to their riding toddlers and we could jump on when the fair-man was busy pumping it into action – and run off again before he had time to bring it to a halt and collar us. Then there was a sophisticated train, to which we graduated with age and a girl whom we could kiss as it went through the tunnel.

But the pride of the fair was the beautiful Merry-Go-Round in the centre, where its dappled ponies in scarlet harness waltzed stately golden chariots through a circle of fluted pillars. It was our Granny Morag's delight, epitomizing all her ideas of style and grace; the baroque and grandeur of the design, the waves of gramophone music, the flying, flowing gallop carrying her over the common herd into a gracious trance. She could not have enough of it and, during the fair's three-day stay, she could be persuaded to leave her favourite seat only for a short visit to the rifle range with Robbie beag.

There, the pair of them had a vigorous annual argument with the range owner over the fixed sights of his weapons. This ended with our grandmother insisting on using her son's rifle, to such effect that the fair-man would finally refuse to give her any more prizes and threaten to close the range if she didn't go away.

At night, the three would get drunk together and, owing to her weakness for flowery plaster vases, we had a collection which threatened to crowd us out of the cottage and could have kept a shop in business for a year.

With Herself happily whirling in a three-day lasso, we were freed into the jungle of trumpetings and screams and gramophones, scrapping like chipmunks, and toffee apples, dangerous as cacti, and looping hoops and crashing coconuts and trailing leaves of striped canvas and hoarse gorillas beating their chests and howling before carrying off the unwary into their caves. The air smelt of sausages and skunk and we swung through it on ropes of fried chips and dreams of schemes.

With enough of us together, we could rig the competition at every stall and the Sturrock twins, putting their identical faces to good use, managed to have two goes at everything for the price of one. At the skittles, Bug Renwick was sent round the side with a stick to sweep them all over each time one of us bowled and the skittle man handed over a goldfish in a bowl, a top and a rubber ball before he discovered what was happening.

At the back of Madam Lola's tent we found a tear and wriggled into the incense gloom to hear whispered consultations and roll out again, curled up with giggles.

'She just telt old Ernie Pate that he's a great trial tae come.'

'Hey, Bug, yis sister's going tae meet a dark, braw laddie.'

'Whit? Again? She's met them a' already, has she no, Bug?'

'I'll bash yis teeth in!'

'Ma Crook's having a right fight wi' the fortune wifie the now. Says she's been ta'en on.'

'If I wis the wifie, I'd be giving Ma Crook back her bawbee afore she turned me intae a moose.'

And, shouting and shoving and squabbling, we were edging nearer and closer to the tent on the far corner of the pitch, a square splendour draped with rugs and mystery from Arabian nights and fronted by a platform, on which gambolled three hawk-faced midgets round a man in a top hat. Closer and quieter and awkward, with the last silver threepenny bits glued damply to our palms and my belly shrivelled and I wish I hadn't come.

'See the most fantastic women in the world! No one under sixteen can see this daring French show. This is a show for men,' bawled the top hat and grabbed me as we arrived. 'You're sixteen, aren't you, sonny?' And Lachlan kicked me from behind.

'Yes, mister.' My voice squeaked, as I stood on tiptoe to gain seven years. The next moment I was inside.

Dark-full of sweating shadows and hands in pockets and the heavy, stealthy anticipation of men waiting. A smell as thick as custard smothered me and I could see nothing, but the others pushed me through dull bumps and impacts, blind and random, like being lost in a stack of cushions; though we reached the front at last and, somehow, the shouting top hat had gained the stage before us.

The three midgets appeared, falling over and cracking jokes and I couldn't laugh. How old their faces were and cruel, as though they were even more vicious to life than life had been to them. I was glad when a gramophone coughed and two women sidled on and the men growled. I thought of Bess Piercy's mother and wondered when it would happen and then, without announcement, it did.

She rode in, backwards and incredibly, on Indian flute music; a double Sophie Tucker, ballooning round straps and over fastenings as she waded towards us. At the edge of the stage she stopped and, still with her back towards us, swayed, dangerously rocking herself off each foot like a tottering grand piano, until we began to retreat into the awe-silent crowd, while she stretched her arms and snapped her fingers and, once, shook the fleece of bleached hair that reached to her waist; and the men grew restless.

'Time ye gave it up, mistress,' came the first call from behind.

'Och no, she'd do fine in the barn,' shouted back wee Bert.

'So long as she didna turn over, lad.' And a big laugh started and cut into sudden quiet, for the woman on the stage had turned round to face us all.

The yellow hair was black at the roots and the eyebrows met over dull, stone eyes – and a great beard, like a blackthorn hedge, bristled from her ears to her chest. She stood with hands on hips and stared at us.

'It canna be true,' whispered Lachlan and I turned and ran, butting through the laugh-again crowd to the air, where I was immediately and violently sick.

The Highland Games took place under autumn hills outside Dornoch and everyone, who was not actually bedridden or our Auntie Annie, went to enter the dancing competitions or show cattle and horses or picnic or buy a big, satin tie from a Glasgow spiv; but primarily to cheer on Drew Heggie (who worked with Lachlan at the Slaughter) in his annual battle of putting the shot against the contemptible, red-haired A. Begg of the south. The result of this competition made or broke our day, for on it our honour was staked.

We set off in the frosted five a.m. night, crashing our way, half-dressed and asleep, through the cottage to the suicidal curses of old Angus and the muffled intonations of the distant blanketed aunt. Potted hough and pan loaves and cold potatoes and tea bread and apples were rammed into bags and bottles into pockets and Deamhan into the peat bucket by our chanting granny as the horn blasted us on to the back of Farmer Gregson's motor tree hauler. God knows how we ever got to the Games before he acquired that machine, because I can never remember those annual outings without seeing myself perched behind its great coils of wire on the back, with Mrs. Gregson and our grand-mother in beside the farmer and my brothers and sisters and crofters' children from miles about set, large ones to the outside, around me. Its motor had no fan-belt (or the belt was always broken) because every mile or so we came to a halt in clouds of steam and had to wait for the engine to come off the boil.

Those mornings had a special scent and feel not found again and never forgotten, beginning in the stars and riding on this mad old waggon into the cool, oyster dawn of the north. It came without twilight, a luminous horizon lifting from the sea and cutting pure across the night, a straight, sunless, silver band, widening and rising, until the whole sky was pearl and only the Morning Star still glinted. It spread down the black mountains, a lavender mist and touched the walls with hoar and changed its border from ivory to honey and rose and jade. Dawn without passion, clear and fresh as spring water; it slowly woke us up with its beauty and carried us on to Dornoch.

Dornoch was hung with banners and flags and early closing shops, for which the women reached, yearning from their seats at perilous angles and darting out to trill over the window displays each time the waggon stopped, which it did frequently, what with the steam and the traffic jams of cars and ponies and traps and late shoppers.

'We'll no get a place if they females dinna skelter,' Gregson would say, dourly, to us through his broken rear window, and we men would agree and shout angrily at our sisters. But there was always a place, of course, and always the same one on the north side of the Games ring, where we could sit on the grass or on the roof of the waggon and see everything.

The Games were opened by an earl, or sometimes a duke, or, at the very least, a sir, who drawled a short speech, which the few select visitors in his enclosure were privileged to hear, but which was inaudible to the crowd: though we all cheered heartily when it was finished.

Then marched the glory of the day, the highlight, which came at the beginning instead of the end, and touched every event which followed with splendour. The pipe bands. Row upon row of kilts and cocked bonnets, sporrans, plaids and gleaming spats, tides of dead colours. Men marching with swing, with the arrogance of centuries, with lungs firing a sound which stirred forgotten gods in Greece and Babylonian pipers and Negro and French ladies, who had danced to silk-clad musettes, and Boadicea and the Irish and which was ours and made us lions. This was the blood and the flame, the deep and wild force which had made fierce clans and drawn Scots to their causes and led the Gordons and the 'ladies from Hell' and the Argyll and Sutherlands and many more to immortal victory. I could feel it moving in my very heart even as a child. Our Granny Morag listened and her eyes blazed. It was the soul of Scotland.

With that, the day pole-vaulted away, high-jumping and wrestling and hill-racing round the platform of competing reels and marches and pibrochs in the centre. Tugs-o'-war groaned and skidded across invisible lines, weaving and heaving it seemed through flying larch trunks, the somersaulting bolts hurled by kilted Zeuses. On the platform, the pipers changed into dancers, challenging each other with pointed toes to jigs and hornpipes, sword dances and the Highland Fling, Strathspeys, as controlled as slow marches or abandoned as fevers, and the graceful, lilting ballet of Seann Triubhas. They twirled like coloured leaves above the rivalling giants. Little girls, pleasing with their dancing earnestness, and below, like fathers swinging small children on a beach, the men whirled round and round with their iron-headed hammers, which finally flew off on their own to land with murderous thud and smash the turf to mud.

They kept us chewing our pies into our fingers without even noticing the difference until, at last, our own Drew Heggie and the redhead from Paisley walked grimly on to the field. I felt as though I was wearing a damp vest and everyone tensed. Our grandmother pointed contemptuously to the Paisley man.

'Yon's no a man, it's a bullock', she snapped, as one who preferred her men to be spare and tough, rather than muscular; though, in fact, there was only a difference in height between the men.

The battle was conducted over the best of three 'puts' each and a groan growled through us as Drew lost the toss for last place, as he did every year.

'That bawbees was loaded fer certain,' Robbie beag muttered, as our man lifted the twenty-two-pound shot to his shoulder and bent all his weight on to one leg for a long, agonizing moment before pushing the stone into the air with a great forward heave.

'Christ! The mannie's playing at marbles,' said Lachlan, shocked, as the stone fell less than twenty feet and everyone from our glen baled unprintable insults, which turned poor Drew puce and must have added at least five feet of confidence to a fine 'put' by the redhead.

And, when Drew stepped up the second time, he stood over the stone, glaring at it till we thought he'd never pick it up, but just hammer it to dust where it lay. Then he was swelling under it again, calves bulging, biceps knotted, the veins in his neck standing out like oil pipes and his face puffed with affront. He balanced and sweated and swelled until it seemed sure he would burst; and then he lunged.

It was a magnificent throw, with the shot catapulting through the air to land over thirty-five feet away and, after it, Drew didn't even bother to take his third try, just waved on Mister Begg and accepted the trophy with dignity.

We carried him off the field in triumph before curling together, like field mice, on the back of the waggon and dreaming that we were champions, too, during the long ride home.

The year, with its folds of surprises and festivals and penniless pockets, began and ended with Hogmanay, a night which other lands celebrate with noisy insensibility, which the English virtually ignore and which for us was, and is, a mystic, fey time full of symbols and hopes and pagan old customs.

Christmas came and went, a day, worked as any other day, with the men out fishing and the village stores open. A few churchgoers went to worship, though even that was considered to be a newfangled, heretic habit. It was cardless and stockingless and we had hardly heard of Santa Claus. Presents were given on birthdays, if we were lucky, and celebration was Hogmanay.

The year's last day was papered in black, with the dark giving way to a gloaming for only a few hours. We were so far north that we had to light our way through the winters with candles and lived like pit ponies for four months of the year.

But, in this long night, there was hoarding and scrimping and the clonking of secret full bottles and the whiffs of midnight baking. To be run short of anything on Hogmanay would have been unthinkable. We had no Christmas puddings, but the black bread was richer and fruitier than a brandy-soaked squire and the shortbread dissolved into sweet, crumbly butter on our tongues.

All day was an impatient hunt for things to do until evening. The girls pressed their dresses a dozen times and Granny Morag and Annie rummaged for old cups and mugs and jam-jars, anything that would serve for the hospitality.

We boys, evicted from the domestic scene, met others to push and loaf with, aimlessly hovering round the harbour or hacking branches off trees with our knives, until it was time to go home and put on our kilts.

At eight o'clock Robbie beag arrived with his woman, Siubhan, and Bert from the farm with his father, and all the tinkers from next door. Even grim Uncle Tómas came with Alice at his heels, blushing and giggling over his once-a-year good nature, and our cousins almost relaxed. The cottage was so full that the walls seemed to bulge and people continually fell backwards over the fender and burnt their bottoms on the range.

Our Uncle Angus and Bert's Da tucked their fiddles under their chins and sawed away like two manic Pied Pipers in a personal struggle that went back to before anyone else in the room was born. They refused to stand together, so pulled us from one end of the kitchen to the other with their music and glowered at each other through the gaps in the crowd. It was generally agreed that Bert's Da had the technique, but auld Angus had the heart.

And, as we buried the old year, memories and regrets and secret vows and hopes joined the wake and the very young grew excited about the new tomorrow and our older brothers and sisters began to exchange long, candy looks and the parents and grandparents and uncles and aunts and friends remembered the years spent together before and welcomed the coming one to them. Good and bad, we loved each other deeply and the midnight chimes began to strike.

One . . . two . . . three . . . four . . . and Robbie beag was pushed hastily out of the back door . . . five . six .. seven . . . eight . . . and everyone began kissing every one else . . . nine . . . ten . . . eleven . . . last second of the old year, first instant of the new . . . twelve! A Happy New Year! A Happy New Year!

The back door was shaking under the pounding from outside and Granny Morag flung it wide open to let our 'first foot' in. Dark and handsome, our Uncle Robbie beag crossed the threshold with his magic gifts for the New Year; a lump of coal to bring us warmth, a piece of black bun to bring us food, a farthing for prosperity and a smoked herring, dressed in coloured crêpe paper, for luck; and a bottle.

Granny Morag took a respectable sook from that and revived her son with a bottle of her own whisky, as he was pulled joyously to the fire.

We sang 'Auld Lang Syne' and the women wiped their eyes and filled the glasses till our throats scorched and Auntie Annie got so carried away that she sang an unrhythmical solo in a forgotten, quavering voice and burst into tears at the end when everyone applauded.

Then it was our turn to go first-footing and we fell gasping from the pupa of bodies into the night pool, blowing bubbles which rose to the sky as wraiths; swept along by the wind, as cold on the outside as if we were naked, but with a whisky lining which kept us from caring. Snowflakes wriggled in our ears like tadpoles and slid over the tops of our gumboots, rubbing raw patches on our calves and trickling down the insides till our toes chattered.

Others passed us in single file, black lumps behind a lantern, on the way to our cottage and the farm and Drew Heggie at the Slaughter.

'A guid Hogmanay,' we called.

'And mony happy ones tae yis,' called back the New Year dragon in six different voices, before weaving away into the dark; and the village came to us, milky blue and window-glowing under the moon.

The doors were open, there was no need to knock. 'Come in! Come in! And a happy New Year. Set yisselves down and have a droppie. My, but the wee'ns are frozen. Ye'll have ginger wine and a bit of shortbread, bairnies, will ye no? That's right, Calum. Help yisself, laddie.'

So we went on from Dollopy Kirst's to the Renwicks, to the Sturrocks, to Teeny-face-Troon and Conn Barnet's, to the canny, who poured out fingers of sherry in the hope that the bottle would do again next year, and to the lavish, who tilted tumblerfuls into our bright-eyed grandmother; and all had a drink from our bottle and we all had a pull at theirs.

We went to all the houses we knew till the light of the first day came and we were muddled and fuddled and mumbling happy nonsense to each other, full of cake and goodwill after the loving night.

For the spirit of Hogmanay was real and tangible. It wasn't just a great overstuffing. It was the smiles on faces normally stern and the friendliness in eyes often hostile. It was the reminder that people are good. It was the hour when everything you wanted seemed suddenly to be within reach; the spell of the promise of a new start, a New Year in which wishes could come true and dreams be caught, when our secret, ideal selves could become flesh-and-blood real, if we kept our resolutions. It was that no one ever said, 'Thank God that's over.' It was Crabbie's Green Ginger Wine and shortbread.

CHAPTER EIGHT

ROBBIE BEAG

Our uncle Robbie beag was not a smiling man. He had a hard, gypsy face, dark and scored by strong lines. His high cheekbones and big, curving nose were our grandfather's, and he had eyes so black that their irises had vanished into the pupils. Sometimes his laugh would shout aggressively, but he was not given to anything as half-hearted as a smile.

There was much secretive and sinister about this man. He was so sprung and watchful. Even the way he walked, so fluidly and quiet, like an animal hunting, made him seem subtly dangerous.

He was hero to me, when I was growing. We saw him supervise furtive distillings in hidden bothies and shoot down the laird's game with deadly precision on full moon nights and mix easily at the bar, or harbour, and we sensed women want him and men treat him with careful respect. He was powerful, called to our house whenever trouble menaced, and we grew up knowing that he could do anything.

Robbie beag's past was obscure. He was so close, never mentioning where he had been or who had been there, and so what I know is only a flotsam of hints gathered from the datemarks of a few yellowed postcards, from half-remembered comments and abruptly unfinished tales and from chancing on one or two people, who had known of him somewhere long ago. Nevertheless, even with its gaps years wide, it is the account of a thriller of a time.

As a boy, our uncle had not been a defiant rebel in the family tradition, that is, he did not deliberately set out to disobey orders merely because they were issued; but there was an aloofness about him, which simply ignored any rules in his way, and this remained a characteristic all his life.

When Rob Mór left for America in 1901, Robbie, his eldest son, was ten years old and, according to our grandmother, was the one most stricken by the desertion. For a long time he hated and missed the old man with equal bitterness and become uncontrollably restless until, four years later, he stowed away on a local drifter.

It may only have been the trip which drew him at first, but, after the angry captain had discovered and set him to work, he jumped ship when they put in at Yarmouth. Fourteen years passed before he was seen at home again.

He must have found work as deckhand on a cargo boat, for among her papers are a couple of khaki-stained notes from Bilbao and Rio de Janeiro addressed to Granny Morag.

Later, comes a line from Marseilles and probably it was only a couple of weeks after that that his vessel docked in Egypt – Alexandria, full of rich squalor and wrapped in a stench, which then, as now, reached four miles out to sea, sucking up stray ships long before the city, herself, came into view.

Arabs in white robes and women hooded by long tarhah and vield in black; muezzin, with their quincuncial daily cries from the minarets, calling the faithful to prayer; the Suq, savage with smells and sights and noise, hot as a furnace, harshly, boundlessly different from the politely pretty Latin markets of before. The first instantly foreign city: glamorous beyond fantasy to the lad from a bleak hamlet on the north-east coast of Scotland. What happened to him then? Did he desert ship again? Or, did he just wander off to explore streets and alleys and become wholly lost in the shuttered, bursting maze? Whichever it was, he certainly did not sail away with his sea-mates on that night's tide.

Dear mother,
    This is a big place and I will be staying here. Write me at the Post Office. Your son, Robert Sinclair.

For some years our uncle Robbie beag lived in Egypt, mostly in Alexandria, I think. Prosaic, non-committal messages, bare as bones, occasionally arrived when he felt duty bound to communicate, as at New Year, or when he moved room. Once, astonishingly, he sent a hand-drawn, tinted picture postcard:

These are things called piramids and I saw some the day. They would be big graves for old kings. The dot I have put on the picture is about the size I would be against them lots of people go to see them.

So he had journeyed as far as Cairo; but he never wrote for help.

How he survived alone in such a bedlam of poverty will always be a mystery. A raw, alien boy could hardly have found even the humblest of work as a water carrier, or a cooked-meat vendor, or a shoe-shine, or a fruit-juice seller in the narrow lanes against the ferocious competition of the swarming poor and, for the same reason, there was even less chance of making a living as a beggar. In those first days, I think he must have discovered unsuspected talent and proved to be a remarkably successful thief in a community of experts.

Later, darkened by the sun, he would have blended easily with the Alexandrians. With a little local knowledge and the crumbs of a few languages, there were tourists to pick up in the cafés on the Corniche and guide round sights, or lure into brothels (robbing them discreetly at the same time).

One can imagine the surprise of those intrepid European matrons to find themselves boarded on to excursion dromedaries by a Scots teenager; and the gentlemen travellers, totally insulated by their Britishness, refusing to believe it and shouting at him in pidgin English anyway.

So several years passed and I think he stayed so long because he was a natural swashbuckler. He wanted to live on the knife spine of life, where all his senses and wits and flair would be overworked to maintain his existence. It was not philosophy or antiquities which pulled him to Egypt. It was this. For all its reputation of indolence, here was a seething potful of life, voluptuous and sudden, hot and sinuous in its turning moods, dressed in golden sand and silver dust and the discarded veils of new women and the sweet smell of hashish. All, with poetic fitness, in the shadow of a great necropolis.

The surprise is not that he stayed, but that he ever left; although, at last, he did.

Soon after I began work, an old Irishman, called what else but

Pat, turned up in the glen and you could tell that our uncle wasn't well pleased to see him, even though he stayed a week or so at the house in the village because they'd known each other in Dublin in 1912. He was a garrulous and interesting old man, always asking and telling about folk we'd never heard of: Murphy and O'Donnell and the Fenian brothers, Hood.

'One of us, indeed ye are, Robert,' he'd say, thumping our embarrassed relation on the back. 'Ah, a great young man, who gave his heart and the strength of his arm to the Irish cause. Ye should all be proud to be the family of him.'

Small wonder we were curious. Until then, none of us had known that Himself had even set foot in Ireland, let alone done glorious deeds there. We flooded the history out of the visitor with large drams, and Robbie beag was only too thankful to see the back of him when he finally moved on, promising that the mere mention of the name Robert Sinclair would make us welcome guests at loyal hearthsides the length and breadth of Erin.

What a strange choice to have made (if it were choice), to go to Ireland, that dreaming green cloud more like a painting, or a fable, than a proper, living land; quastar against the star of Egypt. Yet, there in County Mayo, Pat had come across our uncle travelling with a Jewish pedlar and selling egg-beaters and clocks. It must have been thin trading on that soil-starved Atlantic crag, where there were barely enough eggs to serve a whisk and little call for clocks, when time, itself, was never called.

Of course, they met in a bar, the pedlar grumbling fatalistically and the morose Robert Sinclair and Pat, who had plans to leave for Dublin the next day. Robert Sinclair went with him.

'Did I not know there was a fortune just waitin' in Dublin for me, who'd lived with ten brothers and sisters and the pig all our days in a house of one room,' recalled the old man for us. 'Wasn't I only making eleven shillings a week, like me father, on the land. How could there not be a fortune in the city?'

But there wasn't. In Dublin, the once elegant Georgian houses had long since become slums, without sanitation and infested with rats and human beings; eighty-seven thousand people in five thousand tenements, whole families hungering on incomes of less than a pound a week. Our uncle and the country worker slid in quite unnoticed, not even statistics in the terrible press.

'Had it not been for the man here, sure I would have breathed me last a dozen times or more, Jesus, the tricks and clevernesses he had to keep us alive.

'Up Grafton Street and Temple Road we'd go, casual like, among fine folk and wouldn't your uncle come back rich, with never a soul knowing how!'

They found work, eventually, at that sprawling, sacred monument to the deep, brown velvet satisfaction of Guinness, St. James's Gate Brewery, padded high with sacks of fat barley, throbbing with mad fermentations, rumbling with brews and giant oak butts, mighty horses, drays and leathery carters; the largest brewery in the world, with a language all its own, full of curious words to be learnt and rattled round the mouth, like crackling: wort and hops, malt and mash, kieves, yeast, resin, grist hoppers, sparging and gyle. Even the recipe for the majestic stout read like an ancient incantation:

> A small quantity of yeast is added
> To the liquid in the tuns.
> The yeast begins to feed
> On the sugar in the wort:
> Slowly the froth begins to form
> Into great creamy masses
> Several feet deep.

Under the sign of the harp on the south bank of the river Liffey was a very suitable place for such a man as Robert Sinclair. Indeed, there seemed to be an uncanny pattern of destiny in his life which turned each step he took into a preparation for the next. So Alexandria had proved to be his training for survival in Dublin, where contacts made and that brewery job were to become the reasons he outlasted later experiences in America.

But, in the meantime, he and Pat were no longer ignored outsiders. They had work alongside others, who'd drink with them at the end of the day in bars, where more would arrive to join in arguments and yarns, and where our uncle listened to fire and caught the smell of Ireland.

For, after twenty-seven years of broken freedom promises, the land was wild with frustration and so close to civil war that it seemed as though the very next word would draw blood. In the city, little fevers and rumours and shiftings flurried the people more by intuition than through whispers. All around, men were preparing to emigrate, or joining the Fenians, or just drinking to hate. The Irish Volunteers, in one year, had gained as many members as 'the grand old Duke of York'. The Irish Citizen Army was formed. There were explosives all over the place and gun-running and plotting and the disaster of James Larkin's General Strike and the rejection of the third Home Rule Bill.

An Irishman could not avoid being roused to it all and Pat was soon possessed. Although they still lived in adjacent rooms in the same building, he and Robert Sinclair began to go their own ways.

'There was nothing else for me then but the Cause and, truly, it filled me whole being,' explained Pat, so many years later. 'But I remember that your uncle became friendly with O'Donnell and his people. They were not at all political, you understand, but great lawbreakers for all that. After, did you not meet family of his in America, Robert?'

'There are a guid many folk in America and I canna recall them a',' returned Robbie beag, curtly, and strode out the back door and busily down to the closet.

'Now, O'Donnell had a way with explosives, which was a very expedient gift to have in those days,' went on his visitor, sleekly. 'His auld one had a nice smithy, where the boy made bullets and the loveliest little bombs – for a bit of a price. Meself, I'd never have used a bomb from anywhere else but O'Donnell's, at all. And, indeed, that's where your courageous uncle comes into it, although he's too modest to tell the tale himself.'

It is impossible to imagine Robbie beag as a romantic, even though it takes a romantic to take risk for another's crusade. And, despite his childhood in an atmosphere traditionally full of loathing for the English, we never knew him to show much interest in politics, apart from declaring all politicians to be double-talking sharks. As a grown man, he was steely, tough and calculating, the last type to indulge in self-sacrifice. But, even into middle age, his one weakness persisted; the complete inability to resist adventure. Confronted by a 'dare', he would turn into the classic *Boy's Own* schoolboy, hero of the fifth, exposer of crooks (his own definition), a sort of terrible, teenage Biggles, insufferably full of dash and derring-do.

So, as Pat said, in the end and for no noble purpose at all, he involved himself with Ireland.

He'd bought an old bike and began to deliver the occasional 'parcel' from the forge, apparently ignoring the fact that he might have been blown to smithereens at any moment of the journeys over Dublin's bumpy side streets.

Pat was now an ardent recruit in a cell of very zealous conspirators, who met, amid a tangle of secret signs, codes, speeches and passwords, in the back rooms of sympathizers' houses, to take impassioned oaths and concoct bloody missions.

So far, they had accidentally knocked down a postman with a runaway donkey cart load of bricks, sent an anonymous threatening letter to the Viceroy, misspelt Carson in a 'down With Carsin' slogan, and garrotted an inoffensive, small dog on a trip wire, set up as the first stage in a plot to kidnap a leading politician. Thus, they were ready for greater exploits and evolved their most audacious idea; the scheme to blow up the old State Lottery Office.

There was something so sinful about the plan to destroy a place of gambling in Ireland that, as Pat well recollected, it seemed worse than burning down a church and some of the revolutionaries had to be forcibly persuaded to give it their vote. But, finally, the reasoning that lottery profits were financing the Ulster Volunteers prevailed and the lad Patrick was ordered to carry out the task. Cheered on by his fellows and in a stagnant green blur of cringing cowardice, he left the gathering and was sick all over the street.

'In them days, I was more of what ye might call a talking man, rather than one for the physical action. Oh, I was an orator at the meetings all right, but a bit inexperienced in the field. So, who should I seek out but your own uncle; him having travelled and knowing the world and all.'

O'Donnell ran them up one of his lovely little bombs, not just the usual hurl and boom! Model, but one with a new innovation. It was O'Donnell's first time-bomb and he was proud as a daddy of it.

Robert Sinclair carried it back to Pat's room on his bicycle and it was then that the plan began to take its own ominous course, for, while examining the weapon, one of them accidentally set the time fuse off so that, at eleven p.m., the two found themselves in the company of a bomb about to explode at midnight.

'It was felt among ourselves that we should carry out my committee's instructions a bit ahead of the hour they had had in mind,' outlined the old man, with dignity. 'So your uncle got out his bike again and, with meself on the crossbar and the bomb tickin' away in the basket, rode to the State Lottery Office.'

There, as Pat was planting the precious explosive in a niche by the door, a policeman came ponderously round the corner, saw him and shouted out.

'It was the luck of the devil we had that night. There was I praying for deliverance and there was the blessed bomb smokin' in me hands and there was the guardie, pointing his revolver at me with one fist and raising the whistle to his lips with the other, when Robert Sinclair, pedallin' like all the fiends from hell, came hurtling out of the shadows and rode him down before me eyes.

'What a magnificent act for Ireland it was. What heroism and courage, boys and girls, and to think he got shot in the leg as well when the firearm went off. Why, there was a local man, O'Doherty, who played the fiddle, who made up a whole song about your uncle's famous feat.'

But what of the bomb? 'Well, it's strange that you should mention the bomb, because would you know that it never exploded at all.'

However, all those heroics provided at least one result. They ended Robert Sinclair's stay in Ireland. A wanted man in Dublin, he was smuggled out of the country amid a group of migrant workers heading for Scottish farms and it was the last old Pat was to see of him for twenty years.

'Until I came searching here to his own home, for old times' sake,' he summed up, leaning back with satisfaction at a fine tale, powerfully told. But our uncle was grinning, too, which makes me suspect that Pat had more imagination than memory and that accuracy may not have been one of his gifts.

However, Robbie beag was obviously involved in some curious

event during the time across the water, and that's as close as I'll ever be to knowing what it was.

Our uncle did not return to our valley until I was born, in 1919. He'd been a boy of fourteen when he left home. Now he was twenty-eight. The years of World War I are lost. He never spoke of them, nor of where he went after landing in Stranraer from Dunleary. Granny Morag said he simply walked into the kitchen one evening, as though he hadn't been further than the village.

'He brought me a bonny shawl of soft colours and the grandest bangle wi' wee, dancing people cut around it, and Annie was fair sick wi' envy and disappointment,' our grandmother purred, with a sly look at her daughter. 'She'd aye hoped he wis dead, ye ken.'

Brother and sister, they'd always detested each other. Annie, under her sanctimonious halo of deceits, surrounded by harpies and prayers and familiars all sizzling like a swarm of midgies; Annie, with her way of turning every movement into a gesture of pious suffering, was a compulsive goad to Robbie beag. They were as opposite as creeping plant and axe.

So, although frosty greetings were initially exchanged upon his return, all pretence at hobnobbing was shortly discarded when our aunt accused our uncle of having deserted during the war, 'while guid men were having the decency tae die fer their country.'

I can hear her now, and his retort that she was no saint, herself, for all her fancy that Catrina had been immaculately conceived; for this quarrel was repeated whenever the two met for the rest of their days. He may have been a cool cat in all other spheres of his life, but the mere sight of our crabbit aunt was guaranteed to send Robbie beag wild.

So, they'd spit like camels and throw crockery at each other across the kitchen, while Granny Morag rode in her rocking chair, hammering the poker against the range and loudly singing, 'I'd Be Far Better Off In A Home', until the slanging trailed off into sniffing and grunts.

It was to happen so often that it turned into a weirdly formal ritual in the end; but, in the beginning, our uncle hadn't been home from his travels for more than a few hours when their aggression was declared and the very next day he left the cottage to stay in one of the rooms at Big Jamie's pub.

Siubhan must have turned into his life soon after then; that quiet, but spirited woman, with the amused smile, my cousin Jenny's mother, whom we called aunt and who became our aunt, eventually. I remember that Jenny's grey eyes and soft, brown hair and firm, little face was just like hers; indeed, Siubhan could not have changed much since her own girlhood. She was not much taller than our grandmother and proud in the rather touching way of some slight women, and, although they were not particularly close as friends, those two fully approved of each other.

Women had always been drawn to Robbie beag. They liked his darkness and that peculiar, primal grace. In turn, he took them and their favours for granted, easily obtained and enjoyable. A middle-aged lady, once quite a beauty and in love with him, told me that he had a way of gently not giving the girls his full attention, which seemed to make them all the more eager to give him their all.

'Your uncle never *courted*, you see,' she went on, with a sigh. 'So we had to try and court him.'

However, she was wrong. He did court Siubhan, perhaps because she was far too reserved and fastidious to make a play for him like the rest.

She had lived alone for some years, an orphan girl, on the village hill in the cottage left by her parents, who had been old and died almost within breath of each other. Several local scouts had knocked at her door and she had walked out with one or two, but it was noticed that they were not invited in and she was known to keep herself to herself, which earned her some resentment, although it was to prove her protection.

Robbie beag must have been deft, for he moved in beside her within a few weeks of their meeting and, within a few weeks of the move, neighbouring matrons were noting her pallor and thickening waist, and sliding 'What did I tell you?' glances at one another as she passed.

But the lovers did not care. As Annie recalled, heatedly, for me years after, 'They behaved without a scrap of decency, just like a pair o' heathen. It was a most fearsome scandal.'

'Aye,' agreed Granny Morag, fondly. 'Thon was a true love match. They couldna stop their dance, no matter how folks frowned.'

A letter arrived when Siubhan was seven months pregnant. It contained a ticket for passage to America and our uncle went white when he saw it. Rob Mór had sent for him at last.

He loved her. What did he say to her? She loved him. How did he explain? I know he tentatively brought her to our house, but she would have none of it, none of the second-hand help, and so she refused to stay. Yet, still he set off for the New World, leaving her behind, and Jenny was born the night after his departure.

Our grandfather, Rob Mór, became a stonemason within a few years of his marriage to Granny Morag and then, not long before he left her, he joined the Society of Free and Accepted Masons.

Thus armed with a trade and a useful union, he landed in America where he progressed in a rapid way, remarkable even for that land of opportunity. He quickly acquired a small building firm and, by the time he sent for his eldest son, he was the head of a large construction business in Chicago.

After their meeting, our uncle was to be even more evasive about this man than he was about himself. In fact, he would not discuss his father's life in the United States, nor mention him at all, unless it was quite unavoidable.

We knew that our grandfather had become very rich, but years later after his death, the only one of his possessions to reach the family was a huge ruby ring, deeply carved with a masonic sign. Yet none of us ever questioned this.

I suspect that Bella found out more about him, while living in Los Angeles with her second husband, although she has not talked of it either, nor have the rest of us inquired. It is as if we all know that, even though their existence was not betrayed, Rob Mór had another wife and children in the States.

Our unconcern is not the incuriosity it seems, but a rum trait of the clan in which, for as far back as I remember, no one, apart from the tactless Annie, ever probed another with any tool as unwieldy as a direct question. Somehow, we have always stalked each other more warily and gluttonously enjoyed sensing out the truffle-like secrets. It is as though we were born into a cabal, each knowing his own part of it, but not that of the others. We wait, like people at a seance, hands spread on the table and touching, for the invisible to be revealed. It is the game our uncle Robbie beag plays best.

He joined his father's firm upon arrival in Chicago, but the merger could not have been very successful, because within a few months, Rob Mór was writing peevishly to Granny Morag that he could not begin to understand his son, who had left the business for a job as barman in some illegal saloon supervised by a pair of Irish thugs in Cicero. The tone of this letter suggested that only our grandmother could be to blame for such lack of dedicated ambition in their son. But perhaps, in the end, Robbie beag was to prove sharper than anyone imagined.

At that time Prohibition may have been American law, but Friar's Inn, the Palace Gardens, Pony Inn, Tony's, Mario's and hundreds of other bars stayed open in Chicago and made the law an ass.

Through his retreat out to Cicero, our uncle struck it lucky and rich. As soon as his employers learnt that he had worked at the St. James's Gate Brewery, he was transferred from behind the bar to one of their own distilleries, which lay camouflaged by a warehouse near the Canals. Rob Mór, who, fortunately, was much less guarded than his son, began to write rosy news of his achievements there, quite forgetting to mention that these were all illegal.

There is still a photograph of the disreputable couple, dapper and prosperous in homburgs, gold watch chains and spats, standing beside the old man's symbolically hearse-like motor car. Life was obviously good.

Like his father to his mother, Robbie beag sent regular money orders to Siubhan, and their generosity demonstrated that his bankroll was not going lighter. This was not surprising at that time and place, when the only man likely to be more in demand than a good bootleg brewer was a good killer.

For a while his work continued comfortably and Chicago nights had fun enough for any bachelor guy. There were cabarets stacked with chorus girls in row after dolly row, like wound-up clockwork models from a department store window; the bars, saloons, speakeasies, bordellos, gambling joints and rent parties served all kicks and kinks, and enough bootleg gin flowed to float the entire State of Illinois into Canada, but, instead, it drowned a genius called Bix.

For there was jazz. To my eternal envy, Robbie beag heard Bessie Smith and Jimmy Yancey and King Oliver and, yes, Bix Beiderbecke, when they were all young and alive and swinging in State Street clubs and the Loop.

There, in that city, our uncle might have become anything from a tycoon to a carcass, but never come home again, had it not been for differences of opinion developed between his bosses and a gentleman known as Al Capone.

These grew into battles of muscle and bullets until, one day, an Assistant States Attorney, two known assassins and Myles O'Donnel of Cicero stepped from the Pony Inn into a tattoo of machine-gun bullets, fired from a passing car. The first three men died and O'Donnel barely escaped.

It was surely no coincidence that the very next day our uncle Robbie beag pocketed his assets, packed his bags and left town! In fact, judging by the speed with which he reached home, he must have run all the way to the coast and swum out to the first ship sailing for Britain.

Perhaps he felt, at thirty-five, that the age for retirement had come, or perhaps it was that the gunpowder had singed his whiskers too closely, at last; the first maxim of a swashbuckler being to stay alive.

Whatever the reason, his decision to leave America there and then was a smart one, which Rob Mór should have taken, too, because, years later, even that coroner's verdict of Accidental Death was not to still the doubts about the old man's ultimate departure. Did he fall off the scaffolding? Or was he pushed?

So our uncle returned home, a rare, rather menacing character, tense, wheeling and turning man. He unnerved me completely when I came upon him that first morning, sitting grimly at our kitchen table, the oilcloth I had never seen before spread over it, and talking to Granny Morag in his five-stones voice. He picked me up, suddenly boisterous, which was even more frightening because he was the stranger. On to his shoulder. I was nearly seven years old. My head hit the door lintel as we bounded under it.

Then melting pot, the moment so delicious that I can taste it again right now. Outside the front door, our front door, there on the track, snooty as a sleek and glossy whale, stood a monstrous, black Rolls-Royce.

My brothers and sisters and I had never seen, could not even have imagined, such a glorious machine. Yet there it was on the same old always track, in front of our cottage. When I think it over now, I know that there was nothing else our extraordinary uncle could have come back with but that Rolls-Royce and the hundred pounds; they were the only possible fruits of all his travels and adventures.

Folk in the valley talk to this day about the spending of Robbie beag's hundred pounds. It hangs like a spangle in the mind, that week all wishes came true: frocks and finery for the women, china dolls with blinking, violet eyes for the girls, sleds, footballs, catapults and roller-skates, and a seven-day rain of sweets, through which we guzzled and vomited and gorged again, greedy as seagulls gobbling locusts.

They say Big Jamie had to keep his 'house' open for twenty-four hours just to serve the first round, a drink for every man within miles. For days, drunks passed out and sobered up on the pavements and staggered back for more, without once reaching their own homes. Some were not seen by their good wives for the week: and then took seven more days to sleep it off. It was the wettest wino week in the history of the glen, and our uncle's personal, right and proper burial to Prohibition.

Our fear of the staccato man from everywhere seeped away in the flood, as he dazzled us with extravagance and carried off our delicious grandmother for glamorous rides round and round the little local world, changed into her idea of heaven by the Rolls-Royce.

We had never had a man-figure of our own before and now, incredibly, there he was, solving impossible worries, shrugging away the crises and conjuring up magic. His severity became that of a moody wizard and his spooky unease was obviously the mark of a preoccupied magician. We understood wizards and magicians. In that sensational week, he became accepted, our uncle.

He moved back to Siubhan quite naturally. Theirs was the most undramatic and private relationship in the family, and they were not to part again; though I doubt whether he realized then that vagrancy really had ended.

So, stationary, if not exactly settled, he was confronted by the problem of how to make an ordinary and legal living. To the inquisitiveness of all, Siubhan had a telephone installed in the hill house. Some of her neighbours took this as a personal affront, until the board was hammered over her garden gate. It read:

ROBERT SINCLAIR   TAXI SERVICE

with the number of the new telephone printed below.

It was astonishing how many people in that underpopulated strath suddenly needed a motor car. Robbie beag's Rolls-Royce not only brought mountain crofters and outlying cottagers nearer, but it also became the major status symbol in the region. Even residents in small towns beyond our ring of hills would send for it to glide them stylishly into their next street, and, of course, Granny Morag was far and away her son's best customer, if also the least profitable.

However, as the first months's ledgers showed, he could easily afford her. In fact, the balance was so healthily in the black that he and three mates set off to Dingwall for a night out to celebrate.

It must have seemed a tame evening to the man fresh from Chicago, but to the other three it was big action. Dingwall was at least thirty-five miles away, the capital town of the next county. It had two fish-and-chippers and many more and various pubs, from inn and tavern to bar. They began at the Station Hotel, had a haggis supper each on the way to the next hostelry and then set to the night's purpose in earnest.

By closing time, all four were singing like stuck bullocks; linked and colliding, like a shunting train, they reached the car and collapsed into its luxury and warmth. When Robbie beag took the wheel, Dingwall was almost asleep, but they pestered it awake with goodbye shouts and kisses and set off lovingly on the long drive home.

Next morning, the wreck of the Rolls-Royce was found at the

foot of a coast road cliff. Inside it, only our uncle Robbie beag was left alive.

The tragedy wounded him in every way and he had many months in the infirmary during which to think about it and about his own life. When he returned to us, the side of his face which had been damaged in the accident, was still queerly frozen. It was never to heal and the impulsiveness, which had kept him chasing after excitement for so long, was dead.

He took work on the fishing boats and dug into the ways of the glen, becoming a good man to Siubhan and Jenny and generously standing in for our various and unknown fathers. He guarded our grandmother and gentled old Uncle Angus. He kept Authority at a distance and all of us fed.

It is true that our uncle Robbie beag's moonshine whisky was recognized as the best in fifty miles and that, when the old itch returned, it took a good night's poaching to soothe it. Then, sometimes, he would take off for a few days, or even weeks, but he was never free to roam again.

Even to look at, he became like a cloven man. It was as though he had made some pitiless vow of atonement, for, after the Rolls-Royce crashed, the wild man tamed himself.

CHAPTER NINE

THE LITTLE MYRTLE ARROWS

It was such a noisy pocket, this childhood of mine, so full of crackles and skirl that it was her silence I loved. She moved wordlessly among the quicksilver witches like a secret, arriving in the winter with her parents, shy and quiet as a snowflake.

I used to watch her through the window, carrying washing, or water, or sticks, with the wind pulling at her thin skirt and blowing pale ribbons of hair across her face. She was as quiet and soft as a little sigh. Caitir, one of Moira the tinker's daughters. She was deaf.

When her work was over, she would go to the deep-coated ponies, or wriggle under one of the carts to where the tired dogs lay and, when I was tired, I went there, too. She would low to the animals, her voice a sad wind in the wheels, and she patted each one of us in turn, like Snow White kissing her dwarfs goodbye.

How serious she was, always searching with those earnest eyes for the sounds she could not hear, for the scrabble of a baby just behind her, or the scruff of a cat by her feet. So careful, so precise. Was Caitir two or three years older than I? I never knew. But, when my brothers and sisters seemed a horde, she was my island – and, when I was six, she stole me.

The summer day had strayed into Christmas, blue and shocking, full of confused squirrels and unrolled hedgehogs convinced they had overslept. All over the hills, hares and ermine were looking at their white coats and feeling overdressed and a late lapwing sat down and thought he was in England already. Caitir had a plan and bread and jam, which she waved at me over the wall.

'Gis a piece,' I said to Granny Morag and she gave me a potato as well. 'Put a ganzie on,' she added jerking down a jumper from the pulley.

Caitir pushed me on to a pony's back and climbed up behind, holding the halter rope. It was like sitting astride a warm wave as we bobbed gently away from the cottages and along the ridge of the coast, passed the lorn cypress tree, so chilling with its bare, scraggy arms, under nets of gulls and round a flock of sheep, whose shepherd waved and said, 'Aye.'

'Where are we going?' I asked once, but, although she pointed to the far mountains, it didn't matter because I didn't know where we were anyway. There were woods, snapping with cross-bills crunching fir cones, and rowan trees hung with feasting ring-ouzels and snails laying silver paths and Caitir, solemnly, soundlessly, curling me against her.

We sat on a wall full of mouseholes and ate and the damp dust of gloam filtered down and the pony squelched stream water through his teeth. His easy morning sway jolted now, and, with each lurch, I chafed and slid nearer to the ground, till she tugged me back.

'Where are we going?' What a long way it was to the far mountains. I wondered why we were going there, but Caitir could only nod and point. I wanted my dinner and then my tea, but she held me in a bumpy, loving dream instead and crooned her tune-less song over the hours and heather and into the dark, until we lost the rattle of the sea and stopped.

It was a cave, or rather a hollow enclosed by a boulder on one side and a bramble thicket on the other and overhung by a rock. We crawled into its smell of rabbits and spread the sack from the pony's back on the floor and, when we looked out again, the pony had walked away; tiptoed across the grass and become the night.

We were alone and the shelter was colder than a pothole, crowded with little fierce winds, which bit and jumped on us and whirred round our heads like moths and plugged our ears with aches. Caitir stuffed me into the sack, but it made no difference, I shivered just the same and she fretted and hugged and stroked my hair, as she did to the animals at home.

So thin, so pale, but she didn't seem to feel the cold, just lay there breathing all her warmth into me and the dark became so full of her anxious grace that I saw her unseeable face beside me all the night. Yet, when they found us in the morning, we were both frozen half to death.

What had she wanted when she took me away? She couldn't tell and nobody listened to her silence, so they beat her and she cried. I knew, in the way children know, but I was too young to explain – and now I am too old.

The loves of this long-before-manhood time were painless and without past or future, unmarked by concern and forgotten, it is true, during the battles and business of boys. But they were none the less real for all that; small, pretty girls, who bounced in and out of one's heart without warning. One had to show off when they appeared, shout louder, run faster, win wars. I tugged their pigtails and called them names because I loved them so and the worst of them all was my cousin, Jenny.

Jenny, Robbie beag's daughter by Siubhan. Although she had always been around, she was in that strange yoked state, half child half woman, when I first noticed her. She must have been about ten and we were on a Sunday School picnic.

How we came to be included in such an outing is a forgotten mystery, because certainly neither of us had ever attended the Sunday School. Yet, there we were amid a swarm of others in a sandy cove on the coast preparing to go bathing before the picnic.

Most of us boys went in in our underpants, but the girls had swimsuits and, when I looked over, my cousin Jenny was self-consciously squirming into hers and trying to hide her non-exist-ent breasts with a towel at the same time. She giggled when she saw me and turned her back to continue the struggle, quite un-aware that her round white bottom was completely bared to view.

I thought how sissy girls were and why couldn't they just take off their clothes and put on their bathing suits without all that daft carry on with towels.

But the giggle lingered on and, once in the water, on the spray-fevered rocks, her new fuss and bashfulness were lost. Caught in sea-rapture, she screamed and dived through the crests of the waves, rolling over and over like an otter, and breaking into possessed, wholly instinctive dances. So straight, so supple, so glowingly wet, all wriggle and somersault and winding, arching swoops, a mermaid Jenny. I couldn't stop looking at her – and she knew.

The whole beach was my cousin's laughter. It gurgled and peeled and chuckled and gusted across the sand, breaking up the shadows and milking our own laughs into it, until we were weakly silly and pushing each other and choking on seawater.

'Look at Miss Maclean's paddling.'

'No, she'll be hunting fer her feet,' and we curled up, holding our aching faces and getting half drowned at the joke.

'Margie Wilson's got seaweed in her lug.' All at once, everything was killingly funny.

'Och thon's been there since last year.' We fell on each other with smarting eyes and sore bellies.

'Warty's lost his drawers.' And everybody collapsed and died.

And, after the picnic, my cousin Jenny was inexplicably everywhere; covert, grey-eyed glances in the playground, running off pink down the street, unravelling that giggle round the harbour, making faces at me through the window. I wondered if I should hit her, but instead I scored goals and beat the ferret-fast Sturrock twins in races and swaggered busily among the fishing nets and climbed Gregson's barn one day just to show her – and broke my leg in the fall from the top.

They set and plastered me and put me in bed with Robbie beag supervising and comics and scorn, and then they left. Jenny sat on the edge of the bed, alone.

'It must hurt awfie,' she said, looking at me in admiring sympathy.

'Och, no, I hardly felt it,' I lied airily, and so she concentrated on plucking bits of wool from the blanket, with the tip of her tongue just showing, while I watched and felt like a hero.

Suddenly, I wondered what a kiss was like. 'Give us a kiss, Jenny,' I said, and it came breathless and swift on my lips, like a salt tear.

Jenny giggled. 'D'ye suck yis thumb?' she asked.

'I do not, so there,' I answered, stoutly, being a year older, anyway.

'I do,' she said. 'See.' She sat and rocked happily with her thumb in her mouth and then she took mine, like a weaning calf. But, after a minute, she gave it back.

'I like mines better,' she said, and went away.

Somehow, we had climbed to the top of a small hill together and played out the first moves of the long sweet game, without even dreaming of all the needs and thirsts and ecstasies and false mirages and goddesses and jealousies and love to come. Trees, leaved with kisses, would grow from Jenny's kiss; our pleasures, our deceits, our work, our children, perhaps our fulfilment, certainly our lives. One tree for her and one for me.

But, until it all started, there was nothing more to do and so we separated down different paths and forgot each other for a time.

Soon Dug and Bug and Cracked Bill and Warty Walter and all the others and I, too, began to swank and boast of conquests never made and experiences impossible to have achieved. Round the back of the schoolhouse, comparisons were made and competitions held which would have made the dominie burn his Homer in despair. Though perhaps he knew; for it had always been so.

During those next years, I swung savagely from misery to hysteria, one minute mooching moodily round the house and the next pelting headlong to the village on Bella's bike in search of company and action; too sluggish to move, too restless to stop. Racked between the need for time and the growing, until it felt as though one was permanently inflamed in dry ice. A gong beat in one's thighs and they smouldered with scorching tingles and thrills, until sleep was a state and reached thankfully during exhausting hungers and unappeasable wants and one woke in a damp, spent flame.

Neither man nor boy, but a bewilderment of each. It was a season of torment and, when Robbie beag removed the fluffy down from my face with a cut-throat one day, he still held me by the ear to do it.

The little girls we had teased and taunted for so long had vanished and the village seemed suddenly crowded with different beings, all curves and shingle cuts and long, mysterious legs. Something had happened to their eyes so that, when they looked my way, I grew hot and knew that my voice squeaked and that I had pimples. They were so knowing and assured, these new girls, that they left me too shaken to speak: though there were some among us who knew what to say and began going on long country walks to say it.

I took to careering from the cottage at all hours to scatter my clothes on the dunes and plunge into the sea, but even she, with her snow-cold caresses, only put out the heat for a moment.

It was there on the beach, while stripping off my shirt one day, that I heard the rustle and the giggle of an age before. I hadn't looked at her for years, but she was there. My cousin Jenny.

'Dad's at Granny Morag's.'

'Aye,' I said, buttoning up my shirt again.

'I was thinking of going up the cove,' she went on.

'Aye.' And I followed her.

She was shorter than I and still long-haired and stockingless, still slender and straight, with the walk and face of a child and only little, round hints to show that she was not. She chattered with blushes and cheek, spilling out the words rapidly, like all our family. She slipped and grazed her knee on a rock and, when we held hands afterwards, they cupped together, sleeping, like a folded leaf.

Jenny was magical, shy and careless as a curious foal. I answered her in monosyllables, wanting to touch her so much that it hurt and left me trembling. In the cove, we sat down and the sand blew over us in white drifts, burying our legs, turning our eyes into oysters crying pearls, powdering our hair into wigs and Jenny, laughing, pressed against me from the wind; soft and firm and scented with sea, stirring under my clumsy hands, kindling me with flares and sparks. Mermaid Jenny, with the silver eyes: suddenly too still, too quiet, and, when I looked down, I saw that she was frightened.

'Jenny!' Her white face tore into the blaze and flayed my skin with sleet. 'Jenny!' Almost in tears because now I was afraid, too, and didn't know what to do.

We stared at each other, numb as ghosts, and she wavered and quivered and seemed to come nearer. Then, in a moment, we were saved – or perhaps lost – for, suddenly, she squealed and turned, and the cliffs barked and honked and gulls scattered above us, like an exploded pillowful of feathers, and I was butted angrily from behind as a whiskered head thrust its way between us.

A small seal looked from one to other of us and snorted. My

cousin Jenny hugged it into her arms and bowled, laughing, over the sand, kicking her legs, delighted and helpless.

'Look how bonny he is, Micheil,' she shouted, and I felt sick and relieved.

'Och, ye're daft,' I said, jerking her up and starting to walk. 'It'll never go away now ye've touched it.' And, indeed it followed us all the way home, bouncing along behind, like a tired, woolly ball, hiccuping crossly when we went too fast, weeping for three days outside the cottage after Jenny left. And it never did go away.

For Jenny grew more and more enchanting and, although there were others who caught my eye along the way, she was the one I loved hopelessly for years; but in every close hush she broke away with her laugh.

'D'ye mind the seal, Micheil?' she would say; as if I could ever forget.

Eventually, a bright, young solicitor, full of initiative, appeared on holiday and took my cousin Jenny off to Edinburgh, where there are no seals, and he married her there.

They were quiet people in our glen (that is, the folk apart from my manic family), deep and reticent, bred with that unique blend of passion and puritanism which gnaws at very Celt. One or two of the girls were bold and bad, but very few. The rest were ruled by their own feeling for the privacy of sex – and, like girls all over the world, by Cossack-like fathers and elder brothers, who had far from forgotten their own youth and were all the more ferocious for the memory.

And the village could be hard on the wayward girl. Cruel ostracism by the women, the sly, relentless lust of the men and, often, complete rejection by her family usually drove her away to live in Aberdeen, or Dundee, or some great city fortress in the south. There was only one Granny Morag where we lived.

So, although they say that more sin takes place behind the lace curtains on a Scottish Sabbath than in all the Spanish brothels, it wasn't so. The wifies were too busy peeping through their curtains in the hopes of spying a passing vice to have many themselves.

On the whole, we married late, after a courtship of years, and stayed married and usually contented. This was probably because, in those days, men and women had such totally different roles in society that there could be no argument. Then, too, the lack of acceptable alternative solutions forced most husbands and wives to work harder at the the business of adapting to each other and living together, and from necessity they demanded less.

There were the exceptions, of course. The wife-beaters, the shrews, my sadistic Uncle Tómas, the couples who systematically goaded each other over the years, the crofter in the hills who spreadeagled his wife on the bed with ropes one night and murdered her with a white-hot poker, and there was a pair who had not spoken to each other in twenty years. Of course they were there among us, these tortured, ill-assorted souls; but they were rare.

I doubt if many of that loud and edgy gang of boys achieved more than a buss and a few self-conscious cuddles in those first rutting days. And my chances were even less, hamstrung by my new, panic-stricken speechlessness: and by my brother, Lachlan.

Lachlan, randy and disgustingly handsome, had been rampaging round the valley like an escaped bull for years and, before I had even noticed that a girl was not just one of Nature's mistakes, it was well known that I had at least one dark infant nephew. Lachlan, with his swift cat walk and blacker than Latin eyes, could hypnotize women without effort and, in true family tradition, he did. His success was phenomenal; and a curse.

Too late, the village mothers looked at him and remembered the effect our Uncle Tómas and Robbie beag had once had on themselves. But, eyeing Calum and me coming up behind, they set the defence warnings early.

That Calum proved to be too immersed in cattle fodder and manure to see beyond the farm boundaries was no help at all to me, for brother Lachlan did not mellow with age. So, while he was still conquering the oldest daughters, the youngest had been taught to 'keep away frae they Sinclairs' and watched me, nervously.

Had I been more sophisticated, I would have known it was a diffidence mixed, more often than not, with interest, but I was far more scared than they and went on scaling mountains and catching fish and gullibly swallowing all Dug Sauchan's tales of his own prowess and going up in a bonfire every night and dreaming tender, brutal, adoring, persecuted, triumphant dreams of unobtainable Jenny.

It was Spring when Bridie and her several brothers and sisters came from Galway Bay to stay with their aunt, Mrs. Mackenzie of the shop. Their mother was taken to the infirmary, they said, for a major operation. The children, poor wee lambs, were to be here for the Summer, they said. Bridie was bonny, they said.

In fact, it turned out that their parents had decided to move to England, sending the children north for the few months needed to settle and find work, and the 'poor, wee lambs' were the wildest set of touregs ever to cross the Irish Sea. But Bridie was truly fair.

There was a ceilidh in the village hall not long after she arrived and, although she didn't know the dances, she danced anyway, nudged and pushed into place by too many partners until, by midnight, the steps were hers.

Our mob had gathered early in a corner to discuss her; Dug and Cracked Bill (not so cracked after all) viewing and giving opinion, like old experienced hands.

'I widna say she was that bonny,' said the first of the two, determinedly cool.

'Och, she's no at all bad, Dug. No bad at all,' contested Bill, taking a deep, mature draw on his Woodbine. 'And, besides, she's Irish.'

Irish! Legends of the wicked, inviting Irish spiked every mind, like darts dipped in carmine. We'd never read *Ulysses*, or heard of Swift's Stella, but we knew about Irish women. Oh yes.

There was a mass urge to the reels and, it being one of those tetchy days, only I was left behind, sullenly holding a beer and glowering with contempt as Bridie moved from one to the next of my simpering pals, who clearly thought she was the year's big experience.

'Irish!' I thought, furiously. 'Women!'

She gave us an Irish jig, with expressionless mask and arms stiff against her sides, weird cross of starch and spring, a mongrel dance. I was not impressed and neither were the others, really, though they clapped at the end like performing penguins.

Is it that the Celtic Irish are even more scourged by shame and desire than the Scots, that even their dances are controlled? And what of the Welsh, who don't dance at all?

At opposite ends of the hall, Bert's Da and our Uncle Angus fought their eternal battle of the fiddles. In the gaslight and the heat and the steady stream of whisky through the veins, the ceilidh unfocused into upraised arms changed into antlers, and faces sweating glass; grenades of howls bursting off the walls, lights and shadows, bunions and old women's toes on the ceiling, and Bridie's blue-black mane.

At last, someone hauled me, semi-conscious, into 'Kelso Races' and, in the change of partners, she was there, dancing ferine and tousled as a sprite opposite me, Cadeam Wood on the violins. Sound of before birth and since. Steps learnt before walking. They came without thought, although I was drunk. What black, deep hair she had. She made me think of someone else, only Bridie's eyes were green. We passed each other back to back, looking over our shoulders, near and untouching as dipping mobiles.

'Will ye go tae the pictures the morrow?' I mumbled, aghast. And she nodded without smiling. I was very drunk.

The morning after, I nursed my head blindly and wondered what I'd done; asking out some toffee-nosed scarlet Irish female. I must have been loony. The whisky! That would be what it was, and my stomach turned over the porridge bowl. Perhaps she wouldn't turn up, I imagined, hopefully, and then remembered that an Irish seductress would most certainly turn up. *I* wouldn't go, I decided.

'That Bridie's a braw lass,' said Lachlan, with slow, early morning contemplation. 'I'm thinking tae take her tae the pictures the nicht.'

So bloody confident, as though it was a foregone conclusion that she was just waiting for a chance in the chummy seats with him.

'Did ye have a word wi' her, Micheil?' he went on.

'I ...'

'No, ye widna, of course.' He hadn't even waited for a reply. That settled it. I would go, I decided; and I went.

The new picture house, built opposite the school, had a back row of double seats, generously constructed for the convenience of couples who didn't want to be divided by a wooden arm. The chummy seats. I had never sat in them before and Bridie had never seen them, yet, with a courage which amazed me, I pushed her in before either of us had time to think. We both sat as far apart as possible and looked straight ahead.

Celluloid images scuttled meaninglessly across the screen, lighting us up in the action and drenching us in sub-titled darkness and, in the entire back row, I'm sure we were the only two who even noticed them. Once, I felt her head turn towards me and my face go crimson. Thank God it was dark. Though, when I looked at her, she seemed engrossed in the film. I wondered what Lachlan would have done. I knew what he would have done. But how?

I closed my eyes tight and grabbed her hand, abruptly, like swiping a fly, and she squeaked with surprise. Everyone in the seats in front turned round and old Mrs. Crook said 'Sshhh!' so loudly that the people in the rows in front of her turned round, too. I wished I was dead; but Bridie's hand stayed in mine and then I squeezed it hard, just to prove that this was not the first time.

We didn't move again. I was too scared and she didn't seem much happier and, however much I tried to keep up, that picture remained senseless to the end. Some turbanned heathen in a tent. 'Maybe I should put an arm round her.' Two more turbans galloping out of frame. 'She might yelp again!' A turban with a wifie skeltering in the other direction. The horse looked beat. 'It's all right for Irish lads. They're used to it. Whit was the wifie greetin' for? Maybe she'd fallen off her horse.' She pushed her bang out of her eyes and I shrank.

By the time it was over, I was wrecked and shattered and lying gasping on a scorched rock.

'I'll no be doing this again,' I told myself muzzily, and then I heard Bridie. 'Thank you very much, Micheil.' Just like a little girl leaving a birthday party.

'I'll be going tae Battie's Den, Friday,' I mumbled, in panic for something to say, and she stood quite still clasping her handbag. 'Wid ye come?' Christ! I hadn't meant to say that.

'Thank you, Micheil.' Why didn't she smile?

'See ye then.' And I left her, still standing in front of the red-lettered board. *The Son of the Sheik* it read. So that was what we'd just seen.

'Fine brither you are, without a doubt.' Lachie was in a murderous temper when I got home. 'Made me look an idjot wi' that Irish quine. "Oh Lachlan, what a terrible shame. If you'd said first, I'd have known it was yourself, but it's with your brother I'm going." '

Suddenly, I felt gigantic, the Don Juan of the Highlands, irresistible to all women. Mirages of pleading harems floated through my head and I went whistling off to bed.

'I thocht the lassie meant Calum,' I heard Lachlan say in puzzled tones to Granny Morag as I closed the door; but our grandmother was tactfully poking the grate.

It was April, time of showers and rainbows, days opening like slow fans to the sun and the salad smell of new moss. Battie's Den was in the pale green mist of Spring, a dingle of hazels and willows, tassled with catkins and honeypots, and the black poplars which Granny Morag annually robbed of twigs for her brooms. A wasp's nest hung like a basket from a branch and the first Bath White butterflies were flickering in the nettles, while birds shoplifted spiders' webs in a last minute rush of house-building.

Bridie and I went nesting, parting grasses where a skylark sat and the leaves round a thrush, finding the domed coconut of a wren hidden in a dark yew. There were five eggs in the black-bird's nest. 'Oh leave them, Micheil,' Bridie called, as I looked down.

She stood below me, translucent in the rain, with reflections and sunbeams and shadows quivering over her face, countless, changing faces, pleasing to me from the morning through drowned eyes. Jade pale girl, milky as a swan; I stumbled, tumbled down the rust branches, rough and sightless and spurred by daggers to stand desperate before her.

What happened next was as quick and silly and classic as slipping on a banana skin, for the kiss was snatched and I was slapped.

And they breed them tough in Ireland. It was a fighter's blow. Whack! Sending me reeling through catherine wheels and snow-storms; a miracle of a blow, for it snapped the choking bonds of adolescence as surely as Calum's attack had pulled me from the cradle years before. In that second, all my cornered terrors were ripped away and I heard the drunk birds and shouting dragonflies and the rushing stems and leaves and barks and shoots and the firing buds. I was stormed by my own forces, husky with the kick of power and Bridie was blowing away through the spray.

'Bridie!' I bellowed and raced after her. 'Bridie!' And caught her.

So light, so fragile, so slender, it was like finding a pain in a flower. So dear and dangerous, there at the end of the rainbow, discovering me with raindrop fingers.

'No,' she whispered once, but so gently that we slipped into the deep, cool grass, down and down through the tarn of ferns. At-lantic girl trailing and tangling her hair in the weeds. Down through the pale green wastes of herbs to currents and eddys and tides never before traced, to unchartered sounds, to where at last there was only the moving fathomless deep of Bridie. And Bridie was me.

All the long day we stayed by the stream in the showers and the hide-and-seek sun, curling our hands through the water, nestling our faces together, cheeks and mouths and fingertips, rolling and tumbling like puppies across the kingcup beds, lying silently close on the sweet earth. Bridie, with green fires in her eyes, turning me to a torch; Bridie cooling me in dark green pools, till I lay in the endless spell of her voice, hearing only a wordless poem of Erin sound; in love. She loved me, too, she said, and we would write to each other every day when she left and I would go to England.

Then we walked drowsily out of the Den and the glen was webbed with crystal and all the way home we loved in the rosy bed of the sky and hedgerow pillows I'd never seen before, and I was the Erl King commanding volcanoes to erupt and unicorns to race and the stars to fall and the sun to stay. I gave her heather and moths and foxgloves and left her at Mrs. Mackenzie's gate and, when I got home, I climbed through the bedroom window and hugged myself secretly, joyfully, to sleep.

Bridie left not long after that and we wrote a week of daily letters and then a month of weekly ones and then a Hogmanay note. So many poor Irish lads there, she said, exiles just like her, and, although I went to work and soon saw Aberdeen and Arbroath and even Hull, the travelling never took me to London town.

Besides, a couple from Inverness had just moved into Nichol's Brae and their daughter was a bonny lass . . .

CHAPTER TEN

THE TOIL

SOMEHOW, out of the disorder of our childhoods, my brothers and sisters emerged as effective, if unorthodox people. Perhaps they had inherited the bite which had brought Rob Mór success in the New World, for each achieved what he wanted in life: Catrina, weaving her dreams and shrewdness in a travel agency; Calum, the big-time farmer; Lachlan, with his butcher's shop; even Bella, after a breathtaking sweep through three husbands, has been settled happily into mink-lined domesticity for the past fifteen years, still with number three; and the only drifter was me.

One by one, they went out into the salty air and haltingly through the garden gate, looking back with more and more astonishment as they moved farther away; but lapped in this beginning to the end. We are lent to our futures by those crafty first years and the web they threaded to each as he left is still being spun. It tugs us together sometimes, to love and be curious over our sameness and separateness, and each one alone has made his pilgrimage back to the stones by the track, just to see.

Lachlan left first, short and stocky at fourteen, turning his back after a long, locked-in-winter to walk away down the road; though not very far, a few hundred yards to the slaughter-house.

Our Auntie Annie pondered over the right reaction, as he pushed his porridge aside that morning, and decided to wail over losing a nephew, while clapping him heartily on the back over gaining a pay packet. Granny Morag was practical to the point of being offhand. Then she went quietly off to the back room to watch through the window as he whistled away.

To us, he didn't seem to be doing anything special, but, from that time on he was changed. He grew no more, but his thick back and man's voice and black stubble seemed to date from that day. I suppose he must have squeaked through fluff and pimples for months, just as Calum and I were to do, later, yet I don't remember. It was as though he left us that morning as a child and returned the same night a man.

And, from then on he was among the chiefs, a provider of food and money, a maker of laws and Granny, with her infallible sense of ritual, confirmed it. The oilcloth was still reserved for Robbie beag, but Lachlan was sat at the top of the table and given his plateful before us all, and so it was until he left the cottage.

The Slaughter stood about halfway between us and the village. It was a collection of stone shacks set in the moor round a cobble-stone yard, where feathers and wool and hair floated in reddened puddles.

There were pens outside where the animals huddled into lumps, unnaturally turning their heads to the wind and shivering at its breath; clotted heather air as sweet and sickening as a bro-thel.

The days of hygienic abattoirs were yet to come and, although the health inspectors and animal protection societies may have managed to supervise big city organizations, they were unheard of in our hidden valley. So, forgotten brains were left to stink in the corners and new-hung hides slapped bloodily against the walls, buckets of offal writhed under crusts of flies, which gorged and bred and collapsed, too heavy ever to fly. Rust-red choppers cut the screams into gurgles, but each gurgle remained a scream and, although the huts were doused with water at night, that was for convenience and the splattered ceilings remained unwiped for all time.

In this dirt and dust and steel and stone, the running animals were changed into long, cold limbs, pale as shells or ruby with strength; reaped muscles overlapping in curves, flanks like mosques and sad, dead lambs, naked as pearls: each one beautiful. After it all, only the veins and sweat of the living men were ugly and their blotted hands.

Sometimes I went there after Lachlan started work, yet re-vulsion is solely in the memory. At the time, I watched the pink, fleeced sheep and baffled pigs arrive and the loner bull, still bel-lowing lust and rage; all to be killed. And I saw with an accepting

140

curiosity, which only broke into nausea when I returned home to be confronted with mutton stew for dinner.

Lachlan, however, was not so fastidious. His back broadened and forearms bulged and, before long, he could work as fast as the men, lifting a ewe on one shoulder from the pens in the yard and cutting its throat with a swift, reflex blow. A bullock was killed and skinned in under half an hour, while the others, ringed to the wall nearby, snorted and shuddered. They knew, and yet each walked passively towards the spot in his turn, with just a moan at the end. Only the sheep fought, raising their bleats into shrieks, struggling and pleading until they seemed indecent and I felt pitiless as I watched. Chickens squawked and fluttered and cast their feathers in desperate fits, hypnotizing themselves with their own frenzy until their yellow eyes died, even before the man's hand reached them. Only the little bullocks left me feeling sad, which was probably unjust.

Looking back, I realize there could not have been so many animals packed and lined up for killing. Ours was a world of a few thousand souls in many miles and market day was once a fortnight, when crofters and shepherds brought their few beasts in from unseen glens. The people were poor and we couldn't have eaten our way through herds of beef. Yet, in my memory, the pens are always full and the men always rushing: and, when the turkey comes in, flaming bronze at Christmas, or the Easter roast sizzles on the table, I think of Lachlan and a long time ago when I went to the Slaughter and saw them die; different animals and birds, but they seem the same on those days.

Lachlan's apprenticeship didn't make much difference to our way of life. Although Granny Morag was always cursing Rob Mór, none of us children had ever been very aware of the lack of money. The single division in our little district was between fishing and hill folks. The rich only arrived during the shooting and the fishing seasons and their children merely visited them for the occasional summer month. We had never met them and among our companions there were few differences. Thanks to our aunt's mending, there were many others much more ragged than we and we accepted the porridge days at the end of each month more as another idiosyncrasy of our grandmother, than as proof of hardship. In any case, our poaching uncles had always kept us well fed and the only great events resulting from Lachlan starting at the Slaughter were old Angus's retirement and a minor weekly splurge on Saturdays.

We felt it far more when Bella went, perhaps because she was the soaring temperament among us. Bella was the young Morag over again and she seemed to have been bussing and beating up us boys from the time it all began. It was Bella who had pulled me into the family with her sweaty little hand, when I was just a toddler; dragging me along behind her, without ever stopping to see if I could keep up, and turning that dayspring into a long breathlessness. Without Bella stuffing the first broth down our throats, we'd probably have starved to death, as our grandmother was far too impatient to stick with it beyond the first two mouth-fuls and Annie couldn't abide the mess. Bella had taught us reels and cheeked the dominie and once brought home a live duck from an inaccessible garden pond and suddenly grown impudently beautiful. Equally suddenly she was 'away'.

Robbie beag had organized Lachlan's job, but Bella arranged her own, and announced it after high tea one night.

'I'm tae work in the morn.'

'Och, aye, pressing the bolster like usual . . .'

'Putting yer hair up, then?'

'She'll be away tae win a bursary tae one o' they universities.'

'Och, ye're all daft. It's a fact I'm telling yis.'

'Where'll ye be starting?' asked Granny Morag, and Bella went red.

'At the Manse,' she said, loudly, with her chin stuck out.'

We all gaped. It was as though she'd just said 'Hail Mary.'

'There's no use in yis all looking as though I'm fer the loony-bin,' she went on, defiantly. 'It's no up tae yis . . .'

And Auntie Annie burst in, yodelling with excitement. 'Well I never, now isn't that just splendid. The Manse! Wid ye believe it! Sic a nice place. Och, I used tae ken the meenester and his wifie well. Sich nice folk, d'ye no agree, Mither?'

'Ye've picked a hard one, lassie,' said Granny Morag, dryly. 'But no doubt ye ken yer own mind.'

So Bella set off the next day with a grim little, 'See yis,' and without a look at any of us. And it was hard.

Old Crabbie, the minister, was a Wee Free fiend, who did his best to illustrate the inferno of the hereafter by creating as near perfect a replica of it as possible on earth. He practised his public Sunday howl in the privacy of his house for the other six week-days, following our Bella through the dark rooms with hourly promises of the furnace to come and glaring at her with mad, red eyes until, 'Ye'd imagine he wis going tae pull a bairn frae his pocket and eat it,' she said.

Mrs. Crabbie Dougal came behind her, too, unexpectedly appearing in unlit doorways to issue instructions in a creaking Cumley Bank voice, or to nod her head over her husband's latest lecture.

She was tall and unbending and frozen with righteousness; a tyrant who had repressed and disciplined herself until there was only a rigid black candle left, which not even her husband's flaming hell could have melted. She stood over young Bella from morning till night, tense as a whip, with fingers which flicked up invisible specks of dust into accusing heaps and a timetable to cover every second.

'You've been five and a half minutes peeling the potatoes, when five minutes should do, girl, and you'd better stay on an extra half an hour tonight as you've been arriving ten minutes late every morning this week.'

Bella would mimic her, after the weary walk home, and make us all laugh; but we laughed with amazement, too, wondering how our irrepressible sister did not give up.

Yet, although it kept her drudging for fourteen hours a day, the presence of Mrs. Dougal was welcomed by Bella. I think she would have scrubbed floors and carried coal and tackled towers of dirty dishes and burnt pans for nothing, in order to avoid those ghoulish moments set aside for the welfare of her soul by old Crabbie.

They materialized about once a fortnight, when the minister would announce that the wickedness of this sinful girl was such that he must make still another effort to drive the Devil from her. With that, Bella would be sent to his study, where she waited with an uneasiness she was not to understand until years later and, throughout the half-hour that followed, she stood, trying not to twist her apron and replying to his questions with movements of her head and without saying a word.

The monologue never varied in form. It began with a rehearsal of the Sunday sermon, in which the congregation was to be transported to the bowels of hell and the church would be filled with sulphur fumes by the power of his words.

Strung with life and carefree, will-o'-the-wisp and not yet fifteen, our sister was bludgeoned with the full weight of all God's wrath: how her tongue would be as smouldering cinders even in her mouth as punishment for her lies and, for her vanity, her body would be scorched through all eternity. If the Lord hadn't put those curls in her hair, Satan would turn them into ashes of inextinguishable flames and a red-hot ember would be set into the very skin touched by that brooch, evil symbol of empty pride.

Then the minister's voice would reason and pry and stumble over hurried questions as he examined his bookcase, where he could see her reflected in its glass, without realizing that she knew.

What did she do when she left the Manse? Did she go straight home? Did the lads talk to her? She must never talk to them. They were vile and damned as Satan's messengers. She must keep away from the black hearts and hands of men. She must keep herself pure for God. Did she know what pure meant? Pure meant untouched – he breathed heavily, as though he had run a long way – clean and untouched, so that when she stood naked . . . when she stood naked before the Lord Almighty, there would be no marks on her body.

He stared at her in the dark glass and pushed the palm of his hand against her reflection – the touch of man would turn into sores in heaven. Did she know that? There must be no marks on her body for God to see. No marks!

And, at this point, he would return abruptly to his desk and Bella would be sent away, leaving him trembling.

'Och, they're both as batty as hornets,' she used to say, after giving us a benefit performance of the latest sermon. 'And ye canna tell which one started it: him, wi' his thousand pokers of fire burning into the flesh fer ever; or her, wi' her 'The Meenester never eats of the unclean beast, so we'll have no meat in this kitchen.' They're both half starving and that as likely explains the whole trouble. Nae doubt they'd turn intae normal folk wi' a good bit o' beef in them.'

But Granny Morag did not laugh.

'I think it's high time ye left that bliddy midden,' she would say, grimly. And, when our aunt once protested over that, she flung an iron at her in blind fury.

'Hud yer tongue, ye grasping, idle slut.' And Annie did. She could have been killed. But Bella went back to work anyway.

There was something about that Manse, planted like a great tomb beside the church, which appealed to her; not the pittance it brought in, nor the little independence it gave her and certainly not the work. Its appeal was in its size and content.

It was one of those large Scottish houses, built of unplaned stone with long, unimaginative windows and walls over two feet thick. It was severe and it was impressive. Inside, the curtains were always drawn, to prevent sunlight from fading the cushions, so that the house was perpetually in gloom. But the curtains were velvet and the cushion-covers were tapestry. There were carpets in every room and a silver tea service and the heavy Victorian mahogany was waxed to the patina that comes to wood only after years of care.

Bella, her grandmother's grandchild, delighted in it all. It was the Manse which set her sights on a future which was to make her an expert and ardent collector of antiques, and lover of paintings – and the wife of three progressively rich men.

However, despite all her efforts, her stay in its sinister gentility was short and the end came in a swift crisis.

On the last Friday of every month, Mrs. Dougal audited the contents of her household. Every single item was ticked off against a list, from the print of Landseer's 'Stag At Bay', to the three walking sticks (two of his and one of hers), to the number of candle-ends stored in the scullery, to the half-full, non-alcoholic bottle left over from last Hogmanay. Only when everything was found to be present and in its proper place did a faint loosening of muscles crumble the face of the preacher's wife and the maid would be given a biscuit.

But, on this, her final Friday, there were no biscuits because a spoon was missing. Bella was sent to search through every room and drawer and closet in the place, with the assurance that she would not be allowed to leave until it was found. Mrs. Dougal, convinced that the spoon had been stolen by our sister, or by that Mrs. Robertson they'd had to entertain to tea because she knew the Moderator, waited in a straightbacked chair and turned to granite.

Though the Manse was large and full of cupboards and shelves, it was also so ordered that the hunt did not take long and, within about an hour, the only room unchecked was the minister's study.

In this caserne of rules and laws, none was more strict than that governing times of entry into this umber connection with heaven. It was open for cleaning, in the presence of himself, in the mornings only and, after midday, not even his wife would have dared to open its door. But today a spoon was missing and Bella went in.

It did not occur to her that this was the first time she had been alone there for more than a few minutes. She ran her hands across the dim surfaces and peered, on hands and knees, round the legs of the furniture. She lifted the paper weight and the blotter and shook out a few papers. She opened the little cupboard, set into the left of the desk, and then each of the drawers opposite, right down to the large one at the bottom. Each was full of a sermon-maker's tools, except that.

To our sister's stupified delight, the last drawer was full of pictures – pictures of women: nudes and half-nudes, buttocks and breasts and parted thighs; saucy and pretty and gross and each one beckoning with lips like plums.

Bella, giggling incredulously, pulled them out; fistfuls scattering across the desk and swirling off the chairs to the floor, overflowing from the bureau and floating past *The Life of John Knox*, sitting and lying voluptuously along the top of *Lamb's Sermons* and giggling back at her. And, just as the last one settled, feet up over the photograph of some long-dead church elder, the minister, himself, opened the door.

Crabbie Dougal looked at his own soul, spread in all its trivial obscenity before him, and the safe brown walls ran purple. For a second, he lunged towards little Bella with arms outstretched, like a monstrous nightmare, and then he fell. Just a dull thud and he shrank before her into a small, helpless old man on the floor.

'My God, lassie, what have ye done?' he gasped, as she ran past him, terrified, to the door.

The minister was ill for some months after his heart attack and, during them, his wife nursed him meticulously. On his recovery, she announced that he'd been ordered a change of climate and they both left for the south, never to return.

His replacement seemed a nice enough man, whose wife was undoubtedly an improvement on the other; but, by that time, Bella was working for two retired spinster sisters, who lived in a mansion above the village and loved her.

In any case, the whole episode had left Granny Morag with a rabid allergy to all clergymen. The new man discovered it when he amiably came to call – and left with the potato peelings, meant for the pig, still clinging to his dog collar. She had never liked the church set-up anyway.

Catrina, the secret one amongst us, went to work later, partly because she was the only one in the family who was given a 'further education' and partly because she was Catrina. She grew unnoticed, without rounding and curving like her cousin. She remained skinny, yet became sinuous, and the smoky reserve of her childhood deepened into mystery, which screened her long, black, contemptuous eyes.

Only the men of the glen looked her way. The boys were far too afraid. But, in any case, she hardly noticed any of them. She was cat-like and, like a cat, Catrina looked after herself.

A long time before, in those early winters of the tinkers, she had examined the valley and concluded that it was too small for her. Perhaps we had all done the same, unconsciously, but for her it was a fact and a decision. She wanted out, with all her independence intact, and a local marriage was not for her.

Unexpectedly, at thirteen, she had begun to go regularly to school; accepting her mother's audible pride as being right and due, and ignoring the teasing of the rest of us. She worked hard and consistently and without pleasure, taking her homework into the icy bedroom for hours to escape from our nightly bedlam and, because she was neither a clever nor natural scholar, everything she achieved cost her effort.

We were not forced or nagged into earning our livings and, although it was vaguely accepted that one started work at fourteen, this was not in any way compulsory. So, when Catrina stayed on at school after her birthday, the adults said nothing and Lachlan only groused a bit about some people being 'toil shy' and it was Robbie beag who decided what to do with her in the end.

'You're a serious kind of a lass, but ye'll no make a good scourer of pots,' he said to her one day. 'So I'm sending ye tae Aberdeen fer a year, tae a college there. Ye'll be learning how tae do accounts and use a writing machine and then ye can work in an office. Have yisself ready tae leave by Friday next.'

Then he and Granny Morag had a brief discussion about stenography, which undoubtedly left her as perplexed about it as ever. In fact, she was so bemused by the whole idea that she kept very quiet for a week. Our grandmother did not risk her opinions where they might rebound to make her look absurd at a later date. Wrong she might be, but ridiculous never.

It was a gruelling week, top-heavy with Catrina and her mother. Their friends descended en masse, drawn by our aunt's telepathic 'currents' (which she was always informing us she could emit). They glared glances of hatred, sharp as hatpins, while Auntie Annie, all aware and glorying, hammered in the news that *her* daughter was to go to business college: just as she'd always planned, of course, and to the best college in Aberdeen, naturally.

She made them all line up with comfort as she wept bravely surreptitious tears, and wondered how she would manage to live without her wee bairn. Then they left – our grandmother outraged, our aunt bland with triumph and the air choked with indignation as far as the village.

And, when there was no one else to talk to, Auntie Annie continued just the same, for a week, for a month, a year and years, reciting Catrina's fabulous future to us all and deaf old Deamhan and the postman and our tight-lipped granddam and the wind. She never got over it, ever.

Catrina was almost as insufferable. During those few days she pinned her hair into corkscrew curls, then balanced the lot over one ear and took to tripping around with geisha girl steps and shrilling over every rut in the road, as though it were an impassable ravine. She set her face into a week-long moue of distaste and addressed the adults in a voice that suggested acute laryngitis. On the whole, she managed to look remarkably like a one-eared pekinese.

We were not spoken to at all; although, on the last day, when the packing and panic were over and Farmer Gregson's mare and trap had cantered us all to the station, just as the train drew in, Catrina took time to step from the pedestal and wish each of us a refined farewell before disappearing into a froth of steam, just as she used to do over the tinker lads in the old days.

So she, too, was gone and her mother, who had braved the fresh air as far as the garden gate for the first time in fifteen and a half years to see her off, retired to bed for a month suffering from exposure and grief.

We missed her, too; the trances and voodoo of this strange little sister, which had been like living with an apprentice clairvoyant, her feverish cold passions, her ceremonies, her veiled intrigues and schemes, which we'd tried to anticipate, but never could; her surprising affection, when she emerged without warning from her privacy and attached herself to one or other of us for a week or so before withdrawing again. She had been the unexpected in our cottage, the one we never knew or understood, but missed now that she was no longer with us.

Letters came, of course, with extravagant descriptions of sophisticated city life and edged with pity for us poor bumpkins still existing in the backwoods. Our aunt's house, where she was staying, had a bathroom, did we know? And one of they new gas geysers that heats the the water, and gas lighting, too. And the longer she stayed away, the longer were the words she used, until her epistles became completely incomprehensible and we merely gathered from them that she was still alive.

Then came the news that Catrina had a sweetheart, a genuine intended, a fiancé, who was all for marrying her and, from then on, the letters were all 'my St. John'.

'Whaurever did he get that name, fer Christ's sake?'

'Perhaps his Ma was a virgin,' said Lachlan. It was the one witticism of his life.

'My St. John' was tall, unbelievably well-favoured and rich. He had his suits made in Edinburgh and owned a motor car and 'property' and he *travelled*. He'd been to Paris, which was in France, for a holiday once and went to London nearly every year. Granny Morag did not approve of that and immediately condemned him as a Sassenach.

However, eventually our sister came home for a holiday, complete with a photograph of this sainted Adonis; and we were all impressed. 'My St. John' was indeed a virile-looking man, with a strong, handsome face and powerful shoulders.

'He's six foot one tall, you know.' And Bella went mad with envy.

'When's he coming tae visit?' she kept asking, and 'Och, let's see his photy again. My, he's that brawl.'

Then, at last, unable to contain herself any longer, she removed the precious likeness, one day when her sister wasn't looking and took off with it to the village, where all the girls had heard of Catrina's lad and couldn't wait to see it.

They gathered and squabbled like birds, scrabbling against each other to get the first view, full of ooh's and sighs – and a shriek.

'But thon's Clark Gable, the filum star,' screeched Margie Mackenzie. And she had been to Edinburgh.

Calum went, as we all knew he would, to Gregson's farm; pulling on his boots the morning of his birthday and setting off with a loaf-and-dripping piece and a pie, as stoically as always, but looking happier than we'd ever seen him.

The farm was his Elysium and all his childhood had been a waiting to reach it. It covered the whole of the only fertile acreage in the wide glen, a freak pasturage that ran in the shelter of the first low hills and, because it was formed like a plateau above sea-level, neither turned to moor nor became contaminated by the salt. Barley and root crops grew on it and, at the end of each summer, half the village women and all the children picked the rasps and tatties there. It had been in the Gregson family for generations and was the only sizeable part of our world which did not belong to the laird.

Gregson himself was a worker and the money which he made

went back into his land, to modernize the equipment and improve his stock. In those days, farmers were all-rounders and, in our district, it would not have been economical to specialize. So the farm fattened bullocks and kept pigs and a small dairy herd of shorthorns alongside the arable fields, and ran sheep on the surrounding hills.

Our Calum had spent all his spare time on this land so, when he arrived officially, Gregson, who knew a promising youngster as well as he knew a good beast, trained him hard.

He had a solid, modern mind, the farmer, informed about all the latest trends in agriculture and, before Calum started, he had taken the trouble to visit our grandmother; though with obvious doubts about his success.

'The lad'll have tae study, ye ken,' he'd said, severely. 'It's nae use his just coming up the farm at six in the morn and stopping at six at nicht. He's an ambitious laddie and there's aye progress on the land which he'll have tae keep up wi', if he wants tae go further.'

And, as bait for her support, he promised Granny Morag the free use of the pony cart once a fortnight, if Calum did well; but our brother needed no encouragement. After the long day, he'd tramp home with the journals and books supplied by his master and grunt over them, like an old boar, until, without knowing it, he collapsed in a great snore of tired muscles and punished brain and it was Lachlan's last chore to heave him to bed.

Great, gentle Calum. The other lads on the farm didn't know what to make of him, so much bigger than they and so clumsy-looking. Yet the horses pulled for him and the cows lowed with content as he milked them. His furrows were matched and straight and the stooks he stacked in the harvest did not blow down.

The others came and went with the seasons, not staying longer than a year or so before moving off to the sleep-till-eight and dancing-at-night cities, but they resented the attention he received from Gregson and, because he talked little, imagined he was touched.

They needled him all day, taunting as he gravely munched his midday pie and interrupting the long minutes when he stood, just looking across the wide earth at its hollows and rises and subtle colours; when he was dreaming – no, planning his own tomorrow's farm.

'Calum! Cal lad! Give us a fight, Cal! D'ye ken ye're soft, Cal? Give us a fight then!'

'Tell us whit it's like tae be daft, Cal! Go on, tell us!'

'Och no, he's no that cracked. He's thinkin' o' the lassies, are ye not, Cal?' said Donal Barnet, nudging Calum, conspiratorially.

'Get away! What wid he be doin' wi' a lassie, when he doesna have one?' Alec Pate was the chief joker among them.

'Aye, he has. He keeps it in his ganzie.'

'Och, ye're right enough, man, it widna', do fer a lassie. It's an auld mare he's needing, like auld Princess there. Isn't that right, Cal?' And Alec rolled up at his own smartness.

Calum would walk away in his deliberate tread, as though they didn't exist; but the words were there, tolling through the weeks and months and baffling him. He was used to the jostling of us against him, like his affectionate, thoughtless farm beasts, but this tormenting was something new. Sometimes, at night, he would stop reading and puzzle over it, shaking his head as though an obstinate fly were heckling him. How could he have understood that they were only lads, when he was but a lad himself.

But, on the morning, they were waiting and on the mornings after, drops of words, dripping insistently throughout the day; harmless, just words, but persistent.

Pitching hay with the late sun cooling the sweat. Listening to blades that cut lime green fringes into paths. Blue above, over the mountains, over the sea and deep for ever, blue. Feeling his own power with pleasure in the working and stretching of his back and the rhythmic flexing of his arms. Content.

'Are ye deaf, then?' Old Bertie was tapping his arm.

'Eh?'

'Get out yis basket, man.'

'Och aye.' It was time to eat.

'Och, dearie dear. I've spilled water on yis piece, Cal,' called over young Barnet, unregretfully.

'Ye'll needs shout a bit louder or he'll no hear ye,' instructed Alec and winked at Donal before going on. 'Deaf besides daft, sic a scunner and ye ken it's all because his ma had him by Bonnety

Wull and there's none as loony as yon. Whit did yer ma do in Glasgae, Cal?'

And our Calum picked up a pitchfork and drove it right through Alec Pate's shoulder.

Of course, there was a real commotion, with Alec taken off to the infirmary in Dornoch to be mended and Constable Duff arriving at the cottage to take notes and the whole family, from Robbie beag to Uncle Tómas, arriving to hold conferences and, worst of all, Farmer Gregson threatening to run Calum off his land for good.

But ours was still a raw glen, where fierce, freakish happenings took place between the men of the sea and between the men of the crofts and their hidden families and the fight between our brother and young Alec was an unimportant incident, which everyone involved dramatized for a while, without the slightest intention of taking it further. Life was rugged in those days, but it was less complicated.

So, Constable Duff's notes were never sent off to his superiors and it never occurred to anyone to sue anyone else and, after a couple of speechless weeks, Calum was allowed to return to work, where he found, to his surprise, that the other lads had stopped their baiting and treated him with a certain respect.

And then there was one. Me: for a long, quiet year of days alone. And, in that year, I discovered a whole new valley of corners and fells overlooked in the noisy race before. Uncle Angus's footsteps had marked the ways and I followed them, understanding him at last and his solitude.

I climbed peaks which, from below, had seemed to be the highest, only to be crushed by still others towering beyond; summits of intolerant sovereignty which shrugged me away to wonder.

It was the year when I learnt to ask 'Why?' instead of 'What?' Why the heights and ocean? Why did sun set and moon rise? Why the order? Why was I? The unanswerable why, which led me later through books and philosophies and churches without reply. It was the year, too, when I learnt that I did not know myself.

CHAPTER ELEVEN

SEA LOVE

Everyone knew that when my turn came I would go to the fishing, though my brothers considered it somewhat disloyal to cast off with old childhood foes and leave themselves behind on the shore. But, ever since I could hold an old tin can, I'd been bailing out puddles of sea from boat bottoms and hanging round the harbour, hoping the men would beckon me to help.

It was a straightforward love of the sea which pulled me to her and I should have gone even without the Excise men, though they were an added attraction certainly. They crept on us by land and water at intervals and I foresaw myself in dashing combat with them and laughing as I made swashbuckling escapes; for those were Mittyish years, when legendary armies materialized out of groups of trees and every hillock was Everest, when rocky monsters and thorny ogres were defeated with the traditional single hand and superior intelligence, and I died my way of malaria and snakebites through impenetrable jungles with a pocketful of diamonds and saved as few distressed maidens as possible.

His Majesty's Customs and Excise Department had various reasons for eyeing our coastline with suspicion: one was the brandy, which arrived from France, barrelled like salt for the herrings; and the other was a number of bothies, which distilled a product locally known as 'mountain dew'. It was cheaper and tasted better than the whisky sold in the bottles and most surely our uncle Robbie beag had a hand in the making of it.

The stills were secret and elaborate and set in heather-covered caves; pipes leading to an underground spring, casks and tubs to which the grain was carried out by pony. They were also changed frequently, so that, when the Customs 'chentlemen' poked through the disturbed heather with their long, iron sticks, they usually discovered only an old site housing a rather startled family of adders.

None the less, when a stranger neared the glen, the word was passed through relays of housewifely whispers and running small boys to those concerned, and everyone went around wearing faces of teetotal puritanism; which is, perhaps, how the Highlanders earned their reputation for being close.

At sea, the system of evasion was one of signs and studied confusion between the boats, with an innocent drifter giving a show of guilt by putting on speed, so that the Customs' steam launch followed to investigate, while the real culprit floated quietly away in another direction. Only in cases of genuine chase was the cargo dumped, as the 'chentlemen' were, unfortunately, equipped with the faster vessels, apart from their authority.

In fact, I don't think anyone was ever actually caught at the smuggling, although there were some narrow escapes and, on one night in particular, it looked as though at least twenty of the lads were about to spend the small hours in Constable Duff's one small cell.

It was one of those clear summer nights, when midnight is only twilight and one sleeps like a Turk under a steaming sheet, twisting it into turbans and shrouds and floor mops and dreaming of being splashed round a boiler and picked out, shrunk as a doll.

The splashing and the soft laughter continued when I woke up and found myself alone in the room. The other bed was empty and, when I reached the kitchen, the whole family was crowded there at the window in the dark.

'Whit in the world wid they be doing up as far as this?' Granny Morag was asking in baffled tones. And, through a bent elbow, I saw that the sea round the point was shadowed with whales, black humps in the moon water which suddenly lit up into rowing boats one by one.

'They canna be ours wi' a' they lights burning,' said Lachlan.

'Amachures! Amachures!' replied our grandmother, in disgust, and we watched them land and the men carrying their flaring paraffin cans and black burdens up the beach. The shouting and laughing were awful to hear.

'It's a disgrace,' quavered Annie, over the illegality of it all.

'Aye, ye widna credit it, ye wid not,' agreed her mother, affronted that such a serious operation should be conducted so carelessly.

But the noise increased, rising into song, until it sounded like a nightclub on the doorstep and we stood, nervously clutching our shirts, while Herself absently downed a succession of drams in sheer disbelief. Yet, even the atmosphere of brewing disaster did not stop us from a combined leap of shock as someone rapped at the door.

'Quick! Away tae yis beds!' she ordered, straightening her nightcap, and we scampered as far as the passage, where we turned and pressed our ear to its door.

'Would there be some disturbance here tonight, mistress?' he asked.

'Aye, ye've just raised me from my bed,' she replied, acidly. 'And that's a disturbance.'

'Ye willna have been hearing onything amiss then,' stoically and, after a pause. 'And ye willna be thinking of going out at all.'

'That's my affair, laddie, and none o' yis and, whit's more, there'll be a stiff complaint tae yer mannie in Parliament in the post by the morn, fer the rousing of decent Christian bodies from their rest.' With all the self-righteous outrage of one who'd swallowed the last drop of untaxed brandy in the house but a minute before.

'Aye, well, I'll be nearby. Good night tae yis, mistress.'

The two had known each other a long time, owing to the remnants of a bothy having been discovered in a corner of the garden some fifteen years before: to her complete 'mystification'.

Lachlan and Calum and I climbed out of the window and ran, crouching, under the wall, over the bank, along the gully and to the beach in silent, sinking slide. The air was so still that we could pick out familiar voices from the uproar in the reeds; the high-pitched one was Billie Kirst and the loudest was Johnny the Baltic. Conn Barnet was there and old man Mulgies and, to our dismay, we heard Robbie beag's laugh, resonant across the sands.

'Herself'll no like this, by Christ,' said Lachlan. 'We'd better get word tae them fast.' But it was too late.

Just ahead, a torch flashed and was answered by another in the rocks and another from the dunes and three dark figures raced down the strand. And the song stopped, as though someone had closed a door.

We crawled to the narest hummock, waiting for a British gunboat to steam round the point with all cannon firing till every man in the village was shackled to the galleys.

'Wid ye be having a picnic then, lads?' the leader of the 'chentlemen' was asking.

'Ye might say it was a reunion of friends,' we heard Johnny the Baltic reply, with tipsy dignity.

'A wee bit comfort for Billie here, whose wifie has left him fer another,' added Soukie Mulgies, rolling about.

And that is exactly what it was.

Dollopy Kirst, a well-known harpy, had gone to spend a week with her sister in Buckie and Billie had decided to commemorate the occasion with a party 'as far frae the women as possible' – and with every bottle labelled.

'It's thirsty work, the Excise, they tell me. Ye'll be having a drop?' he said, generously, after the laughing had stopped.

'Aye,' said the chentlemen, wearily, and were as drunk as the rest within a half-hour. Then the toast was drunk.

'The wifies,' shouted Conn Barnet, swaying to his knees, and the reunion fell about at the joke.

'Aye, aye, the wifies. Never more sweet than when they're asleep.'

'Ye've no seen my Teenie at the snoring or ye widna put it like that.'

'Wid ye not, Conn Barnet,' came a woman's voice from the dark. 'And just how wid ye put it?'

And down the bank they strode; Teenie frae Troon and Mistress Mulgies and Bauchie Nell, two or three more and poor Billie Kirst's eldest daughter, dismounted from a herd of bikes to prove that not only the Customs can trace a celebration on a still Scottish night.

The men did not even put up a fight, just loaded the women into the boats and rowed sheepishly home.

The incident confirmed two decisions for me. I would go to sea with the men against the 'chentlemen' and . . .

'Whit a disgrace,' said Lachlan. 'Ye widna see me being ordered so easy by a wifie.'

I was not so sure. 'Well, no woman's going tae get me tae a marriage,' I said, stoutly determined to avoid the risk. But one did.

My first skipper was an extraordinary and wonderful gnome, known as Bonnety Wull. He was about four and a half feet tall and most of that was head. The head was topped by a tartan tammy, exchanged for a gold-braided cap on Sundays, and a large, blue-black growth of beard grew up to his eyes. He ruled his ship by a mixture of evangelism, poetry and biblical oaths, and he never washed at all.

I went to see him on my fourteenth birthday and found him sitting on a large bass drum alone on his old drifter, the *Roane*.

He looked through me to the jetty for a while.

'Whit d'ye think o' mackerel, laddie?' he asked, still gloomily out of focus.

'They're bonny fish, sir,' I replied, tentatively.

'Right enough. Bonny they are and I dinna care the same fer the herrings.' It was said with sharp decision and a nod of the beard. Then, 'We'll be putting out at nine the night.'

When I was halfway down the jetty, he came to the rail.

'Laddie! . . .

Avoid the reeking herd,
Shun the polluted flock,
Live like that stoic bird,
The eagle of the rock.'

His voice boomed past me to the harbour, and I was a new-fledged man and going to sea tonight and it seemed quite right that he should say it. Besides, hadn't I seen him banging the same drum and shouting 'Hallelujah!' through the village since I was a boy, and, though he'd seemed loony then, he didn't any more.

'Aye, aye, sir!' I called back and rolled across the harbour like a lifelong seaman and loved him.

We cast off on the turn of the tide, the *Roane* and her sister, the *Mona*, kicking over the waves, like two middle-aged matrons hell-bent for holiday vice in Paris. There was nothing sedate about either of them and the *Roane* was the worst. Creaking in her stays she might be, but she never let up. It was knees up and bucking, us thrown across decks and Bonnety Wull into a miming, mouthing fury for two hours or more, until the lights of the village had fallen behind a new horizon, like matches, and the *Mona* was long out of sight.

The water unfurled from the sides of the ship in opaque fans, trailing into white spots on the black cat back of the sea, and the fleet of nets dotted ahead under their entrail of floats. Shoals of slim shadows, risen from a deep green daytime, slipped by in the wash. As they reached the waves, their curious 'swim' would begin, the nightly scattering of the herring across the surface on which our living depended. No moon this night, only stars, brighter away from the matt land, reflecting in the ocean glass a billion years beneath. The running cough of the engine had stopped and we drifted head to wind. There were cocoa and bully beef and jacketed potatoes below.

For a mile and a half or so the nets unwound, dropping fifty feet down the sea to form a deadly curtain across the tide which the fish in their restlessness could not see. Like flocks of scaled birds in a liquid sky, they veered and swerved together, never touching, yet never apart; unable to separate, not even one; follow my leader into the mesh. We ate our supper and the twine caught in their gills and snared them by the hundred.

The cry to haul broke up our sleep between midnight and dawn and we hunched blearily on deck to where the sea slapped us hard awake. Every one of the crew was needed now to wrench our nets and, God willing, our catch back from her: skipper in the wheelhouse, mate by the jinny, cook in the warp-room and the rest of us changing places during the rasping, muscle-tearing struggle, which would last for the next three to seven hours.

To me, that first drawing in of the nets was so unexpectedly punishing that nothing at sea ever seemed so bad again. It was like a vicious and endless and totally useless tug-of-war with the very claws of the deep, which hooked and snatched at the sole-rope until my hands were branded with burns. Behind me, the other five men groaned great rhythmic grunts in time to the strain of the nets and it seemed that, however stoutly we heaved, the task would never be done, so slowly, slowly, sullenly did the lint drag over the rollers to the hold.

Then, at last, I saw them, quivering in the first strands of mesh, the living tears of the sea; a few at first, then pendant showers and a silver stain, a sheet and then each fish was just a scale on the monster body of the net. The men were scudding the herring from the lint; bodies leaning backwards to draw and lift together, till the net leapt and fell in a thrashing, heavy throb and the fish were shaken to the deck to twist and gasp their dance of death and beat their tails against the wood, until it sounded as though we were drowning in torrential rain. Through the bunker lids they spilled with rattling steps to the pounds below, to rumble like a passing tumbril, a distant war, a buried Africa; even the roar of the sea was masked by the terrible final drumming of the fish.

In the morning, we gutted and bedded them in salt and, through the day, the nets were 'cleaned' and the *Roane* scrubbed and oiled, as our wily old skipper set her course for the next night's fishing grounds, sensing out where the herring would rise.

In those days, there were no echo-sounders, or radar, or other gadgets, apart from a simple plankton indicator and a feeling wire, to help him find his catch. A drifter skipper relied on his own blend of experience and indefinable instinct for the movements of the shoals, the instinct to find the phosphorescent fire of the herring and 'get right': a few yards could make all the difference between a ton shimmer and empty nets – 'a feast or a famine'.

Three days after leaving the harbour, we'd return with an average catch of ten or eleven cran.

My life settled into a tidal flow of a day at home to two or three away; and the day at home was usually spent line-fishing from a rowing-boat. Sundays, too, were spent on land as, unlike the heathen English, the Scots driftermen preserved the day of rest, and do so even now.

On board, I served my turn at everything, as spare hand and galley boy and stoker, sweating below, to shivering watch at daybreak. We steamed to Faeroe and Rockall and Aberdeen and Yarmouth, through grey days over grey waters, which were churned into diamonds at night to hit our faces and melt back into brine. Sea-serpents wound behind us, sinuous and amber-eyed. Long-wrecked galleons shivered under our passing and the barnacled skeletons of their crews lolled and sighed drunkenly in the depth charge of our wash. Down there, the fishes nested in dead marble hands and weeds were hung with jewels and blackened gold. I saw them. Through the windowless night ocean I saw them all and Roane, the sea-princess, guarding and following in her sealskin to see if one of her earthborn sons sailed with us. Who would have believed me, had I told them?

Sometimes, aurora borealis lit the navy sky above us, lime-green arcs floating slowly from horizon to horizon, the faint, white searchlights flickering across the planets, flashing on and off, changing shape, rising higher and higher until tinged with red and vanishing as suddenly as they had come. I'd seen them all my life, the Northern Lights, always beautiful and perhaps our compensation, because we lived in cold clouds and rain and so far from the sun.

It was during my first year at sea that the strange thing happened in our waters, which emptied them of fish for many weeks and left many a family hungry round the coast when the men were laid off the boats. We'd been sailing for two days and, of the tiny catch we'd hauled, half had had lumps torn from their sides. Supper that night was a sullen meal, with the crew morose after their useless labour and the skipper absent from his place. Later, on deck, we saw him aft, alternately quoting God's threats to the sea and praying to her, because to him she was equally divine.

I wandered to the foredeck, to where the buoyant corks bobbed away into the dark and the white foam endlessly lathered the bows. But, when I looked this night, the foam was pitch with bubbles, like floating, black eggshells crowded on the surface.

'Jack!' I called to the 'driver'. 'Take a look at this.' And he did and then the others and the mate and, finally, Bonnety Wull, himself, came down to strain his eyes over the rail.

'It's no usual. It is not,' he grumbled, looking at us over his beard, as though we were responsible.

'It looks like oil,' suggested the mate, dubiously.

'Nothing of the sort, mate. It's no a bit like oil.' The skipper stumped off, angrily.

We shone a searchlight over the water and through its beams the black stain ran farther than we could see above the nets. The haul began and, as the first patch of lint emerged, I saw, with sick surprise, a long, wet tentacle clinging to its edge.

Squid! Dozens and hundreds of squid, coiled and contorted in the nets, looping their long arms round every object, ravelled together in black ink. They tied themselves to the rails and the warp, some spanning more than four feet, with their parrot-like beaks opening and shutting in the air and their motionless eyes staring over the ship in blank rage.

The crew jumped through them, hacking off the tentacles that caught round their legs as they passed and cursing, as though they were merely annoyed by the invasion. After all, we had all seen the occasional squid before. But there was something inexplicably repulsive about this mass of clinging, sucking limbs and, as we stabbed them furiously to death, I knew I was not the only man scared by the sudden swarm.

Throughout the whole of the summer, the squid stayed and harried the shoals beyond our range, so that there was no longer any point in trying to fish. Their eggs clustered across the top of the sea in forgotten mops and their half-eaten quarries were washed up on the shores.

The men sat on the harbour wall and stared bitterly at the water, or stoned the odd, ten-armed body which fell out of the waves. The women dolefully hinted that it was all a trick by the men to give the men excuse for sitting on their backsides all day and then it was rumoured that the plague had been secretly dumped there by the Germans in revenge (the Great War had not been forgotten). But no one at all thought of eating the squid.

It was during those months that I built my first rowing-boat under the guidance of Bonnety Wull. We laid her keel in an old shed near the quayside and bound her larchwood ribs and stringers with copper nails, till she looked like the marvellous skeleton of some prehistoric monster awaiting discovery in a lost cave. We corked her with hemp and then she was pitched and literally drowned for a week in the harbour, until her timber swelled up and tight against each other and she was ready for painting and proud launching and christening – the *Morag*, of course.

It was while we had worked together on her, that the old skipper told me the tales of his life at sea and true fisherman's yarns they were. He'd sailed the oceans of the world, had been wrecked on an iceberg in the Arctic and, the only survivor, had lived off the dead body of a whale for three weeks, until the berg floated past another whaler, which had picked him up unharmed and none the worse.

In the Indian Ocean, he'd escaped from a killer shark by thrusting a great rock into its mouth, just as it was about to take the first bite. Off the coast of Australia, a forty-foot octopus had reached into the ship and plucked him over the side and he'd had to cut off each of its eight limbs in turn before he was free. But, most wonderful of all, after being washed up on a deserted island off Africa in a storm, he'd trained a dolphin to bring him fish and, in a year, to speak; then he'd sent it to fetch help from the mainland and, as he left, the dolphin followed the rescue ship, crying.

'It fair broke my heart, laddie,' he said, and I knew it was true. Bonnety Wull saw the same vision and heard the same sea songs as I, and many more. So the pictures of his adventures filled my imagination with plans to discover all the straits and secret channels of every forgotten sea for myself, one day.

I listened to him for hours, and, between the stories of his past, learnt many things. He taught me how the herring lays her eggs at the bottom of the ocean, although she, herself, lives at the top, and migrates on seasonal group honeymoons; and how the dogfish lays just one egg, protected by a horny shell, and the salmon breeds in fresh water, but lives in the sea, while the fresh-water eel breeds in the sea and lives in the rivers.

He showed me a hidden graveyard, centuries old, for ship-wrecked Danish sailors, a place so surrounded by superstition and fears that no one else would go there, but the history of great storms and foundering ships came alive again through him and I often went there afterwards.

He taught me, too, about boats and tides; and how to survive them, and each piece of advice was marked with a poem, or a text. Without doubt, he would have known what to do in Jonah's place; but, equally without doubt, on land he was quite mad.

He lived with his sister above a junk shop, which never sold a thing because she refused everyone entrance. She hated the sight of Bonnety Wull as well and regularly threw water over him, as he stood under her window banging his Sunday drum. His Sundays were immutably patterned, commencing with the drum and ending when he and Wee Stuart, the joiner, both thoroughly drunk, sang 'The Lord's My Shepherd' in harmony.

At sea, Saturday, the traditional Sabbath, usually summoned the crew to a service unique in its content of confused Bible-readings, pure fable and outlandish ritual, filched from various religions across the earth and ended with 'The Lord's My Shepherd' sung by the captain, alone.

His mother, wife and daughter were the *Roane*. He knew every notch in her timbers and understood her every creak and had not left her in twenty years. He talked to her and coaxed her and swore at her and hid in her and ruled her and dressed her in paint and polish and bitterly blamed Archie Macpherson, the engineer, for the inevitable fact that she was growing old.

The two men never spoke. Archie had joined the ship only a year after her master and immediately, so the latter proclaimed, her engines had begun to falter. The feud had developed from there to the point where bridge and engine-room communicated only through whistles and third parties.

'More steam,' the skipper would growl.

'Skipper wants more steam,' the nearest man would shout, and, from below, Archie would snarl back, not too loudly, 'Tell the holy auld fool he canna have it,' which was tactfully translated into, 'We're at full steam already, sir,' a reply which left old Wull gibbering through his beard.

The master of the *Mona* was a younger and saner soul and came from beyond our village to use the *Mona* as a stepping-stone to a more sophisticated vessel. He'd taken her over a short while before I went to sea and, three years later, he left her for a Grimsby trawler. He left before a replacement had been found and while her mate was down sick, but in one of those calm, moonless weeks just right for the herring.

Bonnety Wull knew very well he could not take the *Roane* out and leave the crew of the *Mona* idle, when the solution was known to all, and so he sat morosely by his anchored ship all day, trying to ignore the sea stretched out before him like a speckled carpet, so light and still that you could have floated to Greenland on a raft, without getting wet. It was more than any good seaman could stomach and, at last, he stalked over to the other ship, leaving our mate in charge of the *Roane* and Archie Macpherson grinning for the first time in years.

All the way out, our skipper stood in the wheelhouse of the *Mona* with his binoculars trained on us, until the two drifters moved beyond sight of each other and the work of the night began. But, in the morning, the *Mona* was back, tugging at our skirts, like a toddler behind its shopping mother, all day and the day after.

The sea was choppier now and the waves burst into white streaks for as far as the eye could see. The clouds bulged downwards until they seemed to touch our funnel. With them came the dark and the *Mona* steamed reluctantly away with her head to the wind.

Everyone was busy shooting the nets, when the inexplicable signal came to haul them in. When we looked up there were no stars and, despite the wind, the air was choking and heavy, as though the sky were pressing it down so hard that it was turning solid.

We headed for home with the wind behind us, but soon the *Roane* was skidding and sliding across the purple water, toppling from port to starboard and back and outracing her own engines in the gale. The mate turned and spun the tiller in a useless effort to keep her straight while behind him the watch was sweating white. It was as though she knew she was without a master and wanted to fling us all from her. We held fast to her rails and gunwale in desperation, too alarmed to go below, in case we never surfaced again.

Archie Macpherson came stumbling and falling from the engine room, weeping with rage. 'Ye loony, buggering bastard,' he shrieked up unreasonably at the mate, and rushed back to his dials and fires.

We saw the water a handstretch away, as she listed under the squall, which densed into a hurricane minutes later, blowing ocean and sky into one and the swell into a wall above us. Ten, twenty, thirty feet high rollers toppled over the decks without time to drain away before the next came fuming down, as if we were already halfway to the bottom.

It seemed we fought for hours, crawling over the flooded decks, securing doors and hatches and working the pumps and, for the only time in my life, I was seasick, the vomit whipped upwards away from my mouth and no time for surprise. With Death gigantic before me, I don't remember thinking much at all, just feeling – violent, physical jolts of fear each time my hand slipped on its hold, or a wave reared to pounce, the sting of a broken rope recoiling into my face; feeling so wet that, like a swimmer, I felt dry, goaded by the fish hurled on board by the capricious water. Above all, there was the mighty sexual need to smash and bruise and crush and defeat the snarling bitch sea and bring her down to a sigh. I screamed at her. I hated her.

Primeval instincts gripped us all and turned some into supermen, thrice as strong as normal mortals. I saw old Dargie Calder drag a full barrel of salt from below to secure a door. It weighed at least two hundredweight, but he had carried it single-handed and, seconds later, it bounced over the side, like a rubber ball.

The rockets went up in the midst of the storm; red and green streaks of distress flaring weakly in the distance above where the *Mona* lay and, all at once, she and her crew mattered more than we and each man thought his thoughts as we turned again. It took an hour to cover the mile and sometimes we dropped to the sea-bed, yes, with starfish like a living cloud around, us, and sometimes we were thrown to the sky along a lightning shaft, faster than sight.

But, when we reached the *Mona*, she was dying, heeled over and shuddering in pillows of surf, hardly visible in the black night and nothing could touch her for the swell. There were cries coming, it seemed from all around, thinner than silks on the wind and, as we nosed blindly towards them, a massive breaker picked up the *Mona* and broke her in half on its back.

She sank quickly, almost gladly, with only a last, quick sucking breath as her head disappeared. She left a gaping whirlpool, then a patch of foam and then it was as though she had never been.

A rowing-boat lurched into sight and we picked up the survivors, most of them old fishermen and crying. Bonnety Wull was not among them.

There was an inquiry, of course, and our skipper, Captain William Douglas Aird, was posthumously commended for his courage in the face of danger and for his refusal to abandon his ship until his crew were safely off. But by then it was too late.

Then the marine surveyors, whom he'd barred for so long from the *Roane*, boarded and condemned her and she was sold for scrap. Archie Macpherson retired and the rest of us went separate ways, some to the trawlers and one to open a shop.

I signed on with a modern drifter under another, more orthodox captain. We had sprung bunks, a trained cook and an echo-sounder, but the catch never seemed much larger for all that and, although later I worked on long-distance trawlers and even, for a spell, with the whalers and fished in all waters and saw the world, the *Roane* and Bonnety Wull stayed dear in my mind, for she was the first ship and he was the finest skipper.

CHAPTER TWELVE

CHANGES

IT was impossible to imagine a future different from my past for, despite talk of fortune awaiting us beyond the mountains, it seemed to me then that the world would always be what it had been; Lachlan and Calum and Bella and Catrina, Auntie Annie, Uncle Angus and me, and Granny Morag in that cottage above the sea. Later (always later), my brothers and sister and I would marry, but we would stay together in the valley. We would not leave. Even Catrina's living in Aberdeen was only one of her whims. She, too, would return when it had passed, I thought, and I was too young not to believe that we were immortal. Death happened to others, not to us.

The days passed in unchanging pattern, waking with agonized yawns, filling their hours with fishing and flirting, squalls and sweetnesses. The bottles of dazzle became pints of beer and the hunger to possess a football of my own transformed, without my noticing, into a longing for a polka-dotted kipper tie. The glen turned through its shadows and the moon through her phases and the sun through his sky-sweeping arc, always different and yet ever the same. And in our home we parted and united with the daily, hourly hugs and hates that went back to always.

'Give us a tune, give us a dance' till the ritual of family supper. How could I have suspected that one day it would not be so while Granny and Annie still warred?

Yet, when she was a child, Morag's hair had grown living and marvellously black to her waist. At fifteen, she had gathered its weight into a glossy coil round her head and each morning, for the rest of her life, wound it into the same style. Nightly it tumbled from its pins in a rushing clean smell to become the cloak in which she slept and I don't think it had ever been cut. Fifteen-year-old Catrina decisively chopped her hair into a shingle cut. Changes.

Our grandmother would have denied them. 'There's no sic thing as change,' she said once, sounding like a quotation from *Reader's Digest*. 'Life just has a few tucks let in or out o' it now and then.'

True, the place did not alter. Of course not. It never will. Lines of modern houses were scribbled across the valley, but eventually the bricks will crumble and the walls be overgrown and the strath will take up its former outline, leaving only a few metal door numbers to be found, like the shattered statue of Ozymandias, to tell the story that man was there.

Soon, indeed, the forest was to be hacked to stubble and the hills left torn and naked as raped children for the sake of another war, but the trees grew again and the woods of my boyhood are back now where they were before, a little faint and, for the moment, pale, but *there*. So, in eternity, perhaps my grandmother was right; the roots, the true form and genesis of reality stay always constant.

But about us, around us, among us, were the nudgings and jostlings of people and happenings which continually compelled us into new positions, sometimes without our even noticing it; for our courses were not altered only by dramatic personal events. Sometimes we were displaced by incidents of which we were completely unaware at the time, or by someone nearby stirring, like a sleeper unconsciously dragging the blankets off his partner.

So the Dornoch clerk, whose stroke of pen closed down the local slaughterhouse, unwittingly turned Lachlan into an apprentice butcher by the same move; and, because the roof next door fell in one Spring, we lost forever our Winter neighbours, the tinkers. The arrival of a young jute merchant, the playing of a casual poker game and even the emerging of new local government policy blindly recast our lives until, sometimes, it seemed that destiny was no more than the child of chance and accident.

To me, these shifts in my own cool, certain present came like a succession of stings from an invisible wasp and I reacted with resentment. It was as though I sensed that the safe familiar stamp of our ways was cracking and being replaced, and I felt bewildered – and afraid?

Curiously, still it was not Catrina's going which first tilted our home, although she was the first to leave. We had long been used to this strange sister's sudden, eldritch disappearances and, I suppose, the move merely seemed like another of them. No, it was the wedding of Bella which started the disintegration of closeness and brought the first isolating of us, one from another. It began, I think, for each of us the solitary, unreachable, untouchable life, which every man must lead once childhood is over.

And the shock of it was not the marriage, but that he lived in Dundee, which seemed as far away as Persia. The nephew of the old sisters who employed her, he had courted our Bella with heavy solemnity during a three-weeks stay, followed by several months of instructive correspondence. His nervous concern with her grammar always betraying the fact that he felt he was marrying beneath him.

He was a dour man, bred in the canny south of a family which had made its considerable fortune in jute. During previous visits to the village, he had been better known for his allergy to buying a round than for his wit, and none of us had taken it seriously when he began to bring Bella home from work and sit, sandy-haired and tight-lipped, disapproving whole evenings at the kitchen table drinking tea. But then came the letters and a Hogmanay attendance, a birthday present and, in March, suddenly he was there again, 'in his best suitie' this time.

All of us, including Bella, were at the lobby keyhole.

'I've bought a fine house, Mrs. Sinclair, and furnished it from top to bottom. It's cost me a fair penny.'

'I've nae doubt,' answered our grandmother, drily.

'It appears to me that Bella would make a good wife. It's a different kind of life she'd have, of course, but my mother can help her and I'm sure she'll settle down grand in a wee while.'

'Aye, but will yis be making a guid man fer our Bella, I'm wondering?' She said it pensively, knowing the answer.

The wedding was a very grand affair. It was the kind of wedding the old lady would have cherished in her dreams for ever, had she thought more highly of the groom. Robbie beag and Herself (in the most inspired of her phenomenal hats) attended; Robbie beag to give away the bride and Herself to sit proudly alone in the side of the church reserved for the bride's family, because there wasn't money for us all to go.

Left at home, the rest of us couldn't really believe that it was happening; but it was. Bella walked up the aisle of the Dundee parish kirk on her uncle's arm and returned down it a married woman.

Granny Morag smiled brightly under the stares of her new grandson-in-law's fine folk and stayed through the reception, until the couple left for their honeymoon, and then she came the long journey home again.

And, all at once, I saw how frail she was, such a brittle little frame, with its thin, defenceless shoulders and fragile hands; it looked as though it might break at any moment. We had never seen her tired before that night.

With Bella gone, a tie had been broken between us and we seemed to drift apart. Calum worked late more often and stayed more nights away at the farm; Lachlan, with his tradition of women-filled evenings, hadn't done more than sleep occasionally at the cottage for years anyway, and I was usually away fishing.

Sometimes weeks would go by without our seeing each other, although we all lived at the same address, and then I might pass one of my brothers in the lobby, or even in the street, or see the hollow where he had slept when I woke in the morning. We were to live this way for more than a year.

The home no longer bound me, nor did our grandmother. The time had come to separate and, although we did not move, we split with the ruthlessness of youth and left her to drift in her own slippery world of dreams. Somehow, when Bella went, we all went.

And then there was another marriage. After ten electric years 'biding in' with our uncle in her two-roomed cottage on the brow of the parish, Siubhan went with Robbie beag quietly to Dornoch one morning and returned the same night, wed. And after that night, although he maintained his sidelines in the poaching and the whisky-brewing, the fierce man changed, mellowed. Never one to discuss himself, probably not even with his new wife, yet he grew more approachable and less watchful. The slightly threatening glare of tension he had always worn faded into the faintest flicker and, married to this, his first and last woman, he became more human.

Eighteen months after their wedding, Siubhan died of cancer. Our uncle Robbie beag returned to his former impersonal austerity, which no one, not even my cousin Jenny, could thaw again.

But my brothers and I were still unaware of real disappointment and uncorroded by failure and we sprang each new experience and emotion with that total, trusting enthusiasm which makes the young so endearing, or hateful, to the old.

Around us, the latest social vogues were seeping slyly into our corner. Widows had replaced their traditional dark weeds with colours, and men decided to shave moustaches out of fashion. A young woman got divorced and ever after was pointed out as 'Aggie Simson-wha's-divorced-but-she-comes-fra-Aberdeen-ye-ken', which explained the extraordinary situation and cleared the neighbourhood of responsibility all in one breath. Revolutions were taking place drip by drip. An American business syndicate rented the shooting on the laird's moors one season and the entire population of the glen nearly died of heart failure at the shame of it.

Granda Soutar actually did die at last, on the gold-filled mattress where he'd lain, cackling spitefully, for twenty-five years. The news of his passing swished under the guard of his suspicious eldest daughter and, suddenly, everyone in the village felt an overwhelming need to pay *personal* respects to the auld de'il's body. All in a morning, the Soutars found themselves trapped without an enemy in the region, which queued (mental cash-registers whirring behind piously reverent faces) at their parlour door, until Ma Soutar could contain her rapacity no longer and publicly slit open the venerable mattress with a kitchen knife, to discover ... ten pounds, seven shillings and ninepence three-farthings wrapped in an old sock. It had been a whole year's wages in Granda Soutar's youth.

Other old, old, forever faces disappeared, to be noticed for the first time by their absence. And the valley seemed to be contracting, just as our cottage garden had done in the beginning time when I first hazarded over its limits. Now the mountain boundary itself was being eroded, dwarfed by our experience.

Gaps appeared in the early classroom design of boys, for the drift south had begun, and Warty Walter went to Rosyth Dockyard, Dunfermline, and Jack Soutar to Inverness and Cracked Bill won a bursary to Edinburgh University and went off to be a doctor.

Lachlan wanted to go, too, and kept testing the idea by resentfully producing arguments in its favour in the bar and the kitchen and the billiard room, recently converted from a church hall as an omen of the future. 'Now the Slaughter was closed ... and seeing as how Drew Heggie didna know the fleshing ... and there are more opportunities in the toon, d'ye see? ...' Was he preparing us, or talking himself into it?

Whichever it was, he made up his mind before long and told us, with worried glances at our grandmother. But the exposed loneliness, which had rushed her face after Bella's wedding, was never allowed to betray her again and she merely nodded him on his way to be, first, an apprentice in Dornoch and, later, a master butcher in Aberdeen.

The age when men dreamed dreams and saw visions, the age of curses and miracles, fiends and angels was being overthrown by the Age of Science. Our old superstitions, the phenomena which had once seemed so impossible that they had to be divine, were shrivelling into commonplaces under the latest glut of rational explanations. It was the swollen pause before the avalanche. For the first time in history, we began to feel superior to Nature; we began to believe that man knew everything.

Up on his farm, old Gregson was reading about arsenicals and spraying them over his fields and crops as a panacea to all problems and ailments. Soon he would wonder at the dead birds on his land and watch half a herd of cattle die after drinking from a poisoned pond. An era was ending and life in our hollow and life across the whole earth would never breathe in its old, slowly repeated rhythm again. God was dying. Soon He would be dead.

Down in the village, the old pecking order changed. We were no longer simply ruled by the established trinity of laird, minister and dominie. With the building of a few more houses and the opening of the billiard room, the village began to think of itself as a town and towns, as everyone knew, have provosts. A provost needs clerk and council and harbours have masters. Even old Duff, the policeman, was promoted to sergeant, with an allocation of two shiny, eager constables to emphasize his rank. And soon, although a lift of the laird's lofty eyebrow still constituted the law, the district had become topheavy with figures of authority, for whom work had to be found.

A police-station was built to replace Mrs. Duff's front room and a crime wave swept the area. In the year following her husband's rise to power, more offences were recorded in our region than in the whole of the preceding five years. It wasn't that the local population had become lawless over night, but simply that the disconcerted sergeant was bored.

Replaced by his young subordinates on those sociable bike rides round the glen, and unable, for fear of setting the same subordinates a bad example, to indulge any more in the occasional unofficial day's fishing, the poor man had entertained himself, during those long months shut up in his aseptic station, by building 'cases', where previously a word of warning or a 'blind eye' would have served.

Word reached Dornoch. Word reached the Chief Constable in Dornoch. Word said that there was a highly efficient sergeant down our way who was *worth watching*. And word reached Sergeant Duff that the Chief had heard that he was a highly efficient man, who was *worth watching*. And the crime wave became a crime tidal wave, on the crest of which the sergeant would eventually ride to the rank of superintendent and out of the valley altogether, to take charge of a new division. And ever since then, the village-now-a-town has had a reputation as the place where highly efficient young men with ambition in the Force are to be found and our crime wave has continued to rise to prove it.

One of our first provosts was Ernie Keir, the wee solicitor man, who'd driven the train to Dornoch during the General Strike. A few of his cronies made up the original town council, which, if the truth must be told, was more of a poker school than a buzzing local government – although they did authorize the extension of the quay to please Drew Chalmers, who'd married Ernie's daughter and been given the harbour-mastership as a wedding present. There had been no need to bother with such complications as outside tenders and negotiations, as Soukie Mulgies, the treasurer, happened to be a bit of a builder himself and agreed to start the harbour job, as soon as his men had finished Sergeant Duff's police-station.

Life might have continued in this comfortable fashion for years had the councillors not grown greedy, as officials often do, and raised the stakes in their card school to such heights that poker became more than just a useful hobby, expediently steering their interest away from local affairs. The game became a drama, so intense that the night Ernie the provost won twenty pounds, he collapsed and promptly expired from over-exposure to excitement.

The following Sunday, Wee Frees and R.C.'s thought and acted alike, as is remarkably common, and pointed sermons on the vice of gambling were preached from all pulpits. The mood of the village was set for action. But perhaps this had been brewing for a time past and Ernie Keir's fatal winning was only the catalyst.

It was a season when the world was dissatisfied and Europe restless. Hitler was massing strength in Germany and the Spanish were fighting their civil war and the women, even in our hidden fold of the north, had resorted to their traditional refuge in times of uncertainty – the knitting of socks for soldiers. The faint twitchings of fear were everywhere, bringing with them the desire for anyone who would make and take the decisions for the rest. Our folk were no different and, on the death of Ernie Keir, they reacted by appointing as the new provost – a reformer.

There are those for whom Joshua Logan remains a saint and those who recall him as an unholy freak; but whichever he was, he is remembered to this day by all, for he rushed power like a scrum half and, thereafter, dusted out our quiet settlement like a demented broom. Joshua arrived in office demanding roads where there were tracks, gas where there was paraffin, and electricity where there was gas. A first cousin to the laird (therefore, likely a cousin of my own), he was tucked away into our community, doubtless for the convenience of the family, whose polite circle then had to suffer the embarrassment of his dissertations on the sewage system and drains only during the grouse season. He was improperly left-wing for a Tory.

However, despite the laird's speech of support, it was not family influence which won him the job of provost – it was obsession. His aggressively thumped out programme of improvements was so impressive that it rammed him into office: most extraordinary of all, he intended to keep every promise of it and scourge the glen into becoming a model society. He was a man who demanded order.

The reforms began with education; arranging for a schools inspector to visit our area from Dornoch about once a fortnight (though on a different day each time, so that the regular truants couldn't organize their absences to coincide with his). The system was a big success; boys were yanked back from hookey round the harbour and in the fir woods, from minding sheep and earning money at harvest for a bike; the girls stopped staying home with the wee'ns and the school register began to look quite respectable.

On the way to the fishing, sometimes, I'd meet the inspector man myself, though never without the conditioned urge to hurtle away to hiding up the nearest close; and, often, from aboard my ship at anchor in the bay, I'd see the roundup of lads; the scurrying and tweaked ears and escapes and yelps bringing back the shivering terror of that day the dominie's bony fist first hoist me over the school railings – not so very long ago.

But in this modern era, Lachlan's place as champion truant was inherited by Wee Will Sauchan, Dug's brother and so tenaciously anti-school that his father was soon hauled before the sheriff's court, to the embarrassment of the provost; Stewart Sauchan being his own town clerk and an unforgiving man.

Fish sheds were rebuilt and the area round them given a concrete surface, which was an improvement, folks agreed; but replacing the cobblestones down Nichol's Brae with asphalt was not – even though one icy morning auld Nellie Piercy did skid from top to bottom, displaying violet cami-knickers to all the men coming up to the pub from the boats. Three new gas-lamps and a pillar-box appeared in the streets and Conn Barnet, the Postie, was given a new cap.

On the whole, these innovations were acceptable enough. They added to the tides and crops and weather and fishing as local subjects for lazy comment by men over their evening jars: one could agree that they were useful amenities or grumble over the unnecessary expense, but they were not sufficiently important then to cause disturbance or rouse feuds.

Had the provost been content with them, no doubt I would have stayed my life in the cup of the strath, where the world of my childhood might even have become my children's world; muddled and slow, yes, unjust sometimes, yet strangely tolerant, with room for eccentrics and idiots and unique individuals with original answers and difference. It was the day before the company man: a day later and we would have been bundled into institutions, and I would hardly have known my brothers and sisters.

Joshua Logan was a missionary; to him the diversity among us all seemed like nihilism, the shapelessness of our shambling society offended him; he saw its ills, yet was too hidebound to imagine that there could be other than orthodox remedies.

His ambitions began to travel beyond the immediate tuft-of-houses-growing-without-pain-into-a-town, to plots of stony, open land and soggy dells and handbuilt dykes, neat as slotted jigsaws, to shepherds' huts and still hollows and monastic, mildewed tarns, disturbed only by birds and dragonflies in their summer moment, and to the secret people in the hills. Official aides were sent, like messengers from Caesar Augustus, to inspect, list and number, register and report, so that the great tidying up of our straggling region could begin and, before long, more officials, experts wearing instruments and airs of science, descended by train from Dornoch to stride across the village and out two miles along the road to the pump down from our cottage.

Huddling together crossly, they cranked the handle, bottled the water, held the bottle up to the grey sky light and bolted away, as though fleeing an unknown plague.

The pump was sentenced, of course, and a week later pulled up and the hole filled in for good. A doctor came to examine us, exclaiming in astonishment that we weren't all rotten with typhoid. Perhaps our aunt's purges had worked after all. He left, shaking his head and complimenting us, but, as no one offered to sink us a well to sweet water, we were worse off than before. Had Farmer Gregson not sent down a daily supply in a couple of milk urns, we'd have had to fetch it from the village, or do without.

So Annie wept and Granny Morag swore it was all part of a personal conspiracy by the upstart provost to destroy our family at last, as revenge for my impolitic blood-relationship to himself and the laird.

For many months before this occurrence, our grandmother had been withdrawing into private hostile exile. Her laughter had become rare and freakish and she had stopped dancing. Bella had gone and we neglected her. There was no one left to dance with, or for. Queer and destructive, even with us: determined to reject before she was rejected. I think, now, that she was preparing to kick us out, because we didn't need her any more; because she needed us. Sometimes, she would snap again through the plastic aloofness with a fast, startling joke, or acid song, and then retreat as swiftly and perhaps for days.

Her enemies loomed larger in that time and she fought them off more bitterly, sending longer and taunting letters, personally 'confronting' local dignitaries in her own inimitable way, shouting in public places and whispering into her nightly drench.

Mother Morag, always so sane about her chimeras, began to believe assassins and hemlock everywhere as her nightmares grew clearer than fact. She waned to a harsh chime, to a hate, to a savage green wind with eyes of flame.

Yet Calum and I noticed nothing then: only Annie was there when she flared down the rooms, repeating housework just completed.

As the complaints and warnings mounted at the other end of the track, we slapped our thighs and roared at the tales of her scandals and insults, usually choice and well-deserved; and collecting her from Big Jamie's seemed an old family custom. We didn't meet each other often enough to discover that helping her home was no longer unusual. Now, unknowingly, we were taking it in turns to carry her from the bar almost every night.

We saw nothing. But others were watching and listening and noting – and smarting: others with long, long memories.

CHAPTER THIRTEEN

STONES BY THE TRACK

OUR grandmother had teased and jeered at local bureaucracy for too long; she had offended far too many people. Years before, when my brothers and sisters and I were children, our little hollow, locked away between mountains and sea, had been too isolated and unimportant to interest any powerful authority. Besides, there had been a world war to recover from and then the years of crippling unemployment. The provincial establishment of that time was far too occupied with inherited problems to make extra inquiry, or implement new ideas.

So we were left alone in our comfortable disorder, with only the figureheads of squire, schoolteacher and preacher between us and anarchy. Men built cowsheds and pigsties without plan or permission; people planted, fished, traded and loved with little legal restriction. Our laws were hardly more than the ten commandments and most of those were unenforced. Our grandmother flourished unchecked.

But now, as I became a man, buses and cars, trains and telephones were turning the government into a next-door neighbour. It was the square decade of box furniture and architecture, with the suburbs on the march. Uniformity was winning at the expense of individual liberty.

With justified pride, Joshua Logan authorized and soon opened the first council house to be built in the district. It was solid and safe and a blessing for the Stronachs, who'd lived with their five wee'ns as many years in the wet, two-roomed wreck behind the picture house. Situated on the northern-edge, it brought the new town a few feet nearer to us and plans were announced for twenty more to join it.

Once again, the bowler-hatted men came polling and perching down the track, chanting logarithms, setting squares and sliding rules past the slaughterhouse ruin and the spongy mound where the pump had been; callipers, protractors and T-squares to our very own cottage, no compasses needed to find it, still patched rainbow from old peacock years; brandishing yardsticks, threatening chains, slithering under the door on worms of tape measures. Then, quick as a space, down the lobby, a callous trigonometry to geld the ghost of the sea-serpent and on to pleasure.

With X-ray eyes they laid bare the dry rot and mouse nests and sent the silver fish scurrying. They measured the rising damp and the ancient icicle in the passage and the gap through the scullery wall and the forest of mould under the washstand; they counted the woodworm holes and how many slates were missing off the roof; turning the outing into a holiday and the exposure of our place into a game, in which points were scored for each discovery of collapse and each evidence of dilapidation; congratulating each other and even congratulating us as they left, at last.

Condemned. For decay and disrepair and death-watch beetles soldiering blackly through the timbers; for age. Condemned. Pink, green and purple years do not count; memories cannot be measured. Unfit for human habitation; 'Do they think we're no human? It's fit for us.'

The surveyors had won their revenge, undoubtedly without even planning one. Hoary Annie wailed and tore at her hair, while Angus whimpered with his crumbling dog in the corner and the rest of us shifted about, awkwardly unprepared for this.

The message man they'd sent stood in the open doorway, tutting and shhhing, trying to explain the inexplicable, jerking the council house with bathroom (especially that bathroom) back and forth along his text, like a wee lad possessively trailing a wooden engine on wheels behind him, unable to understand that nobody else wanted it.

'But a *council* house, a modern council house . . .'

'Ayeeeee Jesus, we're being turned out intae the icy wilderness. We're a' tae perish, a' tae perish. Scoundrels and black-hearted brutes. Send doon yis torments and hell fire on them fer the sin o' it.'

'Ye've nae water here, woman, nor yet room enough. There's *three* bedrooms in the council housie, three, d'ye hear.'

He disapproved of us something terrible, but, to give the man his due, he tried.

'They say there's dry rot here and mind how the roof leaks in the rain and, man, ye've not a soul biding by fer miles. Yis'll have other folks, neighbours, in the council house.'

'No!' Out of her rocking-chair, blinking and bloodthirsty. 'Ye can stick yis neighbours, interfering auld sluts, up the lum o' yis council slum and work yisself up wi' them, fer I'll no budge frae this house!'

Herself, she was back with us, dusting down quavering Angus, rousing Annie from her girning and sending the provost's courier skeltering for his life; she was ordering ink and paper and Robbie beag, tugging and mauling us together and with her into the scrap. Gleeful and gaudy again, gremlin grandmother of my boyhood, thumping out mutinous slogans and discharging epistles like missiles into provost and laird and county council, to Sir John Simon, the Home Secretary, to Minister of Health and Prime Minister.

By return post, Notice of the Demolition Order was served on the remote landlord we had never seen, and Notice to Quit was hurriedly delivered to us by his factor, in person.

A letter, which took a chaotic week of family participation and shout-ups to phrase and rewrite, was sent to the King, in whom Granny Morag had implicit and abiding faith. The King would ride into our village in his coronation coach surrounded by the Household Cavalry and a brigade of Guards, who would seize the laird, the councillors and anyone owning a tape-measure and fling them into the dungeons at Balmoral Castle, where they would perish in irons and shackles. The King would save us all.

A reply came from a private secretary at Buckingham Palace. Granny Morag was over the moon.

'Read it, laddie. From the King. Whit does it say? Crivens! He's passing my letter on, och michty me, tae be dealt with by the appropriate authority. There now, d'ye see, did I no say the King would put it all right. He'll teach thon Joshua Logan tae put a wifie oot o' her home. The King is having it *dealt with* – and, nae doubt, he'll be dealing wi' they measurement mannies in his own good time.'

She slapped us all generously, peppered Uncle Angus with snuff and opened a celebration bottle.

We heard no more from the King, but very soon the local authority applied to the sheriff for a warrant to have us ejected. The scuffle had become war.

Our grandmother, flanked by Robbie beag and Tómas, rampaged into Dornoch for the hearing, but she had never been a good listener and her persistent verbal raids on the public health officer's evidence about the state of our house quickly brought the court to disorder.

'Havers! That's whit you're speaking, Bealie Mustard, a load o' havers. There's no been a worm or beastie come out o' one o they holes in the wood, not in twenty year. Man, they holes is in that kind of wood when it's cut frae the tree, ye ken. They're breathing holes.'

'Silence in court!'

'And whit's a' this about drains? How would we be having drains, when we dinna have the water? Laddie, laddie, its time ye got back tae minding measles and pox and left us healthy bodies in peace.'

'Silence! Silence!'

'Aye, aye, it's ay silence when it's a poor wifie having a word, but no when it's one o' the provost's gimpy clerks.'

'Mrs. Sinclair, if you interrupt these proceedings again, you will be removed from this court.

'Dinna raise yis voice taw me, Donald Maclean,' she turned on the sheriff. 'I mind when my cousin Vina stood ye up for thon joiner frae Buckie. Ye were daft enough then and I doubt ye've no changed, for all yis bit wig and goon.'

How could she plead or win sympathy? She knew them all too well – and they knew her. There was no legal aid then, no free advice, no glib, professional lawyer to speak for her, and this was the town in which the last witch in Scotland was burned to death – in 1722; not so very long ago in terms of the nature of man. Granny Morag was escorted firmly from its courtroom under the castle tower, and the Warrant for Ejection by the sheriff's officer was granted. Before it took effect, we were given two weeks to leave the cottage, the minimum time allowed by the law – but the maximum month would have made no difference.

Our uncles came home snarling and seared, crushed by the day and the way they had let their own mother be humiliated, the way they had just stood by and let it happen; two grown sons, choked to helplessness by their best suits and the bored contempt they had sensed around them in the court; the shame of it.

That night, they screwed up our inherent dislike of official-dom to tight, punishing hatred, far beyond reason, and we all got drunk brazen and sang martial Scots songs and staked great swearings of loyalty over the disgrace. The lamplit hours drowned in talk of blood and killing and we began to prepare to die for our stone square of dreams and gentle shades; for our dignity.

Then Uncle Angus walked round and round the kitchen, shaking each of us by the hand and Annie began to weep with real emotion and Granny Morag sat up, ruler straight, to stare at us with glowing eyes and we all began to kiss each other, con-vinced that we'd won the battle already and sent the provost and his bandits to hell. So the glorious victory was baptized with style, until we fell into an unconscious heap on the floor, fondly beside the warm range.

The phoenix Joshua Logan rose again out of our ashen waken-ing to confront us. In the shaking, aching morning, he seemed almighty and only Herself refused to believe he was invincible. She whirred about, like a clockwork jinnyeh, dispensing tea and tots and stirring talk, before chasing Tómas away home and Calum to his work and Robbie beag to the kitchen table to scheme.

There till noon, the two blueprinted plans of defence and the call-up papers went off to Dundee, Dornoch and Aberdeen by the afternoon mail.

They came home. Bella discarding her dour husband without regret; Lachlan typically bringing along meathook and cleaver, and Catrina fussing in crossly from the granite city. For the first time in years we were all together, a crammed, racy, vintage broth in the steaming kitchen, singing and bawling the first night, whispering and plotting the nights after that, pleased and excited by each other, the familiarity, the return of our wild honey time: burrowing and gathering, during the short while left, a hoard of inspirations, special supplies and deterrents; whisky, salt mutton, barley and tea; a couple of shotguns and barrowloads of sandbags.

Herself bowled through these days high with delight and bouncing out impossible brainwaves like ping-pong balls to be pursued round the rooms and burst under sensible comment. A giant catapult would be erected on the roof to fire massive boulders at the invaders, she stated, and we compromised by laying in a more practical supply of hand-size rocks. A thirty-foot-tall wall could be built round the cottage; after prolonged struggle, she was persuaded that there was not enough time for such construction. A moat then? No! Dynamite? Robbie beag threatened to withdraw his expert support and our grandmother flounced into the scullery, convinced she'd bred a bunch of niddering sissies.

But she was appeased by the delivery of final contributions to the war effort: three buckets of cow dung, delicately collected by Uncle Angus, and some crates of bottled urine, the thoughtful gift of Tómas and his tribe. Our wash-house arsenal reeked and rumbled more than Frankenstein's laboratory.

So then, fast, it was the night before, with our cousins creeping in under beginning light to help us shutter windows and pile up sandbags, lock the back door and jam our great-grandma Kirsty's mighty walnut wardrobe against the front door.

Then it was the morning of the fifteenth day after the granting of the warrant. Robbie beag was setting us all to our posts and sending Calum scrambling over the rafters in the roof to the tiny, dormer window set in the slates, to serve the first watch; and I was gulping and quaking, like a bairn again, remembering times when my ears had listened so hard for attack that they'd flown off in fright – and now they were wincing again, for the sheriff's force would come over the stony horizon at dawn.

So it did, slow and stately, Calum hoarsely reporting the progress past the Slaughter, around the pump, over the hillock and to the gate in our dyke.

We tensed our trigger-fingers round ropes of seaweed and bucket handles and paint-filled jamjars, and aimed through holes and punctures which lanced the walls like portholes. Our grandmother swirled up the ladder to join Calum, as the door rattled.

'Now, now,' quavered a voice. 'Open up there.'

'Och,' said Calum, disappointed. 'He's just but the one wee man.'

'The bigger fool then,' hissed Granny Morag and briskly tipped a basin of soot out of the window.

The sheriff's officer gave a yelp of shock, pitched blackly backwards with rolling eyes to his bike and careened off, like a cloud of wailing gnats, to the village.

It was a preposterous anti-climax and, feeling too silly to look at each other, we began to tidy away our weapons. Herself snuck down the ladder, slid self-consciously across the room and was suddenly very occupied with the stoking of the grate.

'My, my, if ye could see yisselves. All that palavering over one wee bit mannie. Ye look right draft.' Our Auntie Annie inevitably could not resist the jeer.

'And whaur were you, ye puddock-faced bitch, when ye thocht ye might have tae defend yis hearth against a bliddy army?' screamed our grandmother, absolutely mad with rage. 'Ye were wetting yis breeks wi' fear in the back room, ye snivelling, peely-wally besom!'

With that, she slammed several lumps of peat and a kettle of our precious water at her daughter with practised and livid accuracy.

'Of course, they'll a' be here before the forenoon,' said Robbie beag, unimpressed. 'So ye'd be as well tae save yis strength, Mother.'

'Now Catrina, get us some breakfast, lassie,' he went on. 'And, Micheil, check that pump ye brought frae the ship. Bella, take over from Calum and mind tae look up tae Gregson's, in case they come by the long way, though I doubt they will.'

Without his experience, we would have been unable to resist hurtling forth, brandishing dirks and claymores in Walter Scott fashion. Instead, he positioned us at the best points from which to guard the cottage, repulse assault and protect ourselves. He organized us, cool and certain from times in Alexandria and Dublin and from Chicago feuds.

In the north, Spring pounces in and explodes over the land with a violence unknown elsewhere, thrusting and stabbing its green daggers up through the diamond soil and blunt, aggressive buds out of dead arms of wood. Curlews and lapwings and linnets are shredded off the long boa of winter and tossed among us, their firework eggs splintering into ravenous beaks. Life, potent and savage, is forced up roots and the channels of trees and veins and arteries. In an hour, winter is obliterated by snowdrops.

Now, as we waited, was that first Spring hour, when the black-cold landscape turned to grass and that silver sorcery, electrifying the earth, changed us into supermen, supercharged. Robbie beag paced among us, generating edge and menace. My brothers and I sensed it all. We became elastic as waiting cats, sprung and ductile. We did not feel silly now.

Now, tough and sure, tough and threatening, gang raw, rough. O.K. ready. Come on! It was torture to wait for them to come to us, for the whites of their eyes, when we were strong and ripe and longing to bomb out over the fells, to burn and devastate and howl.

The morning grew stiff, jerking us through its meaningless time-machine and, as the short, flat afternoon lay in view, we ate without tasting and sat, like a tableau of waxworks, speechless from the strain for action. Soon it would be dark and too late. An open mouth would have screamed and Bella's whisper from the tower blew our minds like a blasting fuse.

'They're coming. It's them.'

Boot studs scraping against the stones and tramping to the door. Sergeant Duff, fortified by his new, button-bright constables, knocked and said ponderously, 'Open up, in the name of the Law.' Just like Ernest the Policeman of Toytown.

In the kitchen, we looked at each other and waited on, while someone outside nervously tried the front handle, although that door had not opened in twenty years.

'Ye'll be doing yisselves no guid in there, disobeying the Law.'

Our grandmother pushed Bella away from the attic window and leant out. 'You listen tae me, laddie. We're nae budging now, nor yet if ye call a hundret more o' yis. We're tae stay till yis all leave us in peace taw stay,' she called down, reasonably; then hooked off one of his constables' helmets with a fish head.

'Mistress Sinclair, ye've just assaulted a policeman in the execution of his duty!' exclaimed the outraged sergeant and landed a fish head for himself across the ear, before she looked out again.

'I have that,' she replied, with satisfaction, and slammed the window shut.

Below, we toppled from our peepholes, crowing and colliding with each other. Outside, the three men withdrew to their bikes in embarrassed helplessness and, suddenly, we realized that there was nothing special about this fight. It was just another rumble, like all the early ones, only this bigger. But Authority would retreat from us in the end, just as it had always done.

'Hoo-oo-ooch!' screeched Catrina, reassured and catching me into a swirl and we jostled to open the shutters, to bawl and skirl happy insults at the uniforms by the gate, and only our uncle Robbie beag did not join in.

The policemen lined up in the path without looking at us, and rumbled down to the door, thudding their shoulders against its wood five times and uselessly, for it had fossilized with age and, behind it, the huge, walnut wardrobe was wedged for all time.

So we swanked and cheered them on and clowned, for it was a grand event, funny as a picture and surely worth the preparation.

They set out stolidly for the back of the house, heads moving slowly past the scullery window, like a rolling coconut shy, impossible to deny, and the large, mottled crab I picked from he bucket thumped on to the last blue chest, where it clung grimly to his tie with one claw and pecked angrily towards his chin with the other. The formation scattered without dignity and Granny Morag, delighted, handed me a large dram and a hug.

'There and whit did I telt ye. Thon'll teach they bawheids that we're not tae be shifted, ye braw loonie. They'll nae be back sae fast after that.'

But, in the distance, a small, black fist grew as it advanced, into a hunch of men, headed by Joshua Logan in his motor car, and Robbie beag was shouting warning from the roof. And, all at once, officials and the sheriff's officer, and reinforcements of police from miles around and even a couple of volunteers were milling about Sergeant Duff on our land. And the provost was shouting through a hailer, with the vast and gusty moor snatching away the sound long before it reached us and blowing it into a distant cry. Then they were spacing themselves along a hefty pine trunk, with Logan waving instructions.

'Get the pump!' ordered Robbie beag, pushing the hose nozzle between the shutters and, as the men outside charged towards the cottage with their battering ram, our jet of sheep dye drenched and buffetted them a bull's-eye blue.

Rehearsals were over. From the attic, Calum and Lachlan were lobbing paper bags full of cowshit and fish scales to burst on the group, like sequin seasoning over a surreal wedding group. Bella and I had opened the window and were bowling the fish heads through it, while straggles of sightseers from the village gradually filled the band at the gate into a crowd.

'Mercy on us, will ye look at it all. Oh my, yon's awfie,' reeled Annie behind us, caught on her knees between tears and praise by our granddam, shadow-boxing round the rooms.

'Whit are ye looking for, ye brainless trollop? Christ, get up and fight the buggers!'

A stone caught Bella on the cheek, biting it open and sending a flame of blood streaking down her neck before she had time to cry out. The caber bashed against the door. Glass was shattering in the windows and ringing to the floor.

'Whit's happened? Whit's happened?'

'Sit down, quine, by the stove.'

The back door was shaking in its bolts as men beat against it and shouted.

'Take care o' her, Annie.' Our uncle and Lachlan ran to the rafters and Calum and me to the open shutter to blitz the bastards with rocks and smash our bottles of piss in their faces.

The old timbers were weakening and pieces of stone, like ancient arrowheads, were snapping from the walls. A man's hand slid round the edge of the window and grabbed my throat. For a second, I was being heaved dizzily out to the ground and then he let go, and Calum battled on beside me with blood forking along his forearm. Robbie beag was cut with glass needles and our clothes were awash in sweat; but, no matter how hard we struggled, we could feel the cottage flinching around us, its frames splitting and its slates loosening, like teeth.

Whole arsenals took to the air, like flocks of metal birds, and the police with their battering ram had turned into an iron machine pounding implacably at the door.

How they must have detested us, the ordered men out there, in the confusion of jars and spattering paints and sticks and fish and steel bars, black soot and whitewash, buckets and black eyes; trapped by our tribal shrieks in the smell of old Calcutta, seeing us breathing and brawling and bleeding all over their tidy images, rejecting their comfy kennel for our own manger. They would defeat us with weed-killer and blow-lamps, if they could.

Lifetimes of hatred, built up between us all through sneers and jangling bells and old moralities and the tawse and wounds we seemed to have been born with and freakishness and long conditioning, erupted in the desperate, primitive action to hold this place this day. For, at last, we understood that *they* would never go away, that this was the ultimate and inevitable confrontation, and we knew that we were going to lose.

'There's folk coming tae help us!' whooped Granny Morag, seeing people she knew restively begin to push in behind the officials.

But then it happened, as the night like a forested womb grew round the old stones, a woman's voice came shrilling, 'Burn them! Burn the place oot!'

We stared at each other through the dusky cottage with shock. Who could have called it? She had to be a stranger. Someone from beyond the glen. But now there were more voices joining her scream. 'Burn the place doon! Burn them a'!' Voices we seemed to know.

'It canna be,' whispered our grandmother, very white. 'They canna mean it.'

'Burn them! Burn!'

Before anyone could stop her, she ran to the front shutters and flung them open, leaning out to search into the dark, and a heavy rock, pitched in from the crowd, hit her powerfully and hurled her right across the room.

'Burn! Burn!' Chanting cry, as she lay bundled in the shadows, iron hammer breaking down the door, slates sliding and sticks cracking, chimney smashing over the roof, stones and glass and blood and old Angus weeping.

189

'We need the doctor. Is there the doctor?'
'Open up, in the name of the Law!'

Our grandmother Morag had a stroke and she was carried, unconscious and paralysed, the four miles to Robbie beag's cottage by the same pony trap, which had swept her in dreaming elegance round the valley all the times since her girlhood. Our women and uncles went with her, and my brothers and I went separate ways to sleeplessness. She died before morning.

Time of anguish beyond hatred, dry heart, blank mind, bleak soul, lungs filled with sadness, leaving no space for breath. The death of my grandmother was a dying in myself, a living limb rived from me and all I could feel was mutilated.

There should have been rituals to give honour to her, some way to let the ache of love, to take the impotence from tears. I needed to wear black and light candles, draw the curtains down and live in half-light for a while to think of her. Laments should have been played and the air filled with myrrh, for she was the great, warm spirit, darling mother of my childhood. I wanted to run after her, calling, 'Wait for me!' Instead, I could only cry, for myself, because she had left me behind.

We buried her in the local graveyard, before my brothers and sisters went away again to their lives. Calum was to live at Gregson's farm and Auntie Annie and Uncle Angus moved into the council house. I stayed there, too, once or twice between fishing trips.

But, down the track, the cottage was tumbling quickly to ruin, the way old places do when we discard them, and somehow the valley, tight in its cage of mountains and seas, had grown too small for me. In it, I felt alien and clumsy with bewildering adult sorrows and sudden strengths I did not yet know how to use. There was nothing to keep me there any longer and so, one day, I set off to wander the world in ships, just as our uncle Robbie beag had done a generation before.

The trawler edged away from the harbour in pouring rain. Ahead, a band of summer sky was lifting from the horizon and we were taking its path. Inland birds followed, like the spirits of home, and, when I looked back, there were rainbows scattered all over the glen.

TOM BROWN'S SCHOOLDAYS
35p

Thomas Hughes

"As on the one hand it should ever be remembered that we are boys, and boys at school, so on the other hand we must bear in mind that we form a complete social body ... a society in which, by the nature of the case, we must not only learn, but act and live; and act and live not only as boys, but as boys who will be men."

A public school in the nineteenth century was a microcosm of a world that the middle-classes of the twentieth century have embraced as a model of prudent, if prudish, society. Reflected in it is every man's dream of England at the height of her power — confident, sure, brash, brutal and oppressive. Television and film revivals of this famous classic bear witness in their popularity to the atavistic pull that the period and the place of Dr. Arnold's Rugby have for the general public. Thomas Hughes' book is a thrilling, virile and humane evocation of England's greatness and also of the seeds of her decline.